X B

Yakima tugged o[...]d
the man out the sta[...]a
swung him around in front of him, and the man pinwheeled again, dropping to the ground on his hands
and knees, wailing.

"No!" the outlaw cried, his chest bloody, his thick
hair dancing about his shoulders. "Someone, make
this Indian stop!"

Yakima stopped ten feet away from the man and just
as the man began to lift up off his knees, snugged the
butt of his Yellowboy against his right shoulder and
aimed carefully.

The rifle leaped and roared.

There was a sharp *whunk* as the bullet plowed
through the dead center of the outlaw's tan forehead,
jerking the man's head violently back and painting
the ground behind him, between the man and the
waiting coach, with red blood and white bone and
brain matter. The outlaw flew straight back and lay
with his arms and legs spread, mouth forming a startled O, his sightless eyes staring skyward.

His right foot, with the hole in its sock, twitched.

continued . . .

Also by Frank Leslie

BULLET FOR A HALF-BREED

Frank Leslie

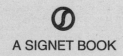

A SIGNET BOOK

SIGNET
Published by New American Library, a division of
Penguin Group (USA) Inc., 375 Hudson Street,
New York, New York 10014, USA
Penguin Group (Canada), 90 Eglinton Avenue East, Suite 700, Toronto,
Ontario M4P 2Y3, Canada (a division of Pearson Penguin Canada Inc.)
Penguin Books Ltd., 80 Strand, London WC2R 0RL, England
Penguin Ireland, 25 St. Stephen's Green, Dublin 2,
Ireland (a division of Penguin Books Ltd.)
Penguin Group (Australia), 250 Camberwell Road, Camberwell, Victoria 3124,
Australia (a division of Pearson Australia Group Pty. Ltd.)
Penguin Books India Pvt. Ltd., 11 Community Centre, Panchsheel Park,
New Delhi - 110 017, India
Penguin Group (NZ), 67 Apollo Drive, Rosedale, North Shore 0632,
New Zealand (a division of Pearson New Zealand Ltd.)
Penguin Books (South Africa) (Pty.) Ltd., 24 Sturdee Avenue,
Rosebank, Johannesburg 2196, South Africa

Penguin Books Ltd., Registered Offices:
80 Strand, London WC2R 0RL, England

First published by Signet, an imprint of New American Library,
a division of Penguin Group (USA) Inc.

First Printing, January 2011
10   9   8   7   6   5   4   3   2   1

For Tom and Tonya

Chapter 1

Yakima Henry ran an oiled rag down the stock of his prized Winchester Yellowboy repeater, then, shoving the rag back behind his cartridge belt, racked a shell into the rifle's chamber. He eased the hammer down to half cock but kept his thumb on it. Ready.

The stagecoach, bound for Red Hill, Arizona Territory, rocked and swayed beneath him. He kept his high-topped, beaded moccasins wedged against the dashboard as he sat in the shotgun messenger's position beside the driver, and stared at the storied and dangerous nest of rocks rising ahead and on the trail's right side.

In the corner of his eye, he saw the driver turn toward him.

He glanced back at the man, Avril Derks, whose cataract-milky, molasses brown eyes stared out from deep in their leathery sockets, out from above the red bandanna with white polka dots that the oldster had wrapped around the lower half of his face to keep the ubiquitous red desert dust out of his mouth and nose.

His skin was black, and it owned the texture of cracked bull hide. Deep lines cut across his forehead, beneath the brim of his weathered, high crowned, snuff brown Stetson.

Yakima saw little point in the bandanna. The old-ster's breathing was already pinched from all his many years smoking hand-rolled cigarettes from wheat paper and the harsh Lobo Negro tobacco he bought in gallon-sized kegs on his whoring forays across the border in Agua Prieta.

"Demon Rock comin' up!" Derks barked out above the thunder of the stage wheels and the pounding hooves of the six-horse hitch.

"I see it."

Derks nodded. The former slave's eyes were serious, cautionary above the bandanna, the tops of his cheekbones spotted with ginger freckles. "Some folks' eyes ain't as good as other folks' eyes."

"You worry about the team," Yakima said. "I'll worry about the rocks."

The driver, whose woolly black-and-gray sideburns ran down into the bandanna, shrugged and turned forward. "Bad place in there," he muttered just loudly enough for Yakima to hear. His voice was dark, brooding, worried.

"How many times were you hit here, Avril?"

"Three times over the past year. The Romans didn't like it one bit. No, sah. Not one bit. And neither did the businessmen that turn their hard-earned money over to us to transport." The Romans, father and daughter, were the chief owners in the Coronado Transport Company, based at the end of the line in Red Hill.

The strongbox on the coach often carried payroll coins for the two big ranches west of Red Hill, as the Red Hill Bank & Trust rarely kept more than a few thousand dollars in its vault at any one time. The reasoning was that even with a fairly effective sheriff and two good deputies, it was easier to rob the bank, a stationary target, than the stage. Sometimes the stage carried no money at all, and it was impossible for would-be thieves to know when it was heavy and when it was light. Unless they were being informed by someone who knew the workings of the line or the banks it serviced, that is. So far, that didn't appear the case.

Derks glanced over his shoulder at the chained and padlocked strongbox riding the stage's roof, then turned forward again. He shook his head slowly as a fresh wave of sand-colored dust wafted over him and Yakima, who preferred his Winchester to a shotgun though a double-barreled Greener was stowed beneath his seat. "I'm surprised ol' Roman hasn't fired me by now. Surprised, indeed."

"Ah, shit," Yakima said, nudging the old jehu with his elbow. "Where they gonna find another driver fool enough to haul this crate between Apache Gap and Red Hill?"

Derks gave Yakima a penetrating look, both woolly gray eyebrows arched.

"Not a chance," Yakima growled, keeping his eyes on the stony escarpment growing before him. "Hell,

I'm a damn fool for takin' the shotgunner's job. Walked right into that one. That 'help wanted' sign in the German Café just looked so innocent."

He shook his head again and squinted against the dust. There were few jobs worse than riding the driver's boot of a southwestern stage. Even one that wasn't plagued by holdups. Hot, sweaty, dusty. When you weren't being fried by the sun, coated in grit, and shaken around like dice in a cup, you were hammered by the sudden rain squalls of a desert monsoon. And there were the dry washes that got wet fast in such a squall, and you either waited for the flood to clear, which could take hours, or you risked getting swept away—team, lockbox, passengers, and all. . . .

As the stage followed the long, gradual bend around the front of the volcanic dyke that had been named Demon Rock by the Mescalero, Yakima removed his moccasin-clad feet from the dashboard and sat up straight in his seat.

Fifty yards . . . forty . . . thirty.

The red rocks, some as flat as planks and shelving in a tall, flame-shaped wedge over the trail's right side, grew closer and closer, so that Yakima could pick out each red rock and the thin, dark gaps between them, the bits of gravel mantling them, as well as the occasional tufts of hardy, colorless weeds that made a home there in that parched jumble of sun-blasted granite, sandstone, limestone, and quartz. There was always the threat that gunmen were nestling in there amongst the diamondbacks, rifles cocked and ready. It would be virtually impossible to see them until after they'd seen you, giving themselves away with a gun blast.

Yakima kept his eye on the top of the formation fifty feet above the trail, and on the nooks and crannies of the inner scarp, as well. No movement yet. No shadows flickering around the rocks, no sun glints off rifle bluing. Even as the stage drew up alongside the perilous jumble of rock and debris, and the flame-shaped crest swept its cool, ominous shade over the trail, Yakima saw nothing but rocks and weeds and sun shadows, with an occasional glimmer of mica chips and the deep umber of iron-rich sandstone. He could smell the dirt and minerals. He winced as the stage lurched back from the chill and impenetrable wall of boulders, as though it were lunging away from the open jaws of some stony, demonic monster.

Above the crest of the wedge, where a gunman might at that moment be lining up rifle sights on the shotgunner's chest, nothing but brassy Arizona sky and the faint brown speck of a high-soaring hawk or eagle.

When the stage had rocked and rattled beyond the snag, a couple of the horses even turning their heads to regard it warily, Yakima eased his grip on the Yellowboy, feeling the soggy sweat inside the fingers of his tight, buckskin gloves. He glanced over his shoulder to watch the formation skid off behind them, obscured by a veil of sifting dust that the rays of the late-afternoon sun now touched with copper and streaked with vermilion.

"Damn, that's funny." Derks rested his elbows

again on his bony knees and glowered over the sweat-silvered backs of the lunging team. "We was due to get hit in there. Been several months. We're due." He spat over the brow of the dashboard. "Maybe next time."

Yakima snorted as he depressed the Yellowboy's hammer. "I'll be damned if you don't sound sorry."

"Yep," the old jehu said darkly, squinting against the dust. "Maybe next time. Bad place in there. . . ."

"Well, we ain't home yet." Yakima lifted his own bandanna now and let the Winchester rest across his thighs. They were about to head across a small playa, an ancient lake bed where the stage's iron-shod wheels would churn up the alkali dust like talcum and work it deep into a man's lungs and eyes so that it clogged the skin pores, and it'd be days hacking the stuff up before a man stopped feeling that chalky grittiness deep in his chest.

This was only Yakima's third run between Apache Gap and Red Hill, a two-day stretch, and he hated that lake bed, which was like a miniature version of the Jornada del Muerto farther south and east. A vexation to man and beast alike.

Later, when they'd crossed the playa and both Yakima and Avril Derks resembled snowmen, they topped a long hill that had led up from the lake bed, and Derks hauled back on the reins, bracing his high-topped, mule-eared boots on the dashboard, and cursing at the general discomfort of that stretch of the run. But the shade of the *bosquecillo* of dusty willows and cotton-woods was refreshing after all that hellish torment under the hot, brassy sun. It was warm for September, when cooler days usually prevailed.

Yakima waited for their broiling dust cloud to sift itself out. Then he poked his hat brim up and looked around carefully. Just because they'd passed the hazard of Demon Rock didn't mean they were out of the woods; the stage had been held up at several points along the trail, and the old Diamondback Station was nearly as good a place as any.

Yakima saw no recent tracks in this broad canyon, however. The San Simon River gorge was a half mile to the north. To the south, rolling brown hills stippled with rocks and saguaro cactus. In the shade between two high bluffs and abutted on both ends by paloverde trees hunkered the Diamondback Station—a low-slung adobe brick shack with a brush roof and no porch to speak of, just a sun-silvered boardwalk fronting the door.

The door was closed.

Yakima turned to the barn sitting right of the shack. Twelve fresh horses milled there, behind the hay cribs and in the sprawling shade of three large cottonwoods. Most were standing near the front of the corral, twitching their ears over the top rail. A couple of others ran circles behind them, kicking up dust and whinnying, eager to get moving. One of the stage's leaders answered in kind.

The barn's small door opened with a squawk of rusty hinges. Chick Bannon stepped out, grinning tightly as he pulled his suspenders up his sloping shoulders. He turned his head to call into the barn behind him then came walking toward the stage, a lock of gray, sandy hair hanging down from beneath the crown of his green canvas hat.

"Afternoon, gentlemen," he greeted as Derks set the coach's brake. "How was the run?"

"Dusty." The jehu tossed the ribbons over the dashboard, then heaved his one hundred and fifty lean pounds to his feet, his knees creaking and popping stiffly. "But quiet around Demon Rock, anyways."

"That right?"

"Yep."

Yakima kept his Winchester in his hand as he climbed down from the coach, on the opposite side from the cabin. He took one more, slow look around at the scrub and rocks shelving down to the river in the north, then at the trees and the few saguaros and boulders defining the station yard's peripheries. Deeming the yard free of would-be dry-gulchers, he shouldered the Yellowboy and stepped back to the coach. Deerskin shades had been pulled down over all the windows to stave off the dust, but he could hear the passengers conversing and milling around in there, jostling the carriage.

"Diamondback Station, folks," Yakima said as he pulled the left-side door open, then set the wooden step in place beneath it.

He stepped back away from the door but continued to hold it open as the lone female passenger, a pretty blonde whom Yakima had thought he'd heard called Mrs. Holgate, rose from her front-facing seat between a gambler and a horse buyer from Las Cruces.

"Come, Calvin," she said, holding out a black-gloved hand to the boy sitting across from her, between two government beef contractors.

As the boy moved out ahead of her, jumping from the carriage without bothering with the step, the woman placed her hands on the doorframe and peered out. For a moment, her hazel-eyed gaze held on Yakima, and he felt a hard pull in his chest, remembering a similar glance from a girl who could easily have been this one's slightly younger sister. One who was dead now, long before her time, buried a good ways north of here, in fact, on the lower slopes of Mount Bailey.

It was an oblique, lingering glance that this woman gave him. When the skin above the bridge of her nose wrinkled slightly, one of the beef contractors said from a now-open window, "For the love of Pete, breed, the lady's waiting to be helped down!"

Yakima's ears suddenly burned. Not only from the old, familiar "breed" insult that he had for the most part learned to ignore, but from his impropriety. Mentally cursing himself for his carelessness—he wasn't yet used to all the summary details of the shotgunner's job, including helping ladies down from unstable carriage perches—he lurched forward and took the woman's soft, glove-clad hand in his own.

She squeezed it as, holding the long skirts of her green traveling dress up above her ankles, she stepped down to the board step and from there to the ground. She glanced at him again, and he was struck by the beauty of her features despite the light coating of dust on her brows and on the small straw hat bedecked with artificial flowers pinned at a fashionable angle atop her upswept, honey blond hair.

"Thank you, Mr. Henry," she said, sliding her curiously lingering glance from him as she released his hand and turned to her boy with an annoyed expression. "Calvin, don't run far—listen to your mother, now!"

"No need to call him 'mister,' Mrs. Holgate," said the dark-haired contractor as he poked his head out the open door, glowering at Yakima. He'd obviously been imbibing during the long ride; he stood swaying drunkenly, and Yakima could smell the sour stench of liquor on him. Yakima remembered his name: Buttercup. Merlin Buttercup. The other one, with long blond hair and a dull-eyed, horsey face was Slater. "He's a damn savage. Look at them green eyes and black hair. Mixed blood—even worse than a *full* blood. Good Lord, breed—don't tell me you're 'Pache!"

Yakima felt his jaws tighten. He glanced at the woman, who was striding off toward her son, who was heading for a nest of rocks on the west edge of the yard. She glanced over her left shoulder at Yakima, and again it was an unreadable expression. And now Yakima felt the inner welt of humiliation grow behind the automatic anger that came with the contractor's comments.

To cover his urge to tattoo Buttercup's face with the brass butt of his Winchester—he needed to hold this job for at least another month—he released the door, doffed his hat, and batted it against his buckskin-clad left thigh.

The contractor dropped down to the wooden step and turned his glower on Yakima again—he was a handsome, dark-haired man in a gray suit and string tie, his shoulders mantled with grit despite the deer hide shades. His brown eyes were dead, and his mouth owned a mocking curl. In his right hand, he held an unlit cheroot.

"I asked you a question, breed."

Yakima pinched his nostrils against the stench of cheap tanglefoot and noted the top of a silver flask protruding from the breast pocket of the man's frock coat.

Yakima squeezed the neck of the Winchester resting on his shoulder but kept a bland expression. If he provoked this gent, he'd have to smash the man's handsome mug, and then the Coronado Transport Company would likely give him his severance pay, and he'd be looking for another job—not an easy task this time of the year. And he'd hoped to winter in the desert.

He'd had his fill of the snowy Rockies last winter in Wyoming.

"No," Yakima said, his Indian-dark features stony, his green eyes set deep in bony sockets hard and bright as sun-washed jade. "Northern Cheyenne."

The contractor stared at him hard. His curled upper lip was just starting to open again when the stationmaster, Chick Bannon, came around the front of the coach as his two Mexican hostlers led the worn team of six horses toward the holding corral. "Cool water at the well yonder, folks! Come on over and refresh

yourselves. No point in lingerin' around the stage.
These fresh horses are a mite jumpy."

The other contractor, Slater, laughed and gave Buttercup a hard shove, and then the two of them marched
off toward the roofed stone well coping, where both
the woman and the boy were winching up a bucket of
fresh water.

Yakima watched the other men—they all smelled
of tanglefoot—saunter light-footed off toward the well,
muttering something about Apaches and that they
were surprised the Romans, father and daughter, would
hire anyone who looked like Geronimo to ride shotgun.

Yakima batted his hat against his chaps once more,
then walked around the front of the stage. The hostlers
were milling about the corral, conversing and tossing
peculiar glances toward the coach, as though they were
waiting for something. Derks was exchanging friendly
banter with Bannon near the coach's sloping tongue.
Bannon was smiling that taut smile he'd worn earlier,
and he was casting quick, furtivelike glances toward
the cabin.

Yakima felt a worm flip its tail in his belly. Standing off to one side of the driver and stationmaster, he
turned his head toward the station itself. His hand
tightened around the neck of his Winchester when he
saw a shadow move behind the dark square of the
unshuttered window left of the closed door.

There was a faint flash there, too.

Like the reflection of sunlight off steel.

Chapter 2

"Still got some o' that firewater in yonder?" the driver asked as Bannon headed off toward the corral, where the hostlers were still curiously milling with the fresh horses.

Yakima turned toward the stationmaster, who still wore that stiff smile. Bannon's gray-blue eyes slid toward the station house but stopped only partway there, as if the shack housed something he didn't want to see, and returned to the expectantly grinning driver.

"Why, sure," Bannon said. "Why, sure I do, Avril. Have I ever *not* had some o' that firewater when you've pulled through?"

"Not that I can remember," Derks said, laughing. "Lettie'll fix me up?"

"Sure, sure. Lettie'll break out a fresh bottle. Tell her I said so. I'm just gonna go on over and see to the fresh hitch." Bannon swallowed, fingered the suspenders bowing over his paunch, and continued toward the corral with a seeming heaviness in his boots, as though the heels were made of lead.

Derks doffed his hat from his bald head and continued in his bandy-legged gait toward the station house, his red bandanna fluttering around his leathery neck. Yakima watched him, then cut his eyes toward the window left of the front door again. Nothing there now but a two-by-two square of deep purple afternoon shade.

Still, Yakima's heart thudded slowly, persistently.

He hurried forward. "Avril!"

The driver stopped halfway between Yakima and the shack's small plank stoop, his previous humor still etched on his full, chapped lips, liquid-brown eyes catching the sunlight angling under the brim of his Stetson.

"What is it, younker? You want me to buy ya a drink? Come on!"

"Nah," Yakima said, feigning a grin and wrapping one arm around the driver's skinny neck as he continued toward the station house. "Let me buy you one."

Derks scowled. "Wait a minute. I didn't think you drank the firewater."

"I don't. You know how Injuns are with the tanglefoot. We get drunk, and the devil takes the hindmost. But since it's such a hot damn day an' all . . ."

Yakima and Derks stopped on the stoop before the front door. Yakima's blood was rushing, the hair beneath the collar of his chambray shirt sticking straight up in the air. Derks was about to place his hand on the door's steel-and-leather latch, but Yakima beat him to it.

"Allow me."

Derks looked at Yakima suspiciously, pooching out his lips. "Now, why in the hell you actin' so strange, all of a sud—"

"Age before beauty," Yakima said as he flipped the latch.

As the door swung inward, he withdrew his arm from around the driver's neck, planted his hand on Derks's left shoulder, and shoved the small man hard.

"Hey!" Derks cried, throwing his arms out as he flew sideways off the stoop.

At the same time, the timbered gray door flew inward. Yakima caught a brief glimpse of a hatted silhouette facing him from only a few feet beyond the stoop before he sidestepped to his left, swinging around and pressing his back to the front station house wall.

Ka-boooom!

The blast of the double-barreled shotgun sounded like near thunder. The entire building jumped. The double-ought buck caromed through the open door, tearing slivers from both sides of the doorframe and spewing them ten feet out into the yard and peppering the side of the stage facing the station house.

The echo of the blast hadn't died before Yakima had cocked the Yellowboy, shifted it to his left hand, and snaked it around the side of the chewed-up doorframe, poking the barrel into the station house. He fired once, heard a grunt inside the building, then turned into the door opening, crouching and racking a fresh shell in the Winchester's chamber.

Squinting, unable to see much but vague man-shapes in the shadows, he fired once, twice, three times, pivoting at the waist while triggering, hearing men shout and scream and try to scramble out of the path of Yakima's lead. Powder smoke wafting in front of him, the half-breed bounded forward, saw the man he'd shot first lying sprawled on his back on the earthen floor ten feet in front of the door, his shotgun lying nearby.

Another man was sliding down the wall beside the building's far, front window, screaming and triggering his carbine into the ceiling above his head and causing dust to sift down from the rafters.

A rifle barked off Yakima's right flank. The bullet burned across Yakima's side, and he dove forward across the scarred puncheon eating table. As he hit the floor on his shoulder and rolled, two more bullets slammed into the top of the table, barking loudly. Another drilled the lamp hanging from a square-hewn ceiling joist over Yakima's head, and glass and oil rained.

Yakima pushed up off the toes of his moccasins and lifted a look over the top of the table. The big man standing in the building's far corner was loudly racking a fresh cartridge into the breech of his Henry rifle, his curly bib beard dancing across his chest. As his ejected shell clanked off the wall behind him, he raised the rifle to his shoulder, but not before Yakima pressed the stock of his Yellowboy against his shoulder and squeezed the rifle's trigger.

The rifle leaped and roared.

The bearded man winced.

Yakima racked another shell and fired, racked again

and fired, and the bearded man triggered his own rifle wild before flying back and crashing back-first through the window behind him, glass flying. The backs of his knees hung up on the sill and his high-topped boots caught on the inside wall, jerking, the spurs tearing at the adobe bricks as he died, hanging there, half in and half out.

Yakima ejected his last spent cartridge. It pinged off the ceiling joist behind him as he racked a fresh one into the chamber and, still on his haunches, swung around.

There was no movement. The gray powder smoke hung heavy in the dark room lit only by the windows. A man on the floor on the other side of the table groaned softly. He was the only one who appeared still alive.

There'd been four, Yakima reckoned. The one in front of the door with the shotgun. The man on the other side of the table now, who'd likely been sidled up against one window when the stage had pulled into the yard. The man now on the floor beneath the far window to Yakima's right. And the man who'd fallen out the window to Yakima's left, near the big stone hearth and cook range and the grease-spattered shelves that held airtight tins and small bags of potatoes that were sending sprouts out their twisted burlap necks.

Behind Yakima, a groan sounded. A frightened female groan.

He swung around, quickly and automatically thumbing fresh cartridges from one of the two shell belts on his narrow waist and pushing them into the Yellowboy's scrolled brass receiver. Before him, in the far wall, was a curtained doorway. He knew from previous visits that this led back into the station house's sleeping area and into Bannon's private living quarters.

He heard the creak of a footstep behind him, and he turned to see Derks leaning forward from the waist to peer into the open front door, keeping his body behind the wall left of the door, a stricken, puzzled look on his craggy features. The driver held his cocked Remington in his right hand, barrel up.

Yakima held up a hand to hold the man, then walked forward. He slid the curtain back with his rifle barrel, carefully scrutinized the narrow hall that was lit by an open door and a window at the other end. Stepping forward, Yakima let the curtain fall back into place behind him and continued slowly, one step at a time, down the short hall, scrutinizing the two doorways on his right, one on his left—both sleeping quarters for overnight stage passengers. The second doorway on his left was the one that interested the half-breed the most, because he'd heard a wooden creak back there, and a nervous throat clearing.

As he approached, he saw that the curtain was partly pulled back to reveal a dusky figure sitting up on a cot. The girl had sandy hair, and she was sitting with her back to the room's far corner. She held a blanket partway around her naked body, revealing one pink breast and the inside of her left leg—a long thigh and slender calf as well as a bare left foot. Her other leg was curled beneath her, only the knee showing from under the blanket. Her head was turned away from the door as though in shame. Her disheveled hair hung down over the side of her face.

Her shoulders jerked as she sobbed.

Yakima put his right foot down in front of the doorway and held the barrel of his cocked Winchester against the curtain covering half of the doorway on the right side. The girl's head swung toward him, and she peered at him darkly through the screen of her hair.

She sucked a bellyful of air and drew the blanket over her exposed breast. Her stricken gaze slid slightly toward Yakima's right, pausing on the wall right of the door. Her eyes seemed to widen slightly, anxiously, and then they slid back to Yakima. She bunched her cheeks and quivering lips, crying softly.

Yakima swung the barrel of his Yellowboy to the right, aiming at the wall beside the door. He triggered two quick shots, the reports sounding like cannon blasts in the close quarters. On the cot, the girl jumped with a start, hair jostling about her bare shoulders.

There was a deep gasp and a grunt, the plunk of a heavy, booted foot.

Yakima bounded into the room and, cocking the Yellowboy, which he held out from his right hip, swung to his right, where a man was staggering out from the wall, and pinwheeled toward the back wall, where there was a low shelf of books below a coat hook and an oval-framed daguerreotype. The man fell back against the wall, dropping his Winchester carbine and planting both hands on the low shelf, sort of holding himself there while two holes in his torso pumped blood out from his chest, most of which was exposed by the open flaps of his long-handle underwear shirt.

He was a tall man with thick, curly brown hair hanging to his shoulders, beneath a tan Stetson with a Montana crease in its crown. An ivory-gripped Colt was holstered low on his right thigh though he wasn't wearing anything but the long-handles, hat, and white socks with a hole in the right toe.

The man's eyes moved to Yakima. A pleading cast washed over them as he panted and winced against the bullets that had torn through him, likely pricking him with slivers from the wall, as well.

"Please," the man rasped. "Don't . . ."

Yakima slid his gaze to the girl cowering atop the cot. Her right cheek and eye were swollen.

Yakima slid his eyes back to the wounded man before him. He took his Winchester in his right hand, tipping the barrel up, then lunged forward and plucked the outlaw's pistol from its holster. He wedged the revolver behind his own cartridge belts then grabbed the man by the front of his underwear shirt. He jerked the man brusquely forward.

The man hit the floor on his knees with a yelp. His hat rolled off his shoulder. Yakima buried his hand in the man's thick hair falling over his left ear, and the man screamed as Yakima jerked him to his feet and pulled him by his hair out the doorway and up the hall and into the station house's main room.

"No!" the man cried, dragging the toes of his stocking feet. He fell again to his knees.

Yakima tugged on his hair again, and then he had the man out the station house's front door. Yakima swung the man around in front of him, and the man pinwheeled again, dropping to the ground on his hands and knees, wailing.

"No!" the outlaw cried, his chest bloody, his thick hair dancing about his shoulders. "Someone, make this Indian stop!"

Yakima stopped ten feet away from the man and just as the man began to lift up off his knees, snugged the butt of his Yellowboy against his right shoulder and aimed carefully.

The rifle leaped and roared.

There was a sharp *whunk* as the bullet plowed through the dead center of the outlaw's tan forehead, jerking the man's head violently back and painting the ground behind him, between him and the waiting coach, with red blood and white bone and brain matter. The outlaw flew straight back and lay with his arms and legs spread, mouth forming a startled O, his sightless eyes staring skyward.

His right foot, with the hole in its sock, twitched.

Chapter 3

"Gries," Avril Derks said, staring grimly down at the dead man. "Tanner Gries. Dangerous damn trail dog. He hit us once about seven months ago."

Yakima ejected the spent cartridge from the Yellowboy's breech, seated fresh, and off-cocked the hammer. Just in case his cleanup wasn't finished yet.

"They didn't give me no choice, Avril!" Chick Bannon yelled just before he crouched between two corral rails and strode toward the driver and Yakima. He threw his hands out in supplication, his face a mask of regret and sorrow. "They told me they'd kill Lettie if I let on like I knew they was here!"

Derks turned to the station house manager, his old eyes sadly accusing. "You was gonna let me walk right on into that ambush."

"They were gonna kill Lettie!"

Derks and Yakima shared a glance. The driver kicked the unmoving side of Tanner Gries. "There's a reward on his otherwise worthless head. Like as not on all his boys." He glanced at Yakima. "We'll haul 'em into town, and you'll be one rich heathen."

Deep humor lines spoked from the corners of Derks's eyes. "Yes, sah . . . likely the flushest heathen around these parts."

Bannon walked up toward the station house door and glanced at Yakima. "Lettie . . . is she . . . ?"

"You better go to her," Yakima said. "Looks like he worked her over good."

When Bannon had gone into the house, Yakima saw the stage passengers—the four men and the woman and the little boy—standing in a ragged line just off the coach's drooping wagon tongue. Their grim eyes were on the dead man. The beef contractor who'd tried to buffalo Yakima earlier was smoking a long black cigar, and he shifted his drink-bright eyes between Yakima and the dead man, the ever-present sneer on his lips.

"Why, you didn't even give that man a chance," Buttercup said, flicking ashes from the cheroot and then using it to point out the dead man. "Didn't even give him a chance to draw his gun."

"Hell," said the man's long-haired partner, Slater, holding the flat silver flask in his hand, "he didn't even *have* a gun. Why, I bet that's his gun there." He used the flask to indicate the ivory-gripped Colt wedged behind Yakima's shell belts.

Yakima looked at the faces of the other passengers. The men were drunk and sneering. The woman, with the boy standing before her, her hands on his shoulders, stared in shock at the dead man, her lips slightly parted. The boy stared down with much the same expression before sliding his squint-eyed glance up to Yakima. The woman absently turned the boy's head toward her with her hand, and pressed his cheek against her belly.

"Careful, Ralph," said the brown-haired contractor, taking a jerky step straight back in mock fear. "I think he's kill-crazy."

Yakima stared back at the men hard. Derks glanced between them; then, as though to forestall a fight, the old jehu stepped forward, holding his arms up. "Why don't you fellas—and you, too, Mrs. Holgate—why don't you all walk on over to the well? As you can see, there's been a delay. We'll give ya'll a call soon as we have the fresh team all hitched and ready to go."

When he had the passengers heading back to the roofed well coping, Derks came back to Yakima, who'd set his rifle up onto the floor of the coach's driver's boot and was drinking from his canteen, letting some of the water dribble down his face. The Mexican hostlers were finally bringing the rigged team up from the corral, the horses snorting, a couple high-stepping and twitching their ears. One whinnied loudly when it saw the dead man and smelled the blood.

"Let's throw the stiffs on board," Derks said. "Take 'em back to the sheriff in Red Hill so's you can draw your reward."

Yakima lowered the canteen and gave the driver a mock severe look. "If you're wantin' a loan, Avril, why don't you just come out and say so?"

The driver gave a snort and turned toward the station, his fists on his hips. "What tipped ya off?"

"Movement in the window there, left of the door."

The driver looked at Yakima. "That coulda been Lettie."

"Could've."

Derks studied Yakima shrewdly, sizing him up as though seeing the half-breed for the first time. He ran his skeptical gaze from the horn-gripped Colt holstered low on Yakima's buckskin-clad thigh to the cartridge belts on his waist and then to the big, hide-wrapped bowie knife sheathed on his left hip. The half-breed also had an Arkansas toothpick peeking up from over his right shoulder, sheathed at the back of his neck. Derks lifted his eyes to Yakima's broad, chiseled face once more, narrowing an eye before turning away and shaking his head ominously.

"Come on, then, shotgun rider," he said with a wave of his arm. "I got me a timetable to keep!"

As the driver continued on into the station house, Yakima drove the cork back into his canteen with the heel of his hand. He'd started turning toward the station house when he saw the woman, Mrs. Holgate, walking toward him from the well, using both her hands to hold her skirts above her ankles while a small, beaded, tan purse dangled from her right wrist.

"Mr. Henry!"

She stopped a few feet away from him. She set those hazel eyes on him, her curving blond bangs and wisps of her hair sliding about her creamy, peach-colored cheeks. There were no age lines around her eyes or mouth. Her neck above her crisp blouse collar, aside from a mole the size of a pinhead, was as smooth as varnished oak. She might not have been much older than Faith, after all, Yakima thought absently. Probably Faith's age when Yakima had put his beloved into the ground on the slopes of Mount Bailey—early twenties. She'd likely had the boy, who was six or seven, fairly young.

A sadness stirred in him behind the pull of the tedious animal desire that was a vague heaviness in his loins. Sadness, regret, a constant torment no less keen for Faith's having been gone now for nearly two years. Two long, long years . . .

As his thoughts returned to the present, he saw that Mrs. Holgate was staring up at him with a faint, curious, probing look in her eyes, her honey brows faintly wrinkled. He realized that he must have been studying her with much the same expression. A warmth touched the tops of his ears, and he lowered his eyes to the ground.

"Mr. Henry," she said again, her voice softer, the words halting. "I . . . couldn't help overhearing. There's a girl in there? A young woman?" She slid her eyes toward the station house.

"Yes, ma'am."

"Is she all right?"

"They worked her over pretty good."

"Do you think I could be of assistance? You know— the council of another woman? If there are no other women around, that is."

Yakima felt the male in him give a little harder tug

as he realized that, like Faith, the woman before him was not only fine to look at, but a good, kind, caring person to boot. It made her doubly attractive. "I reckon it couldn't hurt, Mrs. Holgate. In fact," he added, wanting to say more, to make a deeper connection with this woman. Because of his innate reserve, he was unsure as to how to go about it, so he found himself settling with "I bet she'd appreciate that."

He canted his head toward the station house. "Her room's through the curtained doorway at the back of the main hall. Second door on the left."

"Thank you, Mr. Henry."

Her eyes lingered on him as she turned away and started toward the station house. He pinched his hat brim to her. She turned away and walked through the door, which Derks was holding open for her.

Yakima adjusted his cartridge belts on his hips as he strode over to the station house and went on inside behind the woman and Derks. As he and the jehu hauled the dead men outside, Yakima could hear the woman in the back room talking to the girl. He could hear the girl's sobs and then, when Yakima and Derks were dragging the third body outside, Bannon hustled into the main haul to rummage around his shelves for a bottle and several other things the woman must have called for, and to stoke the cookstove and ladle warm water from the reservoir.

When Yakima and Derks had all the dead men lined up on the ground beside the stage, Derks climbed up onto the luggage rack on the roof. Yakima back-and-bellied the first corpse up to the old man, who grabbed it around the shoulders and, grunting and cursing, wrestled it up over the brass rail and onto the roof at his feet. Despite his protests, Derks was as tough as whang leather. They had all five dead men on the roof and tied to the rails with rope in less than twenty minutes.

Two of the dead men were so tall that the tops of their heads and their feet hung over the sides of the stage. All together, they nearly completely covered the roof, blood from their wounds glistening in the sunlight and already attracting buzzards. The large, ragged, bald-headed carrion-eaters circled the stage from about a hundred yards in the air—slow, lazy, ominous circles. A couple of hawks had found the dead men, as well. They perched on near tree branches and fence posts, staring toward the stage with sharp-eyed interest, dun feathers fluttering in the mounting breeze.

As Mrs. Holgate was still in the station house with the girl, while the male passengers kicked around in the shade of a cottonwood, assuaging their impatience to get moving with a second flask of liquor, Yakima walked over to where the boy was milling around an abandoned outbuilding with a stick. He was a small, round-faced lad with a splash of freckles across his pudgy cheeks, and large round eyes the same dark red as his straight hair.

He wore a shabby suit coat, though he'd outgrown the sleeves, with a crisp white shirt underneath, and knickers and high-topped boots. He seemed a bashful, soulful boy capable of occupying himself, creating his own little world in his head. The stick was obviously a spear, and he threw it at rocks while talking in low, theatrical tones and puffing out his cheeks to fabricate sounds of fighting.

"Them Injuns are having a time of it," Yakima observed, stopping near where the boy was playing beside the old wagon shed. He cocked a foot and hooked his thumbs behind his cartridge belts.

The boy looked at him, eyes snapping wide with a start. A slight, self-conscious flush rose in his cheeks, and he picked up the stick he'd thrown and tapped the tip on a rock. "Not Injuns," he said, squinting an eye at Yakima. "Stage robbers."

"Stage robbers, huh?"

"Yeah. They're all dead."

"I reckon there's nothing good about a stage robber." Yakima tossed his head toward the stage to which the team had been hitched and stood feisty-footed in the traces. "You ready to head out?"

The boy looked at the station house, the roof of which the sun was finding as the large, lemon orb edged westward. Even from here, flies could be heard, buzzing about the grisly cargo topping the stage.

"Where's Ma?"

"She'll be along soon."

"You sure?" The boy looked up with worry in his eyes. "I wouldn't want to leave without her. She's all I got now with Pa dead."

"Oh, we wouldn't leave without her, son."

"I hope not."

Yakima placed a reassuring hand on the boy's shoulder as he headed toward the stage, glancing over his shoulder at the drinking men. "You can board up now."

He turned his head forward, but he heard a couple of the men scoff or snicker. One ran forward as though anxious to follow the half-breed's orders, then slowed down and laughed over his shoulder at the other men, who were donning their hats and hitching up their slacks and squinting their owl eyes against the harsh afternoon light.

"What happened to your pa?" Yakima asked the boy.

"He was a soldier."

Yakima glanced down at him, one dark brow arched. "Injuns kill him?"

The boy nodded slowly, eyes on the ground before him. He turned a quick look up at Yakima, vaguely troubled as he took in the half-breed's long hair and distinct Indian features but with the incongruous green eyes of a white man.

"Half, boy," Yakima said. "I'm half Injun. And I'm right friendly . . . as long as you're not a stage robber, that is." He lifted the corners of his broad mouth in a teasing grin. "You ain't, are ya?"

"No, sir."

"That's good. Hop up there, now."

When he'd helped the boy into the stage, he turned to see the woman walking toward him from the station house. She held the straps of her beaded purse in her teeth as she pinned her hat to the rich golden hair piled atop her head. The male passengers sauntered toward the stage from Yakima's right, and he guardedly kept them in the periphery of his vision as they approached the stage.

The boy said through the window over Yakima's left shoulder, "He's a *good* Injun, Mama."

The woman's face flushed slightly. She stopped before Yakima, lowering her hands from her hat and taking her purse in her hands. She gave her lower lip a brief nibble and swallowed, ignoring the boy smiling through the stage window.

"I'd like to thank you, Mr. Henry. Those men were vile. No telling what else they might have done. . . ." Mrs. Holgate's eyes lifted to the roof of the coach.

"Is the girl all right?"

She nodded. "I think so. The mental wounds will take longer than the physical ones."

"I reckon they usually do."

Her eyes met his and held. She lifted her hand, and he took it as she climbed into the stage. When she and the other passengers were settled, Yakima closed the door and climbed up onto the stage beside Derks. He glanced back at the chained and padlocked lockbox, around which the dead men lay—the jewel in the crown they'd striven so hard for and had fallen just short of.

The box somehow seemed to mock them all, Yakima included.

Derks followed Yakima's gaze to the box, then gave a rueful chuff, released the brake, and shook the ribbons over the team. He yelled and hollered, and the six-horse hitch lunged into their collars and bolted off their rear hocks, and the coach caromed on out of the yard behind them.

Beneath the din of hooves and wheels, the voice of Buttercup rose from below. "You got that wrong, boy. The only *good* Injun is a *dead* Injun."

He and the other men laughed.

Chapter 4

The buzzards followed the stage through the rolling desert, over the low bald hills, and through dangerous creases between the craggy peaks of the legend-haunted Sierra Coronado. They retreated only slightly when the stage rocked and thundered into the little town of Red Hill nestled amongst shelving red bluffs and mesas.

The valley between the mesas was known as Slaughterhouse Gulch. Bits and pieces of bison bones, visible in the light of midmorning and late afternoon, littered the slopes of both bluffs from when ancient Indians drove the herds over the sides and then feasted in the camp that, over the centuries, slowly grew into a rough-hewn hiders' rendezvous and then into what the town of Red Hill was now, a ranching and mining supply settlement awaiting a spur railroad line to link it to civilization. Until then, Delbert Roman and his daughter, Rae, would continue to operate the Coronado Transport Company—a small lone stage line that serviced south-central Arizona Territory.

A few of the buzzards settled on the roofs of the two- and three-story buildings lining Red Hill's broad main street, and watched in frustration as the coach was brought to a halt on the street's north side and roughly in the middle of the town, on a corner between the Red Hill Bank & Trust and a drugstore.

"That right wheeler, Roxy, needs her left rear hock wrapped with mud and whiskey or she'll be lame by this time next week." Avril Derks gave a grunt as he pulled the brake handle back into its locking position, then jerked his bandanna down from his cheeks. "I told them hostlers two days ago to do that, but do they listen to me? Too busy thinkin' about the *putas* over on Bayonet Creek."

Yakima held his rifle across his knees as he looked around at the near-empty street. The stage was no great curiosity, as it ran twice a week between Apache Gap and Red Hill, hauling mostly drummers or horse-less cowpunchers, and of course the U.S. mail, so there was no crowd gathering for the occasions. Just the usual bored youngsters with dogs nipping at their heels, running out of alley mouths to gawk while kicking horse apples and dirt clods. A couple of apron-clad shopkeepers poked their heads out their doors or peered through windows.

The sheriff, Frank Rathbone, stepped out of his office directly across the street from the hotel. The tall, black-clad lawman with a longhorn mustache sweeping up beneath a broad, sunburned nose, was flanked by his two duster-clad deputies, the tall, broad-shouldered and black-bearded Cordovan Stall, and the wiry, muscular half-Mexican Lonnie Silver. All three of the Red Hill lawmen looked as hard-faced and evil-eyed as the bad men they occasionally hauled into their jail from the saloons or from the slopes of the outlying Coronados, which were haunted by all stripe of frontier criminal on the run to Mexico from evil doings farther north. Hard as they were, and as gun handy, Rathbone, Stall, and Silver seldom wandered far from town, however.

Even the most capable lawmen, U.S. Marshals included, were known to disappear in the vast, rough country that surrounded the town. Judging by the conditions most of the lawmen's bodies were found in, their deaths hadn't been easy or quick, and that couldn't always be blamed on the small bronco bands of Mescalero that still haunted that wild, sun-blasted sierra but who were seldom glimpsed except from a distance by prospectors, mustangers, and the occasional desert rat.

Just the same, Yakima never felt easy in town. Even with Rathbone on the scout. The stage could as easily be bushwhacked here by the right brand of desperado. He always took a careful survey of the rooftops and alley mouths before he off-cocked his Winchester and set it down at his feet. He did that now and, as Derks berated the three hostlers—a middle-aged man and two young ones—moving up the gap from the big barn flanking the hotel, stepped down the side of the stage and opened the door facing the gap between the hotel and the bank.

He helped Mrs. Holgate down, and then the boy, and then he went back to the rear luggage boot to remove the woman's steamer trunk and carpetbag. "Can I haul your luggage somewhere for you, ma'am? The hotel, maybe?"

"That won't be necessary, mister," a male voice said behind him.

Yakima turned to see the man who owned the mercantile just up the street from the bank and the hotel, standing off the coach's left rear wheel. He was a tall, gray-eyed, severe-looking man in his late forties, with a broad, flat face bearing a thimble-sized mole off the right corner of his mouth. He was all decked out in gray, pin-striped slacks, button half boots, and a long, butterscotch-colored Prince Albert coat. The shoes were freshly polished, the coat and his matching top hat freshly brushed though both showed signs of wear and closet wrinkles.

He blinked behind his round, wired-framed spectacles and held a bouquet of paper roses out toward Mrs. Holgate with a courtly bow and fawning smile. His long hair curled over his coat collar though Yakima knew that the top of the man's head would have been as bald as an egg but for the hair combed over from the right side.

"Mr. Seagraves?" the woman said, a flush rising in her cheeks that had lately gotten a little too much sun.

"Mrs. Holgate?"

"Yes."

"These are indeed for you, then, ma'am."

The woman took the roses a little awkwardly. Seagraves looked at her son, who stood peering up the street with a faintly lost look in his squinting eyes, one freckled hand worrying the hem of his wool coat. "This is the boy—Carl?"

"Calvin."

"Ah, yes, Calvin." Seagraves grabbed the handle of the steamer trunk and turned back in the direction of the big three-story, spruce green mercantile a half block west and on the south side of the street, where a heavy-shafted Murphy freight wagon was parked behind a four-hitch team of dun and gray mules. "Let's go and get you settled in, then." He crooked his elbow.

The woman hesitated for a moment then shifted the roses to her other hand and hooked her left arm through the mercantiler's. "Come along, son," she said. "Will you grab the carpetbag, please?"

As the two walked away arm in arm, the boy following with the carpetbag bouncing off his knees, Mrs. Holgate glanced over her right shoulder, then jerked her head forward again as Seagraves said something to her and canted his head proudly to indicate the store looming before them.

"Oh, yes," Yakima heard her say. "It's a very handsome place, indeed, Mr. Seagraves."

"There's much work to be done."

"I've never fainted from work, Mr. Seagraves. And neither has Calvin—have you, Calvin?"

If the boy responded, Yakima didn't hear what the response was. They'd all drifted out of hearing, and now the beef contractor, Buttercup, said, "A mail-order bride." He whistled. "Can you believe that? I wonder how far that old coot had to advertise to get the likes of her."

"She ain't so much," said Buttercup's partner, Slater, grabbing his carpetbag and leather accordion satchel out of Yakima's hands as the half-breed continued unloading the luggage boot. "Not with the boy an' all."

"Yeah, but you gotta admit," Buttercup said. "Without the boy . . ."

Yakima had just turned over the last of the luggage, and the male passengers, suffering from the aftereffects of the alcohol they'd apparently run out of somewhere along the last stretch of trail, were staggering off toward the hotel. The bank president stepped out of the bank's double oak doors and scowled up at the top of the stage. He removed the fat stogie from his mouth, blew out a thick smoke plume, and said, "Good Christ! What am I running here—a goddamn meat wagon?"

"We got hit, Mistah Roman." Derks was on the stage roof, unlocking the padlock that held the box's chains to the rails. Neither he nor Yakima had a key to the padlock itself.

"Demon Rock?"

Derks shook his head regretfully. "No, sah. It weren't Demon Rock. Diamondback Station, Mr. Roman."

Roman scowled. He was a big man with a florid face, bushy gray sideburns, and a penchant for custom-made suits and stout pinky rings, though whom he was trying to impress in remote, rough-hewn Red Hill was anyone's guess.

"Bannon?" he asked, genuine worry in his eyes.

The man was first and foremost concerned about his money, but Yakima had sensed that he did have heart.

A banker's heart, but a heart just the same.

Whereas his daughter, who was probably in her early twenties though she sometimes appeared thirty or so, seemed solely concerned with business.

Derks didn't want to go into it. He handed the mail pouch down to the banker, and muttered, "He's all right."

As two men in dress suits—a teller and the young loan officer, Elmwood—strode out of the bank and over to the stage to take custody of the strongbox, a plain-faced young, dark-haired woman stepped out onto the veranda behind Roman. The banker turned his head to one side. "You'd better stay inside, Rae."

The girl walked out onto the porch beside her father, a cloth-bound ledger book in her arms, a pencil in her right hand, the fingers of which were ink stained. She held the book tight against her chest, and while her dress was conservatively cut and she wore an old lady's knitted white shawl, the book still pushed her breasts up high, visible between the shawl's flaps, pinching off her cleavage.

Rae Roman's dark brown hair was gathered in a tight double bun atop her head. Her brown eyes were customarily cool, businesslike, her nose long, her lips broad and serious. When her gaze found the dead men atop the stage roof, it widened, and her cheeks colored slightly.

She frowned with reproof at both Derks and Yakima, who were both handing the strongbox down to the teller and loan officer, who stood near the stage's right front wheel, arms outstretched.

"Oh, my God—what happened?" she asked in a fateful tone.

"Rae, please," her father gently chided her.

The girl held her place there at the veranda rail, waiting for an explanation. Roman, apparently accustomed to the young woman's casual disobedience, turned back to Derks as Yakima climbed up into the stage's driver's boot. Derks had worked for the stage company for several years, and thus he was better equipped for handling the bosses.

"What about the box?" Rae Roman wanted to know, though she had her eyes on the strongbox now as the two bankers hauled it up onto the porch, each carrying a hide handle attached to an end. "You were hauling payroll money for the Lazy Eight, and their foreman is due to pick it up this weekend."

"They didn't touch the box, Miss Rae," Derks assured the woman, holding his hat in his hands and staring up at the queenlike vice president of the Red Hill Bank & Trust.

She might have been pretty, Yakima thought, if she smiled more. If she ever smiled at all. She certainly had a figure—heavy-breasted and round-hipped—though he doubted any man had ever seen it. Her eyes were crusted ice over brown rock, and he doubted those pinched lips had ever been kissed. They likely wouldn't be until she'd married some poor, soon-to-be hard-suffering son of a bitch.

"No, sir—ol' Yakima there didn't let 'em get close to it," the driver continued. "You got you a good shot-gunner in him, Mr. Roman. Miss Roman." He chuckled deep in his chest, bemused. "Though it's that Yellowboy he seems to prefer."

Mr. Roman now stood with his hands on his hips, mailbag slung over a shoulder, watching Yakima loosen the ropes that tied the dead men to the brass rails around the roof of the stage. "Good Lord, Henry—you took them all down yourself?"

"Yes, suh," Derks answered for Yakima. He gave a nervous chuckle.

Yakima knew how he felt. Would the banker and owner of the Coronado Company approve of having his money saved from trail thieves or disapprove of the obviously bloodthirsty savage he'd hired to defend it? Only, unlike the old jehu, Yakima wasn't nervous. If he got nervous every time his job was in trouble, he'd have long ago been locked up in a funny house, scratching on the walls with rocks between his toes.

Let the chips fall where they may. All he could do was keep his mouth shut and hope he could hold on long enough here for a grubstake to take him somewhere else.

He'd remained atop the stage. Now he grabbed Tanner Gries's shoulder and rolled him over the far side of the stage from the bank. Gries hit the street on his side, and dust puffed up around him.

Behind Yakima, Derks and the two Romans continued to converse, but Yakima didn't hear what they were saying as he rolled another of the Gries bunch over the side of the stage and into the street next to the dead man's expired leader.

"*Reward?*" Rae Roman exclaimed suddenly. "We don't give our men rewards for doing their jobs! They're not *bounty hunters!*"

Yakima chuckled and rolled another body over the side of the stage and into the street. The crunch of boots and the *ching* of loose spurs sounded, and Yakima lifted his gaze to see the sheriff sauntering toward the coach, claw-hammer coat pulled back behind the butt of his ivory-gripped .45.

"Well, I'll be damned," Frank Rathbone said, peering down at the dead men. "Didn't know Gries was working this far west. Figured him to be strictly a west-Texas and eastern–New Mexico outlaw." He looked up at Yakima. "Where'd you bring 'em down?"

"Diamondback Station," the half-breed said with a grunt, and another carcass hit the street about five feet in front of Rathbone's polished black, high-heeled, undershot boots with large, cruel, silver-plated spurs.

The sheriff glanced over his shoulder at his two deputies still standing on the jail office porch, both holding rifles. Rathbone called for Silver to fetch the undertaker.

"Anyone hurt?" the sheriff asked, turning back to inspect the dead men. "Besides these fellas who done ate their last slices of apple pie, that is?"

"The girl at Diamondback Station. Lettie."

"Dead?" Rathbone squinted an eye as he stared up at Yakima, the tips of the first two fingers of both hands buried in the pockets of his brocade vest. "Or ruined?"

Yakima glanced at the tall, broad-nosed sheriff over the top of the brass rail and couldn't quite keep the irony out of his voice as he said, "Ruined for decent men, I reckon, Sheriff."

Rathbone nodded at that, apparently not having noted the subtle venom in the half-breed's reply—or having noted it but had chosen to ignore it—and lifted his head to inspect the *zopilotes*, ominous Mexican buzzards, preening on several of the tall facades around him. With a devilish glint in his gray-blue eyes, he slipped his .45 from its holster, rocked back the hammer, and squinted down the barrel.

The pistol barked loudly, echoing. One of the big, shaggy birds dropped from the top of the bank's facade to land with a rustling thud on the shake-shingled porch roof.

"Sheriff Rathbone!" Rae Roman admonished, stomping an exasperated foot on the bank's veranda, a look of supreme disgust on her haughty, regal features.

"That you over there, Miss Roman?" the sheriff said, walking around the back of the stage as he flipped the Colt's loading gate open and plucked the spent shell from the wheel. "Oh—I didn't know you was out here. That mess the half-breed rolled in ain't for a woman to see."

As Yakima climbed down the side of the stage facing the bank, the sheriff appeared from the back of the unloaded coach and plucked a fresh shell from his cartridge belt. "I do apologize for the noise."

"Not to mention a dead bird on my porch roof," Mr. Roman said, turning his anger-pinched eyes on the arrogant lawman. "What's the meaning of that? What about our ordinance against firearms being discharged within the town's limits?"

"Didn't see you, either, Roman." Rathbone thumbed the fresh shell into his Colt's wheel, closed the gate, and spun the cylinder. "I was just keepin' in trim with the forty-five. Wouldn't want the local law dog to get rusty, now, would you? Besides, there's vermin on the bank, Roman. Vermin on the roof, vermin in the street." He glanced at Yakima and gave a slow, meaningful grin. "*Sometimes* they're necessary."

Roman slid his glance between Yakima and the county sheriff. Derks stood to Yakima's left, the jehu continuing to hold his hat in his hands and to keep his eyes on the ground. Yakima only wanted to be dismissed for the day, so he could head over to a cantina for a girl and a cold beer. Aside from Derks, there were few Red Hill citizens whose company he suffered.

He preferred a cheap whore and then afterward to be alone. Since Faith, he could go weeks without a woman, without talking to anybody.

Mr. Roman only scowled as though befuddled by the situation.

Rae Roman glanced at her father, then, seeing the indecision in the man's eyes, hardened her jaws as she spoke to the local lawman. "Well, it is not acceptable to break your own city ordinance, Frank. Don't forget my father is also the mayor of this town."

She slid her cool, commanding glance back to her

driver and shotgun messenger, like a schoolmistress with two misbehaving boys who'd had to stay after class to clean chalkboards. The hostlers stood silently nearby, dully awaiting orders to lead the coach and team back to the barn.

"And, while I do appreciate the safe arrival of the strongbox, especially during these troubled times"— her eyes flicked toward the blood-smeared roof of the coach—"I see no reason to pay out rewards to men whom my father and I are already paying a reasonable wage."

"Forget the damn bounty, Miss Roman," Yakima grunted, wheeling. He grabbed Derks's arm and turned the oldster around, as well. "Come on, Avril—I'll buy you that drink I promised at Diamondback Station."

Derks glanced at Yakima warily as both men headed at an angle across the street, the old jehu a step behind Yakima.

"Say, there, breed," the sheriff said peevishly behind him. "Watch your tone. That's no way to speak to Miss Roman."

"Go to hell, Sheriff." Yakima couldn't help grinning. If they wanted his job, they could have it.

Rae Roman gasped. "Why, that savage!"

Yakima turned and pinched his hat brim to her, then continued toward the Queen of Hearts Saloon.

"Lawdy," Derks grumbled. "Law, Law, Law. . . ."

Several buzzards, now perched atop the stationary coach and looking down at the dead men in the street beside it, echoed the sentiment.

Chapter 5

When Rae Roman got home from the bank that afternoon, she had her and her father's housekeeper—a curiously sullen but capable and seemingly trustworthy Mexican woman—pour her a hot bath in the large copper tub.

The woman, Sumah, then steeped some tea and poured it into a bone china cup. When Sumah had cleaned up the kitchen and straightened Mr. Roman's study according to Rae's specific directions, Rae released the woman from further duties that day. She and her father wouldn't be having their traditional sit-down dinner because Mr. Roman had a meeting with the town council and would likely follow the meeting up with poker and God knew what else. Probably a soiled dove, which he was prone to do. Rae knew this by the stench that often followed him home.

When the Mexican woman had gone, Rae took her steaming teacup into her humble bedroom in the second story of her and her father's plain, frame, two-story house on the northern outskirts of Red Hill. She let her hair down, brushed it out, and got undressed, watching herself in the mirror as she did so. She was pushing twenty-eight, but she still had a good body.

She could tell not only from her own appraisal in the mirror but from the glances she drew from the men about town. She had nice full breasts and a flat belly, well-rounded hips, and strong legs. Her face hadn't yet been too badly weathered by the desert sun. Of course, none of those men who eyeballed her ever showed any serious interest, because she simply didn't invite it despite her father's protestations that she should—as he put it—let her hair down on occasion and maybe even smile at one of the male bank customers.

Especially one of the men from the wealthy ranches west of town. The owner of the Lazy 8 was a widower, after all. He had been for going on two years now, and word had it he was "on the prowl."

Rae chuffed now as, standing naked before her mirror, her hair shining down around her shoulders, she cupped her sloping breasts in her hands and flicked her thumbs across her nipples. She curled her nose.

No stockman would ever heft these in his hands, or run his parched lips across her mouth, toil between her legs. She was reserving her true affections for an eastern man, a gentleman. For when she could get back East to find one, that is. A man like the one she'd nearly married before her father wrote her, telling her that he'd gone broke—this was before he'd reclaimed some semblance of respectability as well as money and bought the Red Hill Bank—and that he could no longer afford for her to live "and frolic" in Philadelphia. She'd have to come West and put her expensive schooling to work by helping him in the bank as a bookkeeper.

Of course, the end of her father's wealth had been the end of her courtship with Stockard Brinkley. In eastern society circles, money married money. If you had no money, you had no respectability, and the Brinkley family quickly doused Stockard's passion for the suddenly down-at-heel Rae Roman, the charming, precocious if a bit conservative girl he'd met at the Academy of Music.

So here she was, she thought now as she stepped into the steaming copper tub, sank slowly down into the water that pleasantly burned the desert grit from her still-tender skin. Here she was in this hellhole called Red Hill, where the air constantly smelled of horses and latrines, and she could hear chickens squawking and pigs grunting at all hours of the day. At night, coyotes yammered so close to her bedroom window that she often woke thinking they were chewing their way into the house.

Here she was in Red Hill because her father had gambled away his small fortune on a Missouri riverboat. That had been the end of Rae's mother, who'd learned—and had been so enraged that she'd even let the bitter information slip to Rae—that during the same cruise Delbert Roman had been literally caught with his pants down by a bigmouthed business competitor in the opulent riverboat quarters of a noted woman of pleasure.

A month later, after word of the scandal spread, Rae's mother, Beatrice, was dead of a heart seizure.

And Roman called Rae out West, to Council Bluffs, which was where he'd been living at the time because he hadn't enough money to go elsewhere. Only enough to bring Rae out to subject her to the same brand of humiliation he was suffering. Although western humiliation was far less venomous than the eastern type. Out West, it seemed, everyone had a scandalous past. Everyone was on the make and on the run. Pride was a very rare and precious commodity.

But Rae Roman would not be running, hiding for much longer. She would leave here soon, when her game had played out. She'd head back East, with or without her father, and she'd return, if not to the life to which she'd been born, at least to one less squalid than the one she was living here. She'd find a man, maybe not one as moneyed as her beloved Stockard, but a man with enough financial backing that she could occasionally take in an opera and spread her picnic blanket in a grassy park under rich, green trees, and feel the soft eastern air caress her skin and make her young again.

She took her time soaping herself, caressing herself— God knew she would get no pleasure from one of the goatish men out here. Finally, she became frustrated by the act, having become heavy and morose under the weight of her loss. She truly had loved Stockard Brinkley, and not only because he'd been wealthy and handsome and enjoyed the opera and fine wine and well-played Bach, but because they'd been soul mates. He, unlike others, hadn't minded that she'd been born in the Midwest, in the small Iowa town in which her father had run first a farm supply tent, then a mercantile, and then, finally, a bona fide bank that had made him wealthy enough to send his daughter to an eastern finishing school.

Oh, what a horror her life had been when Stockard had jilted her, almost literally abandoning her at the altar.

Rae weakly dropped her fist to the side of the tub. It made a wet, squishing sound. She lowered her chin and heard herself sigh raggedly. She heard something else, then, too, a split second after the sigh.

Her head came up. She stared across her small room with the four-poster, canopied bed over which she kept a star quilt. As she pricked her ears, listening, a curious frown wrinkled the skin above the bridge of her long, pale nose.

From downstairs rose the dull squawk of a slow-opening door.

Rae turned her head to the side to call out the open door behind her, "Father? Home so soon?"

Silence.

Faintly, through the room's two darkening windows, one of which was partly open, she could hear the rumble of a distant wagon and the crowing of Mrs. Chipodie's rooster. She drew short, shallow breaths, feeling her pulse begin to quicken.

The back door off the kitchen had come open. She'd recognized the sound of the hinges. Maybe Sumah hadn't closed it. No. Rae remembered locking it just

before she'd headed upstairs. She always kept the
doors locked when she was here alone. There were
many, many depraved men in this town.

With a sudden, frightened gasp, knowing what could
happen to her if an intruder were indeed in the house,
Rae lurched up out of the water and stepped quickly
out of the tub. She grabbed a thick towel off the back
of a nearby chair, wrapped it about herself, tucking it
under her arms, then opened her bureau drawer. She
fished around under her silk undergarments, the last
of those she'd carried out here from the East—they
were threadbare and badly faded, but she couldn't bear
to part with them—until her hand came down on a
lump of cold steel.

She raised the small, silver-plated, pearl-gripped,
.32-caliber Smith & Wesson, liking how reassuring its
solid weight felt in her hand.

She padded barefoot to her open door and looked
down the hall toward the stairs. The green-papered
hall was lit by a single gas lamp bracketed to the left
wall. There were mostly shadows.

"Father? Is that you?"

Her voice sounded strange. Lonely. Desperate.

No response. She wasn't sure—her heart was beginning to thud in her ears—but she thought she heard
the squeak of a floorboard somewhere on the first
story. Squeezing the gun tightly in her right hand, Rae
turned at the top of the stairs, stared down for a moment, then, seeing no one below, started carefully down.
Her bare feet were silent, but the staircase groaned

beneath her weight, as did the railing until she removed her hand from it.

At the bottom, in the hall between the parlor and the formal dining room—if you could call it formal, she often thought with a silent scoff—she stopped and looked back toward the kitchen. The house was eerily quiet. She could hear only her heart beating in her chest and ears.

She held the gun partway out from her belly with one hand while she held the towel together at her left side, and walked slowly down the short hall and into the kitchen. She stopped just inside the kitchen door, and her eyes widened, the sharp light of fear glinting in them. Her lips pinched until they turned nearly white.

The door leading to the backyard was open.

She gave a silent gasp. Her heart fluttered. Her hand was sweaty around the neck of the gun handle.

She looked around the freshly scrubbed though simply laid out kitchen with the dry sink, cutting table, and four-burner range with the black flue doglegging up against the ceiling and then angling out the far wall to connect with the brick chimney outside.

"Is someone here?" Rae said, her voice thick and trembling.

She licked her lips and raised her voice. "Who's here?"

She heard only the rooster crowing and the breeze rustling the cottonwood in the backyard. The draft through the door chilled her still-damp body. She sucked a deep breath, bolted forward, grabbed the door, and slammed it closed. Taking the gun in her left hand now, she turned the key in the lock with her right hand.

She froze, looked down at the lock.

When she'd locked the door, she'd hung the key on the rack of brass hooks attached to the sideboard.

Rae's ears rang.

She felt the displaced air behind her before a hand snaked around her from behind and was clamped harshly across her mouth. It was a big hand, and the callused palm raked her lips, held her firmly against the man's broad chest. The other hand raked her breasts harshly, and she gritted her teeth against the pain.

The man laughed wickedly. "Hello, Rae. Been waitin' for me?"

She recognized the voice. Then Sheriff Frank Rathbone ripped the towel from her body with one hand, nuzzled her neck, raking her skin with his mustache, then laughed again as he picked her up in his arms.

"What do you say we have us some fun?"

"Goddamn you, Rathbone!" Rae squealed, reaching back to batter the man's head with her fists, dislodging his hat. "Put me down this instant!"

Rathbone laughed as he carried her back down the hall.

"Put me down or I'll scream!"

"Oh, I don't think you'll scream, Rae," Rathbone said mockingly as he started up the stairs. "I don't think you'd want anyone runnin' in here and seein' us together, learnin' what a wonderful partnership we've formed."

Upstairs, he tossed Rae onto her bed. She bounced, rose on her elbows, and scowled savagely at Rathbone. "I told you, you son of a bitch. That was the one and only time. And you *agreed*!"

Rathbone ripped his string tie from around his neck. His lust-bright eyes raked the exquisitely well-formed, naked woman sprawled before him. The fury in her eyes only stoked his desire.

"Yeah, well, I lied about that."

When Rathbone had taken his pleasure and rolled off her, Rae lay writhing with the aftereffects of the savage coupling.

Rathbone plucked a cigar off the bedside table and stuck it into his mouth. As he snapped a lucifer to life, Rae pushed up on her elbow and swatted the cigar from his lips. She pushed up farther and slapped the side of his head four times hard with her open hand. He dropped the match and looked at her, indignation in his eyes, his hair mussed, one ear glowing red.

"Hey, goddamnit. You can't tell me you didn't enjoy that!"

Rae hit him one more time, and Rathbone raised an elbow to defend himself, leaning out over the side of the bed, his eyes shocked, indignant.

"That's for your friend Gries!" she barked at him. "I thought you said the man was dependable."

She sat up, leaned back against the oak headboard, and drew the sheet and quilt over her chafed breasts. Her own hair was badly disheveled, hanging in tangles down both sides of her face and over her shoulders.

"Well, hell." Rathbone dropped a bare foot to the floor and mashed the match into the rug, making sure it was out. He leaned down to retrieve his cigar and poked it back into his mouth. "He was dependable. Hell, I ran with him once in the Brazos River country. He must've got overconfident. It happens."

"He got so overconfident that he got not only himself but his entire gang killed by one man."

Rathbone grabbed another stove match off the bedside table, and raked his thumbnail over the top of it. As it flamed to life, he glanced sidelong at Rae, who now sat with her arms crossed on her chest, a sour look in her eyes. "All right. I underestimated the abilities of yours and your old man's shotgun rider. What do you want me to say?"

"I want you to say that you're going to remedy the situation as quickly as possible." Rae turned her derisive gaze on the lawman. "That was a hefty amount of payroll money in that strongbox today, Frank. Not only would it have taken me a long, long ways away from here, the loss would have come very close to ruining my father."

Rathbone puffed smoke as he lit the cigar. "I thought we were going to run away together, conchita."

"Forget it." Rae waved the smoke away from her. With a wicked curse, she got up and tramped naked over to the room's single window, opened one side of the curtains, and raised the window to let the smoke out. "I've had about enough of you, Frank. You're a brute."

Rathbone grinned and raked her naked body with

his gaze. "You like it more than you let on. You got a lot of woman in you, Miss Roman. That woman don't get satisfied all that often."

"You're a whoremonger. I know where you spend your evenings."

"Yeah, well, they don't make demands. And they don't harp. Okay, forget the *us* in this equation." Blowing a thick cloud of smoke, he removed the cigar from his mouth and used it to poke it at Rae, who continued to stand at the window, deriving an undeniable satisfaction in displaying herself to this man who obviously appreciated her physical wares if little else about her. "I'd like to know just one thing," he said. "Aside from greed, why is it you want to ruin your old man so bad?"

"That's personal."

Rathbone glared at her through his wafting cigar smoke lit by the room's single burning lamp.

"Suffice it to say, he's a man not unlike yourself. It's time he was made to suffer the way he's made others suffer, including his wife and daughter. Once he no longer has the bank, his future will be up to him. He can either accompany me back East or stay here and swamp saloons."

"You're a piece of work, Miss Roman." Rathbone's grin brightened again. His eyes roamed over her like groping hands.

"One more good holdup should finish him."

Having had enough of Rathbone's lecherous eyes, she pulled a wrap off a wall hook, drew the garment around her shoulders, and plucked a brush off her dresser. Beginning to brush her hair, she said, "The Lazy-Eight payroll would have done the trick, but the holdings of the next strongbox might even be more lucrative yet. The Sand Creek outfit sold a horse herd in San Angelo last week, and the funds were wired to Apache Gap. The cash money will be sent here either on the next stage or on the one following. If that money is stolen, I've little doubt that the Sand Creek manager will turn his business over to a bank in Tucson. It'll be farther away, but he's already threatened the move if we keep having holdup problems. He lost a rather large payroll just last year, and it wasn't insured."

"You got her all figured out."

Rae wheeled toward the bed, half consciously allowing her wrap to open. "How are you going to handle it?"

"Don't worry. I have more friends in the Coronados, Miss Roman. Gries was only one of many."

"And the half-breed?"

"Don't you worry about the dirt-worshippin' savage. He might've already been taken care of, in fact." Rathbone drew deep on the cigar. His eyes crossed as he ogled the woman before him once more. "We got time for one more go-round?"

"Certainly not," Rae said, giving her back to the man. She resumed brushing her hair.

"I think we do."

Rathbone stepped down from the bed and strode slowly toward her—a stalking mountain lion. Rae watched him in the mirror and couldn't help smiling inside as the predator headed into her trap.

Chapter 6

Yakima sipped his second beer of the night, one he'd been nursing for nearly an hour as a preventive measure against his getting drunk and going "savage" on the saloon, which he was wont to do.

Even he himself admitted it though he hated the stereotype. He didn't think it was so much his Indian blood as white men and full bloods alike regarding him like something that a buzzard had deposited on a boardwalk. Whatever the case, he drained his second beer and set his poker hand on the table before him, where the five other men he'd been playing with for the past three hours could see it.

"Straight flush." The half-breed ran his hands back through his hair and looked at the other men's hands as they laid them down on the table.

Derks had a flush, the man straight across the round table from Yakima had a straight, and the man to his right had three of a kind. Yakima's hand won.

"Goddamnit," said the cow-eyed, bowler-hatted man to his right. He had a brown-eyed blond in a skimpy red and black dress standing behind him whom he'd ordered to knead the game-stress from his shoulders. "That's the third hand in a row you won."

Yakima scooped the pot into his hands—about seventy-five dollars to round off the top of the small pile before him. About a hundred and seventy-five dollars' worth. Not a great haul but impressive considering he'd played only when he had a modicum of disposable cash on hand or a somewhat steady job. He wasn't sure how steady his current job was, or if he even had one now, but he'd built up a few dollars to play poker with when he had nothing else to do.

And he had some money to spend on a woman.

He separated the coins from the folding money on the table before him. "Can I help it if you fellas play like drunk cow pen swampers?" He sighed and folded the small pile of greenbacks and stuffed it into the breast pocket of his shirt. "You had several straights you could've filled into a flush, amigo."

"Don't tell me how to play poker, mister." The cow-eyed man stared hard at Yakima as the girl continued kneading his shoulders but whose bored expression was beginning to change to one of nervousness as she glanced down at the man before her. "It just so happens I was building up my straight before you called."

"If you're gonna start cryin' about your straight," Yakima said, "I hope you'll retire to the nearest rain barrel, *mister*."

Yakima stood. He'd sat out one round to return his saddlebags and rifle to his rented room, and to check on his stabled stallion, so he stood freely now and donned his hat, leaned forward, and removed one of the girl's hands from the cow-eyed man's shoulder.

"Hey, she's mine tonight, breed," the cow-eyed man said.

He was glowering now, puffing his plump cheeks out. He'd had several shots to go with his own two beers, and while he'd been holding it so far, the anger was beginning to ignite the coffin varnish. Yakima knew how that felt, but he'd be damned if he'd walk cautiously around this tinhorn.

"Did you pay her yet?"

The cow-eyed man shook his head. "I was just about to do that."

Yakima had had a feeling the girl hadn't been paid. He proffered a ten-dollar gold piece now, and she grabbed it while casting a faint look of defiance at the cow-eyed gent. To Yakima's left, Avril Derks grinned as he lifted a shot glass to his lips.

Yakima slid an arm around the girl's waist and began leading her toward the stairs rising at the room's rear.

"Yakima," Derks warned in his low, gravelly voice.

Yakima wheeled, saw the gun the cow-eyed man was just beginning to swing up and around, and kicked out with his right foot. The toe of the half-breed's moccasin connected with the gun.

"*Yow!*" the cow-eyed man exclaimed as the gun was torn from his hand. It rose in an arc to bounce off the ceiling and land atop a wagon wheel chandelier several feet away. It got hung up there in the spoke, and stayed.

The cow-eyed man clutched his right hand in his left palm, then, glaring up at Yakima, bolted out of his chair and swung his right fist like a sledge. Calmly, Yakima grabbed the man's fist in his left hand. It stopped the punch cold. Yakima held on to the fist and squeezed.

His hand was large and strong, and his knuckles bulged and turned white as he continued squeezing until the cow-eyed man's own knuckles began to crackle and pop. Yakima's expression was stony as he held the cow-eyed man's exasperated gaze, the man's own eyes sharpening, the corners crinkling as bones started to crack.

Slowly, Yakima stepped forward. Continuing to grind away at the man's hand, he pushed the man straight back into his chair. He released the hand. The sudden release of pressure hurt the cow-eyed man even more, and his lower jaw dropped as he screamed and took the battered hand in the other one and leaned forward, cursing.

The dozen or so other drinkers and cardplayers and sporting girls were silent and staring toward Yakima and the cow-eyed gent. Derks was leaning forward on the table, chin low, his rheumy brown, white-spotted eyes bemused.

Yakima turned to the girl, who stood staring at the cow-eyed gent in shock, and crooked his arm out for her once more. Slowly, dumbly, she hooked her arm through it, and Yakima resumed his trek toward the back of the silent room and mounted the stairs.

He and the girl stopped at a door on the second story. The girl fished a key out of her corset and opened the door. Yakima walked in ahead of her, and she pushed the door closed and, folding her arms behind her, pressed her back to it. Her eyes were anxious.

"You done made a bad enemy in Clell Ogden, mister."

"Call me Yakima. And he done made a bad enemy in me, Miss . . ."

"Janelle. With two *l*s and an *e* at the end."

"Miss Janelle with two *l*s and an *e*." Yakima glanced at the porcelain-lined bathtub on the rope rug between the pedestal bed and the mirrored dresser. The water was filmy, with a few diaphanous bubbles riding its surface. "That yours, Miss Janelle?"

She regarded him darkly, drawing the corners of her mouth down, still edgy over Clell Ogden. She glanced at the water, frowned, and nodded uncertainly. "The houseboy hasn't thrown it out yet."

"Good for him."

"I used it," she said, impatience in her voice.

"Miss Janelle," he said, tossing his hat on the dresser and unbuttoning his shirt, "you're talkin' to a man whose last bath was in a horse trough."

He skinned out of his clothes so fast, leaving them inside out and piled up between the tub and the bed, that the girl sank back against the dresser, chuckling incredulously. Yakima stepped into the tub, dropped into the water, sucked a deep breath dramatically, and submerged his entire body. He came up blowing and shaking his long hair, water flying in all directions and the girl giving a scream as she jerked back from the shower.

"You're crazy, Yakima!"

"Been called far worse. Come on over here and scrub my back for me, will you?"

She grabbed the long-handled brush propped against the outside of the tub, lathered the bristles from the butter-colored cake in the soap rack, and leaned a hip on the edge of the tub as she went to work, scrubbing his back.

"Harder," Yakima said, raising his knees and leaning forward.

The girl scrubbed harder.

"Come on, Miss Janelle," he encouraged. "Put some gut into it!"

"I'm gonna scrape the hide right off your back!" she said, grunting and laughing as she lowered her head and put some muscle into the scrub job.

"Ah, that's better," he said when she finished.

She straightened and glanced over her shoulder at him as she walked over to the bed and began untying her corset. "Where you from, anyway?"

Yakima leaned back in the tub, resting his arms on the sides. "Here. There. Everywhere."

"I done heard that story before."

"You?"

Janelle laughed. He liked her laugh. It was husky and unbridled and bespoke a jolly soul despite what was obviously not an altogether easy existence. If her life were easy, she wouldn't be here, kneading the shoulders of men like Clell Ogden even before she'd been paid to do it. Or hauling smelly half-breed shotgun messengers to her room, Yakima thought.

"Tucson by way of Nevada."

"Follow a man here, did you?"

She removed the corset, tossed it on the floor, then sat down on the bed, and, with her pert breasts swinging free, began unsnapping her garter belts and rolling her long black silk stockings down her long, pale legs.

"I thought he was a man." Janelle shook her head and pooched out her lips. "But he was just a boy," she said fatefully.

When she'd stripped, she draped a sheer, flowered wrap over her shoulders though it hid nothing at all, and, pulling the pins from her hair and letting it tumble across her slender shoulders, she walked over to the dresser. She picked up a wood-handled brush and began brushing out her hair, throwing her head back and tossing her hair behind her shoulders and reaching behind her head to groom the back.

Yakima watched her, and suddenly he was watching Faith brush her long, thick blond hair out while standing in the bedroom of their cabin. A fist tightened around his throat as he watched the girl's hair fly back over her pale shoulders and slide across the slender back, the sheen in the locks growing with each stroke of the brush.

Through the wrap he could see several tiny moles

and blemishes, and one became the one that Faith had had on the edge of her right shoulder. A blemish, not a mole. A small red birthmark in the shape of a ragged-edged summer cloud. He could see Faith's shoulder blades flexing through the wrap, hear her voice now as she asked him which horse he was going to gentle today—the grulla stallion or the sorrel filly?

"Gonna work some more o' the green out of that grulla."

The girl turned to him. Yakima felt his eyes hood with a frown. Now it was not Faith looking at him but Mrs. Holgate from the stage. And he realized that beyond that both women were blond, they looked only vaguely similar. Faith's features had been slightly longer, while Beth Holgate's face was rounder, her cheeks a little fuller, and fewer lines radiated from the outside corners, making her look less shrewd but also less passionate. Beth Holgate's eyes were more innocent and demure, whereas Faith's, owing to the fact of her having escaped from the savage pimp and roadhouse manager Bill Thornton in northern Colorado, had a sharp jadedness to them that took nothing away from her overall beauty.

Beth Holgate stared at Yakima now, holding her brush frozen against the side of her head. The skin above the bridge of her nose wrinkled, and she tilted her head to one side. "What was that, Yakima?"

He realized he'd spoken that last about the horses out loud.

"I said." He cleared his throat and realized with an embarrassed flush that his eyes were wet and that his heart was swollen to twice its normal size. "I said you're gonna brush the color right out of your hair, you keep goin' at it that hard."

Her frown deepened. She set the brush on the dresser and rested an elbow on it as well, turning toward him and hooking one foot over the other, squinting one eye cautiously. "You're not crazy, are you, Yakima?"

He grinned. "Even crazy men need to make the mattress sing with a good-looking girl, now an' then."

He pushed up out of the tub, water rippling off his broad, dark red frame, and stepped onto the floor. The girl tossed him a towel, and he quickly dried himself, rubbing the towel hard through his hair, then walked over and picked her up in his arms. She gasped with a start at the ease with which he'd scooped her up, and wrapped her arms around his neck.

There was fear in her eyes. But also a faintly skeptical delight.

He kissed her.

She returned the kiss, running her hands through his long, wet hair, and he felt her body slowly going pliant in his embrace. He kissed her a long time, holding her there against him.

When he pulled his head away, she was leaning her head far back, eyes closed, lips still parted and waiting. Her pale, smooth hands now rested slack against his shoulders. Her small breasts stood out firmly from her chest, the budlike nipples pebbled, waiting.

Yakima laid her gently down on the bed, and he spread her legs with his own. He lowered his head, pressed his lips to her long, smooth thigh, then her knee. She reached down between his legs, and wrapped her hand around him. She smiled, stretching her pink lips wide.

Yakima grunted.

She whimpered as he mounted her.

Chapter 7

Yakima fell asleep in the girl's bed and didn't awake until a distant pistol shot flatted out briefly across the slumbering town.

There was no threat in the distance-muffled blast. The shot had likely been triggered by a pie-eyed cow-puncher leaving a cantina on the Mexican end of Red Hill, giving one last salute to the girl he'd been reveling with as he started back toward his ranch.

The girl groaned and rolled over as Yakima climbed out of the bed, wincing at the ache in his haunches and the tightness in the backs of his legs. Derks padded his side of the hard wooden stagecoach seat with a heavy horse blanket. Maybe Yakima should try that. If he still had a job. He reckoned he'd find that out sometime in the next day or so, before the stage made another run the day after tomorrow.

He dressed quietly in the dark room lit only by a wedge of moon that shone gauzily through the window curtains, hovering over the ridge humping darkly north of the town, blotting out the stars. He glanced at the girl as he donned his hat. She lay sprawled on her back, one bare knee poking out from beneath the blankets. Her head was turned away from him, her hair fanned out across the pillow.

What was it about a woman sleeping that warmed a man?

He'd thought that he and Faith would have a life-time of slumbering nights together in the protective shadow of Mount Bailey. But then Thornton had sent bounty hunters to retrieve his prized whore, and Yakima hadn't been able to save her. She'd died in Yakima's arms in Colorado, with Thornton's own rancid carcass burning up in the roadhouse behind him, in a fire so large it had made the night look like day.

More than Thornton had burned up in that road-house.

All were ashes now. . . .

Yakima left the room and strode quietly down the Queen of Heart's outside stairs. When he gained the backyard that was as dark as the inside of a glove, he tramped around to the front and stood with a shoulder against the building's front corner, digging into his shirt pocket for his makings sack. Slowly, listening to the night sounds and enjoying the caress of the high-desert chill, he built a quirley.

The town was quiet. He could see the lit windows of a few saloons up and down the street, but the only sound was the yammering of coyotes on the surrounding red ridges that had given the town its name. A slight breeze rattled paper refuse in the alley gap be-

hind him, shepherded a tumbleweed across the street
before him.

Yakima struck a match on his shell belt, touched it
to the quirley. He took a couple of deep puffs, ignoring the remembered chastising remarks of his old mentor, George, who'd told him that tobacco, like women,
dulled the senses and weakened the lungs.

George had been a Shaolin monk, though when
Yakima had known him, they'd been laying rails together in Kansas or eastern Colorado—they'd never
really known where they were at any given time, and
hadn't cared—making their way west. George had
had a Chinese name, but no one in this hemisphere
could pronounce it, including Yakima, so the old
monk had simply settled for George. In their spare
time, George had taught Yakima how to fight in the
Eastern manner, using the mind as well as the body to
hone his limbs into deadly armaments every bit as
effective at close range as a Colt or a bowie knife.

Yakima took another deep drag on the quirley, then
held the half smoked, tightly rolled cylinder up to
inspect it. He scowled, dropped the stub in the dirt.
"Damn it, George."

One stormy night, he'd found George hanging from
a cottonwood after winning a large poker pot at an
end-of-line camp. The monk had been beaten, stripped,
and lynched. Dangerous for a slant-eye to win too big
a poker pot when playing with white men. Yakima
had cut the old man down and, weeping openly, buried him in a wash and covered his grave with stones

large enough to hold the wolves and bobcats at bay, or at least to make them work for the monk's old bones.

Then he'd hunted the men who'd treated his friend and mentor so shabbily, and had killed them without mercy, and he'd cursed over their torn and bloody carcasses.

Killing had gotten a whole lot easier after that. . . .

Yakima stepped out from under the saloon's porch roof, noting that the windows were dark. The Queen of Hearts must be the only watering hole in town that closed before three or when the last customer left. Hooking his thumbs behind his cartridge belts, he headed up the street, habitually staying close to the one side, in this case the south side, where the building shadows would hide him. He had more than his share of enemies on the frontier, and he hadn't forgotten about the one he'd made earlier in the evening in the cow-eyed person of Clell Ogden.

The name had no sooner flitted across the half-breed's mind than a sound rose behind him. It had been too faint for Yakima's brain to identify it but loud enough for his ears to pick it up. He swung around, stepping behind an awning support post and dropping his right hand to the stag-horn grips of his low-slung Colt .44.

The street was wide on this side of town, the sides uneven, a couple of the buildings widely spaced. There was a warehouse on the right, kitty-corner from the Queen of Hearts. Beyond it a mud brick saddle shop with a wooden shed attached to the front. Between the warehouse and the saddlery, a dark shadow, nearly blending with the shadows of the buildings, moved into the gap between the structures. There was the briefest, dull blue flash, like starlight or moonlight reflected off steel.

Yakima closed his hand around the Colt's grips but left the gun in its holster. He stood farther back behind the post, peering out around the left side of it. From behind him, on the east side of town, there came the occasional sounds of drinking, laughing men and the muffled thuds of horses. Otherwise, there was only the breeze rustling trash and tumbleweeds and making shingle chains beneath boardwalk awnings squawk.

A cat stole out from beneath the high loading dock fronting the warehouse. Keeping low to the ground, the cat crept out into the street, making for the alley on the far side of the Queen of Hearts. Yakima watched the cat. It made the alley without looking harassed. The half-breed removed his hand from his pistol grips.

Maybe just blown trash that he'd spied back there. Or his overcautious imagination.

With one more, slow look around the street behind him, he turned around and resumed his journey toward his boardinghouse, where he shared a room with Derks. He hadn't walked much over a block before he drew up again abruptly, and turned toward the mercantile on his right. He heard a wet sound, and now his eyes adjusted to the dark front of the store. A woman sat on the broad wooden steps about halfway between the boardwalk and the door. A slender, blond figure in what appeared a cream housecoat and slippers.

Just as Yakima noted that her head was down, it came up quickly, and while he couldn't distinguish the features of her face, he heard her gasp.

"Oh, please," she said, and began to jerk awkwardly to her feet and turn toward the store.

Yakima stepped forward. "Mrs. Holgate."

She stopped, turned back to him. "Mr. Henry?"

"Is there anything I can do for you?"

It was her turn to answer a question with a question. "What are you doing out here? I thought everyone was asleep on this end of town."

Yakima shrugged. "I was heading that way. I reckon you haven't headed to bed yet yourself." Best to talk around the reason she'd been sitting out here, crying. He didn't want to pry into something that wasn't his business, though he couldn't help feeling both curious and concerned. "Your new situation . . . uh . . . treating you all right?"

"My situation?" She chuckled without mirth and sat back down on the steps, fiddling with a kerchief in her hands. "You mean my marriage to Mr. Seagraves?"

"That was a might quick, wasn't it?"

She continued to fiddle with the handkerchief as she sniffed, then brushed her wrist across her cheek that he could see now, having moved closer to her, was wet. "Mr. Seagraves invited Pastor Hoagland over this evening. Mrs. Hoagland was our witness. If Calvin and I were going to stay here—well, it wouldn't have been appropriate for Mr. Seagraves and myself to retire under the same roof together unless, of course, we were man and wife."

There'd been a dry, ironic tone in her emotion-husky voice.

Yakima set a moccasin up on the edge of the board-walk and poked his hat back off his forehead. He knew the question was impertinent, but he asked it, anyway. "I 'spect you didn't know the man before traveling out here."

"He had been a friend of my brother's. They owned a saloon together in Kansas. When Paul died—my husband—I was lost, Mr. Henry. A woman with a young boy to raise on her own . . ." She shook her head and, looking down at the cloth in her hands, continued softly. "I saw the ad in the Grand Island newspaper, and Mr. Seagraves and I exchanged letters for a while. Then he proposed."

"And you accepted," Yakima said. "And now you're out here on your wedding night. . . ." He let the sentence trail off, then hardened his voice slightly. "Did he hurt you, Mrs. Holgate? I mean . . . Seagraves."

She looked up at him suddenly. "Oh, not at all. No."

"The boy?"

"No." Mrs. Seagraves drew her wrap tighter about her shoulders, sniffed, and glanced behind her as though to make sure no one was observing her from one of the store's dark windows. Yakima assumed the living quarters was on the second floor of the broad building, the big sign over the facade announcing simply SEAGRAVES. "He's just rather brusque with Calvin.

He doesn't so much speak to my son as lecture him." She shook her head suddenly, embarrassed. "I'm making too much out of this, Mr. Henry."

"Yakima."

She looked up at him again. "Yakima." She lowered her eyes once more and drew her shoulders together as though chilled. "The situation is just so new to both Calvin and me. You see, Calvin and my husband, Paul, were very close. Calvin remembers his father quite clearly, and misses him very much. Paul was not a perfect man, but he was a loving husband and father."

She paused, took a deep breath, and set one of her slippered feet atop the other. "Mr. Seagraves and I will grow together in time, and he'll grow to love my son, just as Calvin will grow to love Mr. Seagraves and accept him as his father."

"I'm sorry, ma'am," Yakima said, not knowing what else to say. "But I reckon you're right about that." She looked so small and lonely, sitting there on the steps of the sprawling mercantile, that he suddenly found himself leaning forward and placing his right hand over both of hers and giving them a reassuring squeeze. "If there's anything I can do, you let me know."

She looked at his hand atop hers, then lifted her gaze to his. She nodded and tried a smile.

"Thank you, Mr. Hen—" Her smile broadened. "Ya-kima." She canted her head to one side, narrowing her eyes pleasantly. "Won't you please call me Beth?"

He pinched his hat brim to her. "You best go inside, Beth. It's gettin' chilly out here, and"—he glanced along the street—"it may not be safe."

She stood. Her hair blew around her shoulders in a chill gust of breeze. "Good night, Yakima."

"Night, Beth."

She rose and walked slowly up the steps and grabbed the door handle. Glancing once more over her shoulder, she opened the door and went inside.

Yakima adjusted the gun on his hip as he looked up and down the street, and then continued his trek westward, wondering why everything had to be so goddamn hard for everybody. He took a well-worn shortcut path through the high-desert scrub, heading for the boardinghouse that stood with a few other rough-hewn buildings, separated from the main part of Red Hill by a narrow dry wash called Bayonet Creek.

He came to the bank overlooking the wash, and started down. Deciding he'd like to sit on a rock and gather a little wool, to clear the cobwebs before continuing to the boardinghouse, he pulled back from the wash and started turning toward the rock on the path's right side.

There was a small red flash on the other side of the wash.

A pistol cracked.

The bullet kissed Yakima's left cheek and creased his ear before barking into a paloverde tree to his left. Yakima dove forward, hit the bottom of the wash on his right shoulder, and rolled, clawing his Colt from its holster and jerking back the hammer.

Chapter 8

Yakima triggered a shot where he'd seen the red flash, then lurched off his moccasined heels and dove behind a nest of rocks and driftwood humped in the middle of the wash.

As he rolled once more, a veritable fusillade opened up on the wash's opposite bank, about thirty yards down from Yakima's position. Two guns, possibly three, ripped the night open as they flashed in the darkness and hammered the nest of rocks mercilessly, spraying shards and wood slivers in all directions.

As the gunmen continued to pepper the backside of his cover with lead, Yakima crawled belly-down to the right corner of the rock mound and inched a look around the side. There were two shooters, he decided. Two sets of flashes from the scrub on the far side of the wash, positioned about ten feet apart.

A slug thudded into the sand and gravel about a foot in front of him, spraying grit. He jerked his head back behind his cover and furiously ground his teeth. Sitting up a little, pressing his back against the rocks, he waited for the bushwhackers to run out of lead. When their fire dwindled, Yakima jerked his head and arm around the side of the rocks, aimed at where he'd seen the two flashes, and squeezed the trigger.

The Colt roared and danced in his hands, flames stabbing from the maw. He fired three shots at each spot he'd seen the gun flashes; then, listening to his own echoes dwindle over the wash, he pulled back behind the rocks and flicked his loading gate open. He could hear the rustle and crackle of brush as the two shooters scurried around.

"I'm hit," one man grunted just loudly enough for Yakima to hear.

The scurrying continued, dwindling off up the side of the wash.

Yakima had shaken all six of his spent cartridges from the Colt's wheel and replaced them with fresh in less than twenty seconds. Now, as the bushwhackers ran off, he rose to his knees and emptied the gun once more, aiming farther up the wash, his gray powder smoke wafting around him.

When he'd squeezed off the last shot, silence closed down over the wash once more. He smelled burned cordite and hot brass. The stars twinkled brightly. Somewhere behind him, in the main part of town, a dog barked wildly.

Fury boiled in the half-breed's veins. He squeezed the pistol in one hand and clenched his other fist as he shouted, "Come on back here, you yellow-livered sons o' bitches. Face me like *men*!"

Standing there, eyes burning, he reloaded. Faintly,

he heard the thuds of two galloping horses, the rattle of bridle chains. Soon there was only the echoing din of the dog again.

"Cowards," Yakima growled, looking around cautiously.

Determining that he was alone out here now but keeping his ears pricked, he holstered the .44 and climbed up out of the wash via the well-worn path. He followed the path for another fifty yards, gravel crunching softly beneath his moccasins. The motley buildings of this leg of Red Hill rose before him—four tall wooden structures and a few adobe brick dwellings with attached stock pens.

He made his way around a goat pen, the goats' eyes following him warily, and crossed the rutted, red dirt trace to the shabby three-story house whose shingle announced MA PRATE'S ROOMS—$1 INCLUDING BREAKFAST. Beneath the larger sign was a smaller one: CLEAN AND BEDBUG FREE! There was more: TAROT READINGS—PREPARE FOR YOUR FUTURE!

The place had started out as a simple frame shack, but it had been added onto so many times it looked like a train that had tumbled down a steep cliff. He walked up to the small porch. A shadow filled the window in the door's curtained upper panel. As Yakima reached for the knob, the shadow turned away and he saw the bulky figure of Ma Prate ambling back toward a couple of oil lamps bracketed on the walls around her small desk beneath the stairs.

Yakima went in and, obeying the admonishing sign tacked to the foyer wall, wiped his boots off on the rope rug in front of the door. He could smell Ma's sickly sweet perfume. She said as she turned toward her desk, "What was all that shootin' about, Yakima Henry?"

Ma hailed from Springfield, Missouri, and had the slow, rolling accent of that woodsy, humid country with a still in every boggy hollow. Every shelf and piece of furniture in the small lobby beneath the stairs was adorned with one of Ma's homemade, elaborately costumed dolls. She seemed to be working on one constantly; she had the outfit of one spread out across her puncheon-topped, red-curtained desk now, with a small sewing kit spilling needles and thread nearby.

Yakima doffed his hat, ran his hands through his hair. "Someone musta thought I needed a lead bath. I reckon they didn't know I'd taken a real one just a few hours ago."

"Shoulda known that clatter involved you," Ma said with mild reproof. She dropped her hefty, gingham-dressed bulk into her swivel chair behind the desk, the top of her piled red hair brushing the wainscoted staircase angling just above her head. "You're a trouble-courtin' man, just like my late husband, Devlin. Follows you around like a hungry cur."

"Better that cur followed me and Devlin, 'stead of the other way around." Yakima set his fists on the edge of her desk, leaning toward her and grinning.

He liked the woman's earthy honesty. There was warmth in her character that was rare in most of the people he'd known. She'd been giving him seven kinds of hell since he'd started renting a room from her, and yet he felt she liked him, maybe even felt an affinity with him.

"You be careful around here." Ma sat sideways to the desk, keeping her eyes on the corncob pipe she was filling from a rawhide tobacco pouch. "Men like you don't last long. I heard from the undertaker's hired man you came in with five dead men riding the top of the stage this afternoon."

"They tried to hold us up."

"Makes no never mind." She tossed a blue hand-kerchief across the desk and indicated the bullet burns on his cheek and ear.

"What's that supposed to mean?" Yakima dabbed at the burns with the cloth.

Ma had stuck the pipe into her mouth, but now she removed it and looked up at him. "Your stars are different from most folks'. Trouble follows you the way bad luck follows an owl. Have you seen a large gathering of raptors lately?"

Yakima chuckled. "Buzzards followed the stage into town."

Ma shook her head darkly, holding the pipe in front of her mouth. "That's the worst kind of luck. When death birds shadow a man, he's in for a long, hard run."

"What was I supposed to do—hand over the strong-box to Gries and his boys and wish him luck spending it down in Monterrey?"

"I'm just telling you that your stars are lined up wrong, and this ain't a good place for a man with bad stars showing. I'll read your palm if you want me to."

"No, thanks." Yakima saw one of Ma's dolls staring down at him from a shelf on his right—a pointed-nosed little man in a court jester's costume, with bells adorning the long tows of his green felt shoes. The beady black eyes seemed to bore through Yakima, flashing red as pistol shots in the lantern light.

"Reckon I'll head up to bed." He dropped the blood-spotted handkerchief down on the desk and started turning toward the stairs.

Ma sat back in her squawky chair and lit her pipe. Between smoke puffs, she said, "Where'd you have your bath, Yakima?"

Yakima stopped at the bottom of the stairs, his hand atop the carved wolf's head newel post. "Why? You'll just read something dark into it."

Ma Prate hiked a shoulder, a look of bemused contentment on her face as she continued to puff her pipe to life. "An old woman gets curious, that's all. Call it snoopy. Can't do much more than snoop anymore," she added with a plaintive sigh.

"Janelle."

Ma nodded approvingly. "The new girl at the Queen of Hearts. How was she?"

"Right spry."

"Enjoyed her, did you?"

"What's not to enjoy?" Yakima narrowed an eye. "Why are you so interested in my cavortin's."

"I don't know," Ma said, sitting back in her chair,

puffing her pipe and staring up at him, her eyes faintly devilish. "I used to be partial to men with the wild savage in 'em, I reckon. My Devlin was Choctaw. Full-blood. If'n I was about thirty years younger, Yakima Henry . . ."

She let her voice trail off, blinking her eyes slowly.

"We'd be keeping your other boarders up nights." Yakima winked at the woman, then turned and started up the stairs.

"Yakima?"

He stopped on the first landing and turned back to her.

"You got a weakness for women. I ain't sayin' that's bad or good. I'm just sayin' you got it. You know that, but mind it. Don't let your guard down." Ma removed the pipe from her mouth and stared up at Yakima darkly. "I was tossing my cards around today, and some came up with the face of a half-breed Indian from the northern plains on 'em. The snake woman, a wretched fornicator and devil worshipper, turned up just behind it. For this man, the cards told of death birds, deceitful women, and hard luck here in Red Hill."

"Deceitful women, eh? You tell me one who ain't deceptive, and I'll blow a horse out runnin' her down."

Yakima chuckled and headed on up the stairs.

Ma slowly, pensively puffed her pipe.

The second-story hall smelled of sweat and tobacco. Snores resounded in rooms off both sides of the hall. Ma catered mostly to retired men with nowhere to go, and traveling stockmen and drummers.

Derks had left the door of his and Yakima's room unlocked. Yakima turned the knob, stepped into the small, cramped room furnished with two beds rammed against opposite walls, and a few other sticks of badly worn furniture. The oil lamp on the upended apple crate beside the jehu's bed was lit. Derks was awake, propped on one arm and looking toward the door. The light shone in his milky brown eyes.

Yakima closed the door and turned the key in the lock. "What're you doin' awake?"

"Just waitin' to see if I was gonna have to spend my day off tomorrow lookin' for a new shotgunner."

"Close."

"Ogden?"

"Most likely him and some hunk of human dung he fished out of the nearest privy pit."

Derks yawned. He punched his pillow, laid his head back on it, and turned toward the wall. "Well, good night."

Yakima went over to the washstand, filled the pitcher from a bucket on the floor, intending to clean the bullet burns on his cheek and ear. "Don't you lose any sleep worrying about me."

Derks snored.

Deputies Cordovan Stall and Lonnie Silver trotted their horses up to the hitch rack of the Red Hill Sheriff's Office, and checked their mounts down in front of the stoop on which Sheriff Frank Rathbone stood smoking a black cheroot.

Rathbone took a deep drag off the cigar, let the smoke slither out his broad nostrils. "You get it done?"

The deputies glanced at each other. Both wore high-crowned hats and dusters. Van Stall was a big, bearded man who wore his hair in a ponytail down his back. Silver was a half-Mex from Silver City—a short, wiry man, all muscle and sinew, with a killer's dark eyes and a straggly mustache and goatee. His right arm hung taut against his side. Rathbone now saw a stain on the upper half of that arm.

"Bad case of misfortune, boss." Stall stepped down from his saddle.

Rathbone curled his upper lip. "What the hell does that mean—bad case of misfortune? Christ, I'm gonna hear bad news, ain't I?"

"I had him dead to rights," Silver said, swinging smoothly down from his ornate Spanish saddle in spite of his wounded wing. "But he pulled back suddenly, and my shot went wide. It was pretty much over after that. That son of a bitch is harder to kill than the bobcats I used to hunt in the Coronados."

Rathbone studied both his deputies shrewdly. "When I hired you two, you assured me I was hiring the best."

"Hell, boss," Stall said, throwing out an arm in supplication. "We was—"

Rathbone cut him off, removing his cheroot to study the burning coal. "Get this inept bastard over to Doc Mangan's, have him sewed up good. We're gonna have us a busy week. Busier now that you went and made a mess of things tonight. I'd hate to know how you'd make out facing this man straight-on if you can't even kill him from bushwhack."

Both men shared another dark glance, then started to turn away, leading their horses.

"When you're done at the doc's, you both have night duty. I'm right tired tonight. I think I'll go on over to my digs and get me a long night's sleep." The sheriff grinned with mockery, then stepped down off the stoop, turned, and walked around the side of the building.

His smile dwindled. He'd assured Rae that the savage would be taken care of tonight. She'd find out soon that the job had been botched. Rathbone ground his teeth together as he moved out past the rear of the jailhouse, angling left toward the Stockmen's House Hotel and Saloon, where he kept a set of rooms.

If Stall and Silver had been his last pair of deputies, he'd have no trouble getting shed of them. But these two were good. Damn good. Better than any other men he'd worked with here in Red Hill, and if he put a bullet through each of their heads while they slept— or hired someone to do it—he'd likely never find their equal. True, they'd botched this job, but they'd done well on the holdups, keeping their faces covered so no one could identify them and also making sure that Rathbone got a half cut of the loot they and the other men were able to haul down.

He hadn't sent them out on the last job because he'd owed Gries a favor, and the desperado from Texas hadn't wanted any men he didn't know riding along with him. Even Rathbone's men. He had, however, assured the Red Hill sheriff that he'd get his cut—a cut that Rathbone was obligated to split, of course, with Rae Roman. Rathbone had trusted Gries to not only take the strongbox but to follow through with the agreed upon split.

That had gone sour, too. The strongbox was sitting, safe and sound, in the vault of the Red Hill Bank & Trust.

All because of the half-breed.

As Rathbone walked up the steps of the Stockmen's House, he ground his cigar out angrily on a white porch post. The half-breed needed a bullet in the worst way. Somehow, he was going to get it. Likely not before the next stage run, however.

That was all right. It could happen then. Rathbone would just need to do a little more planning, that's all.

It wasn't like the man was invincible, for chrissake.

One more holdup, one more amply filled strongbox, and he could pull his picket pin, fog the stage the hell out of Red Hill. Only this time, Rae wasn't getting her cut. He'd be damned if he'd give that uppity bitch more money for doing nothing but letting him know which stages would be running "heavy" as opposed to "light."

He walked through the hotel's carpeted, dimly lit lobby and glanced into the saloon opening off the left. Only a few horse buyers in there, gambling and smoking and enjoying their time away from wives and children. There was an old ranch couple in the dining room on the other side of the lobby—a hardy-looking though gray-headed man and wife, two of the county's first settlers behind the Apaches. He'd heard the Chiricahuas had burned them out twice, killed all their children and stock, and still they survived and would probably live another ten, twenty years.

Christ, how did they do it? Rathbone couldn't wait to head for San Francisco and run wild and fuck to his heart's content. If he had any money left over after the high-priced whores, he might invest in a saloon or maybe one of those fine coastal ranches around San Diego. He'd work up no more of a sweat than he would riding around the place on a Sunday afternoon, admiring his holdings.

Rathbone pinched his hat brim to the pair chowing down on T-bones, which they were washing down with nothing stronger than coffee, then headed on up the broad, carpeted stairs, his silver spurs *chinging* softly. His room was on the third floor. It was a three-room suite with a bed the size of two prairie schooners parked side by side. He couldn't wait to get a drink in him, count the money he'd saved from the holdups, and drift off into a deep, well-deserved sleep.

What was it about spending time with Rae that always exhausted him?

The woman had the most incredible, voluptuous body, but her demeanor was gravestone cold, with eyes like granite. He enjoyed taking his pleasure from her, but afterward he always felt as though he'd been the one who'd been mauled but never quite measured up to what she needed.

God, he hated women.

Rathbone chuckled as he closed the door and lit the lamp atop his large oak bureau. He poured a cognac, then doffed his hat, hung his gun and shell belt on a brass hook by the door. He stripped down to his long-handles, then pulled a chair over to the safe, twisted the knob, and opened the heavy iron door.

His eyes shone in the lamplight.

There it was—the two pearl-gripped Colts that he himself had taken from one holdup, and four even stacks of greenbacks and a pale white burlap sack filled with gold coins. He reached for the money, stopped suddenly.

He'd heard something.

Heart thudding, he half turned to glance over his shoulder. He only caught a brief glimpse of the heavy, hide-wrapped bung starter swooping toward him before it crashed into his temple, and everything went black.

Chapter 9

Yakima slept a few hours, then woke at his usual time.

While Derks continued to snore into his pillow, Yakima dressed in the vague light of false dawn, grabbed his saddlebags and Winchester, and headed downstairs to enjoy one of Ma Prate's stout breakfasts— eggs scrambled with ham, biscuits and gravy, and black coffee served hot in thick stone mugs.

Ma did all the cooking and serving herself, shuffling her tall, heavy frame between the kitchen and small dining room cluttered with more dolls of every shape and size. At this hour there was only one other customer, a tired-looking, bald-headed salesman of windmill parts down from Laramie.

Yakima didn't speak to the man. He preferred a quiet, solitary breakfast. When he'd finished, he stood, smoothed his hair back, donned his hat, adjusted his single shell belt around his lean hips, and headed out into a chill, quiet morning. He raised the collar of his denim jacket and, stopping on the boardinghouse's front porch, sniffed the breeze.

There was the stony smell of rain in the air. The clouds were high and purple, edged with the yellow light of the slowly rising sun.

Yakima shouldered his saddlebags and rifle and headed for the Federated Feed Barn. Inside, he lit a rusty hurricane lamp, then hooked it on the pole at the head of the large stall in which he housed his prized black stallion, Wolf. The light washed over the stall door. Inside, the black was down on his side, his rib cage expanding and contracting slowly.

"For chrissake, hoss," Yakima growled. "Look at yourself. Still sendin' up z's with the sun on the rise!"

The horse pricked his ears at the familiar voice. He gave a loud blow, then lifted his big black head with the Florida-shaped white blaze on its face, snorting, eagerly sniffing the air. Wolf rolled over stiffly, turning his head toward Yakima before sitting up and resting a moment on his haunches, his big lungs raking air in and out excitedly, nostrils working like a bellows, when he saw Yakima grab the bridle and saddle off a tack rack on the other side of the alley.

"Time to work some of the stable green out of you, feller."

Yakima dropped the saddle and blanket on the floor fronting the stall, then, bridle in hand, opened the door and stepped inside. Wolf lunged forward over his white-socked front feet as he unfolded his hind legs and pushed up to all fours, stomping and grunting and switching his curried tail with *whoosh*es of displaced air, raking it loudly against the stall's side partition.

As Yakima approached, the black lowered his head and rammed his snoot a little too hard against Yakima's chest, and the half-breed grabbed the horse's ears and, chuckling, pushed the big head back away from him.

"Sorry to have you holed up in here, you wild cuss. Damn fresh hay, though, wouldn't you say? S'posed to be the best barn in town." Yakima slipped the bit through the horse's teeth, ran the bridle straps up and over the stallion's stiff ears. "Now, it's time to run some o' the grain out of you. Gonna get the green heaves before long. What do you say to that, boy? Huh? What do ya say?"

The horse jerked its head up and stomped. He stood patiently as Yakima threw the blanket and saddle on his back and, true to form, sucked a gutful of air as Yakima started to reach under his belly for a latigo strap and buckle.

"Ornery cayuse!" Yakima rammed his knee into the horse's belly.

Wolf released the pent-up air with a loud *whoof* Yakima pulled the cinch tight and buckled it. When he had the second strap secured, he tossed his saddle-bags onto the horse's rump, behind the saddle cantle, then, taking the reins, led the horse out of the stall, down the alley, and out the barn's open front doors and into the gradually lightening street.

He mounted up, and the black was so eager to get going that he bolted to his left and almost threw Yakima over his right wither.

"All right," Yakima said, grabbing the apple. He

eased his hold on the reins as he crouched low in the saddle and stared east along the broad, abandoned street. "Go!"

The horse lunged off his rear hooves and threw his front legs forward. He tore off down the street, and Yakima grinned at the exhilaration, long overdue, of having the morning air in his face and blowing his hair back away from his shoulders. In less than a minute, the last of the town's shacks peeled off behind them, and Wolf was lunging off down the two-track trail that traced a pale, serpentine course through the low hills of cedar and sage, heading straight toward where the yellow sun was rising through ragged tufts of purple clouds.

Suddenly, the smell of privies was gone, and Yakima realized that after his month in Red Hill, he'd gotten so accustomed to the perpetual stench that he rarely ever smelled it anymore. That and horse shit and man sweat and the smells of cook fires and the perpetual sounds of milling humanity—the clang of a hammer on a blacksmith's anvil, yells, shouts, children's screams, horses neighing and thudding down the street, wagons clattering, mothers calling for their little ones to come home for their noon meals or nightly baths. The occasional crackle of gunfire.

Out here, there was just him and the wind and the sage and the gradually lightening clouds, the smell of rain when the breeze switched.

He could feel Wolf's muscles expanding and contracting beneath his saddle, hear the horse's powerful lungs pushing and pulling at the morning wind that seemed to be intensifying as the sun climbed away from the silhouetted horizon beyond a low, long jog of chalky buttes. When he passed the occasional *bosquecillo*, he could hear the wind churning the leaves, see the occasional dust devil spin off across an open stretch of prairie.

Weather was on the way, he vaguely speculated as he kept his head low over the black's stretched neck. How much weather and what kind of weather was anyone's guess this time of the year and in this neck of the high desert. Snow might be coming to the high country around Bailey Peak with a couple of inches of the wet wool on the ground by late tonight. Here, south of Tucson but at a slightly higher elevation, they'd likely see only rain. Rain and wind. It could be clear and quiet again by tonight, but damp and chilly, and men would drift between saloons clad in fur coats, and their breath would show, and the cedar and mesquite fires would perfume the air over Red Hill.

The horse was enjoying the run so much that Yakima soon turned him off the trail and put him up a long, gradual rise. There was nothing like a good uphill climb to get the blood of an eager stallion pumping. Wolf put his legs into it, and Yakima could hear the horse chuffing and groaning in appreciation of the workout, of the luxurious feel of blood-engorged organs and muscles, and of the time away from the cramped and lightless stable.

Wolf hated stables about as much as Yakima hated towns, but the two went hand in hand, and at times they were necessary. At least until the half-breed could earn enough of a grubstake to get them back up in the high, lonely reaches for another good stretch of rejuvenating quiet and isolation, where the only sounds were the coyotes, the wolves, the creeks, the breeze, and the rush of the wind in the pine tops.

Hawks, jays, bugling elk, and the occasional lonely whine of a love-searching bobcat.

He and Wolf climbed into the canyon-slashed foothills of the Coronados. This was expansive country, and he stuck to the game and wild horse trails that meandered around mesas and bluffs and steep pinnacles of ragged, time-gouged rock, towering monoliths that, as the day progressed, slid shade from a weak sun around their bases.

On open stretches, he allowed the horse short bursts of ground-eating lopes. For the most part, because of the dangerous terrain, he held him to trots. In some cases, when they came to steep, rocky slopes deep inside box canyons, Yakima dismounted and led Wolf up the perilous passages rather than risk a fall or a gash to one of his hocks or cannons.

Several times Yakima came upon the remains of strategically placed campfires and small piles of discarded airtight tins, some so old the labels had faded away and the tins themselves had turned to rust. In the box canyon in which he'd stopped to give Wolf a blow and to eat his lunch of jerky and hardtack, he discovered human bones poking out from a mound of red dirt that had collapsed or been kicked down from the cutbank above.

He'd bet that if he uncovered the body he'd find a

couple of lead slugs, possibly delivered by some law-man or posse rider, embedded within the moldering bones. The man might have been buried here in this makeshift grave by his desperado partners who couldn't take the time for a proper funeral on their fast ride to Mexico.

Or maybe north out of Mexico and headed for the far flung reaches of the Coronados or the Chiricahuas beyond.

After noon, he was riding back out of the moun-tains, heading for the stage road that would take him back to Red Hill. There had been a brief shower while he'd been riding the canyons between low ridges, but a chill wind had picked up since, drying the land and kicking up dust and bits of dried brush and flinging it every which way.

As he topped a gravelly hill under a red scarp that jutted over him like a massive pointing finger, he spied movement on the flat below. He drew back on Wolf's reins and automatically slid his right hand down his thigh toward the brass butt plate of the Yellowboy jutting from its sheath.

He stayed his hand as he stared down the hill. The rider, astride a skewbald paint, was trotting toward a low, spinelike ridge to Yakima's right. As horse and rider moved out of the arroyo, moving away from Ya-kima, horse and rider stopped suddenly.

The man jerked in his saddle slightly, lifting the reins high against his chest. The horse lurched back-ward, then reared, lifting its front legs high. The rider was already falling off the paint's left hip when the horse's indignant whinny reached Yakima's ears. As the rider fell out of sight behind lime-colored brush, the horse wheeled sharply left and went galloping off across the desert, buck-kicking and trailing its reins, empty stirrups flapping like wings.

Yakima raised his hand from the rifle's stock and heeled Wolf on down the hill, giving the horse his head as he galloped a serpentine course through cedars and mesquites, occasional flat-topped boulders. Yakima spied a faint trail and followed it into the arroyo, the bottom of which was bathed in an even layer of fist-sized white rocks, and up the other side. He drew rein when he saw the rider on his back, squirming and kicking as though in agony.

Yakima leaped out of the saddle and dropped Wolf's reins. "You all ri . . . ?" He let his voice trail off when he saw the blond hair, the hazel eyes narrowed in pain, the lush body clad in men's black denim Levi's, red plaid shirt, and brown leather vest.

The new Mrs. Seagraves was up on her elbows, staring with more frustration than pain at her left foot, on which she wore a soft leather riding boot. The cuffs of her denims were stuffed into the tops of the boots. She glanced at Yakima, and surprise mixed with the pain and frustration before she turned back to her foot and said, "I've never seen a snake move that fast."

"Diamondback."

Beth nodded. "I think he slithered back into his hole after he gave my horse a good scare."

Yakima crouched over her. "Where you hurt?"

"Ankle." She winced and flexed her foot, and stretched her lips back from her white teeth. "I think it's broken. Boy, I'm in trouble now."

Yakima moved around to her other side and dropped to both knees. He glanced up at her pain-racked face as he set his hands on her boot. "Mr. Seagraves know you're out here?"

She shook her head. "It's your fault."

"How's that?"

"I saw you ride out earlier. You gave me the idea. I've been Mrs. Seagraves less than twenty-four hours, and I'm already entertaining the notion of taking my son and riding off into those mountains yonder, and spending the rest of our lives in a cave."

Yakima snorted and gently moved her foot to each side. "That hurt?"

"Yes."

He moved it up and down, and he couldn't hear or feel any bones grinding. "That?"

"Not as bad as sideways."

"Can I take your boot off?"

Her eyes met his for a moment before sliding back to her foot, and she nodded. She grunted softly as he gently slipped her boot off her foot, then peeled her sock off and dropped it atop the boot.

She had a long, fine-boned foot. An altogether nice-looking foot, as far as feet went. It felt good in his hands but he tried not to show it as, resting her heel on his thigh, he leaned down and sideways to inspect her ankle.

"Not coloring too bad. I'd say it's only sprained, but you better have a sawbones take a look at it." He lifted his head to meet her gaze, keeping his hands on her foot. "Not going so good, huh?"

She shook her head and squinted off toward the Coronados, wisps of loose hair blowing in the wind. "I made a mistake, I'm afraid. As much of one for myself as my boy. I was a fool to come out here. When I saw you this morning, riding so freely away, I decided to rent my own horse. I was raised on a small ranch. I love to ride." She turned to him sharply. "I wasn't following you."

"I never said you were."

"You just gave me the idea."

"All right."

"I put Calvin in school this morning and afterwards I took some of the money I still had saved—money which Mr. Seagraves tried to confiscate last night when he was going through my trunk—and rented Earl there for the morning." Beth turned the corners of her mouth down. "I didn't know Earl was so afraid of snakes."

"Most horses are."

"I'm from Nebraska. We don't have diamondbacks in Nebraska. Just garter snakes, mostly."

"Why was he going through your trunk?"

"He said he was going to help me unpack, but he was snooping. He found a tintype of my husband and Calvin and me on the shore of the North Platte, and he tried to take that, too, saying it was time to say good-bye to the past." Beth hardened her jaws as well as her eyes. "He was going to throw it in his incinerator. My money, he said, would go into our joint account at the bank. I said, 'Oh, so you'll put my name on the account, as well as your own?' To which he replied with a condescending little laugh, 'Don't be silly, dear. Whenever you need money from the account, you need only ask me, your husband, and I'll be more than happy to consider your request.'"

She spat to one side and looked into the brush beside her. "Can you imagine that? Taking my money as his own and requiring that I ask him when I want some of it? I took all of it, hid it where I know he'll never find it, then told him I was going to take a ride to clear my head."

She narrowed her angry eyes at Yakima once more. "Of course, he wasn't going to allow that, either, as this is outlaw country and no decent woman rides out alone, anyways, and especially no wife of his. Ha! The old fool can't move fast, so I got away before he could track me down."

She looked down at Yakima's hands on her foot. "He probably wouldn't appreciate our meeting up this way, either."

"Don't doubt it a bit." Yakima caressed her foot and regarded her darkly, his own long hair now whipping around his head in the wind. She watched his thick brown hands moving over her foot—slow, gentle strokes. She raised her eyes to his once more, and she leveled an oblique, vaguely troubled stare at him.

He set her foot on the ground and reached for her at the same time that she reached for him. She leaned forward, and he grabbed her, wrapped his arms around her back as she wrapped hers around his neck. Then her lips were against his—warm, pliant, hungry.

She groaned.

Slowly, kissing her, he laid her back on the ground and began unbuttoning her shirt.

She did nothing to stop him.

Chapter 10

"*Bang, bang,* Sheriff! I gotcha! You're *dead!*"

Rathbone had drawn his pistol when the kid had bounded around the abandoned brick stable he'd been crouched behind, pressing his back to the crumbling west wall. Now he cocked the pistol and aimed at the kid's laughing face, gritting his teeth as his heart thudded.

Rathbone, in no mood for children, snarled, "Go on, git outta here, you smelly little privy rat, or I'll drill you between your beady little eyes!"

The kid's suntanned face bleached. He let the "rifle" stick he'd been aiming at Rathbone droop in his hands. He backed away, the frayed laces of his badly worn brogans slapping about his feet.

"You tell anyone you saw me here, I'll cut your ears off," Rathbone yelled into the hot wind that had started blowing just after sunup as though to purposely increase the pain in the sheriff's already aching head and eyes. "You hear me, you little cur? Not one word!"

He doubted the kid had heard that last. Letting one suspender holding up his baggy denim coveralls drop down his right arm, the kid tossed his stick away and ran straight off across the sage-covered lot behind the stable, arms and legs pumping hard, his carelessly cropped hair blowing in the wind. As though to avoid lead buzzing toward him, he caromed off toward the abandoned stone shack of one of Red Hill's original and now-deceased dwellers, and disappeared in some cedars.

Rathbone depressed the Colt's hammer and lowered the piece. Squatting on his haunches, he pressed his back once more against the stable wall. He grimaced as the pain kicked up across the front of his head, just behind his eyes. Fingering the goose egg on his right temple, he gave a savage curse, knowing the howling wind would cover it.

He'd regained consciousness just before sunup, just in time to have the rising wind add to the pressure inside his head and to increase the tolling of cracked bells in his ears. For a time, he wasn't sure where he was or what had happened, and then, when he saw the open safe gaping like a great toothless mouth before him, all his hoarded loot gone, he remembered the hammering blow he'd received earlier.

"That bitch," he raked out through gritted teeth. "That bitch . . . that bitch . . . that bitch. . . ."

He hunkered there, edging an occasional look around the corner of the stable every few minutes. A path from the main street of Red Hill had been worn into the brush, angling northeast toward the frame house where the banker and his cool, plain-faced, lush-bodied daughter dwelled on the town's ragged fringe.

Every afternoon around four, Rae Roman took the path home, holding her purse in one hand and lifting her skirts above her expensive leather side-button boots. Rathbone had seen her countless times though he'd never really paid much attention to her route. He hadn't thought he'd ever need that knowledge.

Now, however, he appreciated the fact that he was an idly observant man.

Earlier, when he'd regained his senses, and unbridled fury had begun coursing like miniature pitchforks through his loins, he'd intended to storm into the bank and shove his Colt down the bitch's throat just to enjoy the sheer terror in her eyes. And the sudden-dawning knowledge that she'd crossed the wrong bobcat.

Then he'd find out where she'd squirreled away the money. After that, he'd shoot her. He'd shoot anyone else who stood in his way. Then he'd take both his own loot and hers and any other money that was handy and ride out of Red Hill to a far, far better life in Southern California.

If you couldn't trust a banker's daughter, who could you trust? It was getting so that even the outlaw life didn't make sense anymore. . . .

He dropped to his butt. The bitch was taking her time today. Probably got tied up berating some poor honyonker who couldn't pay his mortgage. Rathbone chuckled savagely and, elbows on his knees, toyed with the gun in his hands, slowly turning the cylinder but barely hearing the clicks above the wind.

He'd be a curious sight if anyone saw him out here. The Coronado County sheriff hunkering before an abandoned stable like some bottle-tipping ne'er-do-well, or a Peeping Tom. Fortunately, few people wandered this empty lot except useless children spawned by whores and left to run amok around Rathbone's fair town. When he saw that kid again, he'd drag him into a wash and give him the whipping a responsible father would give him, if he had one.

Occasional gusts swept dust, prickly goatheads, and other grit at him, and he closed his eyes and lowered his face against it. When she finally came, it took him by surprise. Suddenly she was before him, angling away from him along the path, her chin down, a powder blue cape flapping about her shoulders like the wings of some evil bird the devil had loosed from hell to further torture humanity.

Rathbone heaved himself to his feet, glanced around quickly to make sure they were alone, then grabbed her arm and spun her around. She gasped and lifted her head to him, eyes shocked. Rathbone didn't give her time to call out. He threw her to the ground at the base of the stable, and just as she opened her mouth to scream he rammed the barrel of his Colt into her mouth. She gagged and tried to fight him, but he pinned one of her arms with his free hands and a knee.

There it was—the horror he'd been dreaming of. Her eyes were nearly exploding with it while her lips fought the barrel and she made gagging sounds, her throat expanding and contracting grotesquely.

"I oughta drill you right here, you bitch." Rathbone shoved his face down close to hers while she flopped helplessly beneath him, gagging and groaning. "Give you a pill to choke on? Huh? How'd that be?"

He let her flop and gag for a time, resisting the urge to squeeze the trigger. She wouldn't be any good to him dead. He'd never find out or get access to where she'd hidden the stolen loot she'd taken from him.

He pulled the Colt out of her mouth and scuttled back, freeing her arms. Gulping air, eyes bulging, she grabbed her throat with both hands and made sounds as though she was trying to speak but couldn't get her vocal cords to work.

"You crazy bastard!" she finally pinched out just above a rasp, tears dribbling down her cheeks. "Have you gone—gone *insane*?"

"Where is it, Rae?" Rathbone pressed the Colt's barrel against her forehead, drove the back of her head to the ground again. "You tell me and I'll *think* about letting you live. You don't tell me, and you don't have a chance."

"You have, haven't you?" She stared up at the pistol in his hands. Her voice was almost calm, resigned. "You've gone crazy. I guess this place will do it to even you, Frank. . . ."

"Quit playin' games, Rae," he said, menace in his voice, spittle frothing on his lips. His eyes were pinched to slits. "I wanna know where you put my loot. I wanna hear it in your next breath or I'm gonna pop a slug through your brain plate."

She looked up at him around the gun in his clenched fist. "The loot? You mean the money from the strongbox?" Her eyes crossed slightly, and what appeared to be genuine exasperation flicked across them. "You mean you lost your cut?"

"No, I didn't lose it. You stole it from me, you doublecrossing whore. You were waiting in my room last night—any skeleton key will work in those locks—and you brained me with a pistol butt. Or something equally as unforgiving. Then you took every last dollar of my loot. Every coin. Even the pennies." Rathgone gave a wolfish grin. "Thanks for leaving the Colts." He cocked the pistol and pressed it down harder against her forehead. "But they're not enough to save you. Where is it, Rae? I won't ask you again!"

She closed both her hands over his fist, dangling her long fingers over the cocked revolver. "Please, Frank. I can appreciate how upset you are. But I did not steal your cut of the strongbox money." Her upper lip quivered, and tears varnished her eyes. "Please, Frank. You have to believe me. If I had done that, don't you think I'd tell you? I don't want to die!"

Slowly, the unadulterated rage in Rathbone's face dwindled to incredulity. He turned his face slightly, narrowed a skeptical eye.

"Frank, please," Rae said, opening and closing both her hands over his and staring up at him with beseeching and terror. She swallowed and pitched her voice with reason. "Think it through. Why would I do something that blatantly stupid? Of course, you'd think it was I who'd stolen your money, and you'd come looking for me. I'd be defenseless against you, as I am now."

He continued to stare down at her, one skeptical eye squinted.

She said, "If I were going to do that—which I wouldn't—I'd certainly do it when I had the best chance of getting out of town fast. Well, I didn't do that, did I, Frank? No, I took the same route I always take home, in fact. And I have nothing on me with which I might possibly defend myself from you."

She ran the pink tip of her tongue along the underside of her upper lip, gently squeezed his clenched fist. "Would you like to run your hands over me to see if I'm carrying a gun? Perhaps a knife?"

"I'll be goddamned," Rathbone grunted, "if you don't have me *startin'* to believe you."

"Think it through, Frank." She caressed the bulging knuckles of his gun hand with her fingertips. "You're an intelligent man. Think it through. I'd have been a total idiot to have tried such a stunt."

Deep frown lines cut across Rathbone's forehead. He angrily bit at his upper lip. Finally, he pulled the gun back from her forehead, and Rae drew a deep, relieved breath as she tipped her head back and swallowed.

"If not you," Rathbone asked as much to himself as her, "who?"

"How should I know?" She glared up at him, her indignation returning on the heels of her fear. "With the brand of men you run with, you're certainly better equipped to figure that out than I am."

"Brand of *men*?" Rathbone chuckled mirthlessly. "What makes you so special? The men I run with I trust. Look at you, Miss Roman. Why, you'd double-cross your own dear father if . . ." He let his voice trail off dramatically, then gave a mock look of surprise. "Oh, wait a minute—you did double-cross your dear old pa, didn't you? Still are, as a matter of fact."

She pushed up on her elbows. "Maybe we should save the morality discussion for another time and place, Frank." She looked around cautiously. "I don't think it wise, us loitering out here where the whole town could very easily see us. If anyone walked up right now, Frank, the game would all be over."

"It is over," Rathbone said. "For you. At least until I get my money back and find out who stole it."

"It was one of your men, of course!" Rae shot him an exasperated look of supreme impatience. "Probably Stall or Silver. Who else?"

"Doubt it. When I left them last night, they were headed over to the doc's place."

"Oh, no."

"Yep."

"They blew it again? I thought I saw the half-breed riding out of town a few hours ago. I'd hoped my eyes were lying. Oh, Frank!"

"Leave it to you to lick your own scratches when I've just been wounded. Wounded big. I'm as penni-less now as when I started this shindig."

Rae climbed to her knees, paused to brush dirt from

her cheek, and then Rathbone helped her to a standing position. "If you don't find the money today, you'll make up for it tomorrow. Father just told me that fifty thousand dollars will be riding in the strongbox of tomorrow's stage. Both the payout from the sold horses and extra cash that the Sand Creek manager asked for, probably to buy out a couple of squatters."

Rathbone had bent over to brush sand and grass from his knees. Now he jerked a surprised look up at her, his big face mottling. "I don't believe it. They've never carried that much cash. Not without an armed escort."

"Tomorrow they are. Father probably thinks that since an attempt was made on the stage yesterday, no one will try it again for a while. Especially not with the half-breed riding shotgun. I think Father might even be weakening, considering giving that heathen the reward that was on the heads of your friend Gries and his useless men. Father really wants that man to stay on."

"Well, I can see why." Rathbone turned to gaze speculatively across the vacant lot to scraggly mesquites and cottonwoods lining a wash, and beyond the wash to the bald Coronados rising in the dusty, wind-howling distance. "Fifty thousand dollars . . ." He turned a cunning grin on Rae, who was making a futile effort to straighten her picture hat in the wind. "I reckon me and my deputies will be handling this one ourselves."

"Are you sure that's wise?" She didn't sound confident.

"Oh, we'll manage it this time. Now that we know

what . . . or *who* . . . we're up against." Rathbone looked toward the Coronados again, grinning.

"Frank?"

"What?"

It was Rae's turn to look menacing. "Don't even think about double-crossing me."

Rathbone shook his head as though she'd injured his honor as well as his feelings. "Rae, now, you see." He pointed an incriminating finger at her. "I wouldn't *do* that!"

Chapter 11

"We're like animals," Beth said, no shame in her voice. It was an amused observation, not a judgment.

She was astraddle Yakima, both of them naked now, Yakima lying back-down on the horse blanket he'd taken off Wolf after his and Beth's first, furious coupling. He'd spread the blanket between two mesquites, and they'd taken their time that second time around, going slowly yet hungrily, bringing each other to a long, gradual, luxurious climax.

She looked around at the blowing branches as though to see if anyone else were out here on this windy afternoon in the tablelands. Lowering her eyes to his big, rope-scarred, work-toughened hands massaging her breasts, she placed her own hands over his and pressed them harder against her. She lowered one to his broad, brick-red chest, traced a knife scar with her long, pale fingers, then pushed the heel of her hand against his bulging pectoral as though she were kneading bread on a butcher block.

"Just like animals."

She hunched her shoulders and squeezed her eyes closed, tipping her head back, groaning and holding her hands taut over his, enjoying the rake of his callused palms against her.

After a time, Yakima lifted his hands to caress her smooth cheeks as he slid her hair back away from her face. He stared into her eyes, and now her green gaze, staring out of a face so much like one that he remembered from Thornton's and from his cabin on the slopes of Bailey Peak, dealt him an unsuspecting blow.

And then it was over. Whatever had happened between them. All gone. Only the hollow pit of longing in his belly remained.

He rose to a sitting position, bracing her with his arms, her body so relaxed, so pliant that he knew she'd fall back if he didn't hold her. "I'd best saddle up and run your horse down. Gettin' late."

She frowned, her hair, which she'd taken out of the ponytail, blowing like a tumbleweed about her beautiful head. "I hate the thought of going back."

"Yeah, well, I got a job. And . . ."

Beth narrowed one eye, a peevish set to her lips still wet from his saliva. "And I have a husband?"

"Don't you?"

She rolled her gaze sideways and slid away from him, rising to her knees, grabbing her camisole and shaking it out in front of her.

Yakima dressed. As he tossed his saddle onto Wolf's back, he glanced at her. She was dressing slowly, her back to him, a sullen expression on her face, her eyes downcast.

He rode off in the direction in which he'd seen her rented paint gallop away, and returned a half hour later, leading the horse by his lariat. Beth's ankle had swollen so that she could not put her boot on, so Yakima lifted her onto the paint's back, and she hooked her bare foot over the horn to keep pressure off it.

"How's that?" he asked her, taking her reins in his hands. "I'll lead you in."

She nodded, stared down at him, her eyes vaguely questioning. "I suppose this is going to complicate things."

Yakima frowned. "Why should it?"

The carelessness in his voice belied the ache in his chest now as his heart thudded heavily. She'd reminded him, in both appearance and situation, too much of Faith. His feelings for her were beginning to resemble his feelings for his dead wife. And he couldn't save her any more than he'd been able to save Faith.

Hell, he was hardly able to save himself. . . .

He wanted to run away, howling. But he stood there off her right stirrup, meeting her forlorn gaze that was one more dagger in his heart.

She said softly, clearing her throat first and pitching it with a toughness she didn't feel: "No, I suppose it shouldn't, should it?"

Yakima turned away and swung up onto Wolf's back. Holding Beth's reins in his left hand, keeping his right hand free for the Winchester if he should need it, he heeled the stallion ahead through the brush, angling toward the main trail.

Neither of them said anything as they headed back

toward Red Hill. Yakima found himself grateful for the wind. It seemed to relieve the heavy silence that was between him and the woman now as they plodded along, Beth riding stiffly behind him, her bare foot hooked over her saddle horn, blond hair blowing behind her shoulders.

Yakima was relieved when the town rose before him in the rocky, sage- and cedar-stippled hills sandwiched between shelving red mesas. He rode on in and saw that it had been a mistake to take the main road. He should have ridden into town from one side and approached the doctor's office from the rear where he and Beth might not have been seen together. Now as Wolf clomped slowly along, men came out onto the boardwalks fronting the stores, strange looks on their faces as they studied the half-breed on the black stallion leading the blonde on the paint.

As they passed the sheriff's office, Yakima saw Rathbone's two deputes, Stall and Silver, milling on the shack's front porch. Stall was sitting in a chair, a steaming tin cup in his hand. Silver had one hip hiked on the porch rail, facing Stall. Stall's eyes found the improbably paired newcomers, and his lips moved as he said something to Silver, and the half-Mexican deputy turned his head toward the street. His left arm was held against his chest by a white sling. His dark eyes widened, and his upper lip curled a sneer.

Yakima turned his head forward, vaguely wondering how the half-Mexican deputy had gotten that injured wing, and angled the stallion toward the doctor's office on the street's north side. He put Wolf's nose to the hitch rack, then swung down, looped the reins over the rack, and walked back to the paint. He snaked one arm beneath Beth's legs and slid the other behind her back, and lifted her off the paint. The horse shifted sideways as the woman's supple weight settled in Yakima's arms.

He glanced around. More men were watching them now—shopkeepers in business suits and aprons, cowboys in battered, dusty trail clothes, even a couple of women who'd been chinning in front of the drugstore.

Yakima glanced at Beth. She was looking around, too, her own face remaining passive as she took in the stares around her. He carried her up the creaky outside stairs of the saddle shop to Doc Mangan's office in the building's second story, and gave the door two kicks with his moccasined foot. Footsteps sounded inside, and a round-faced man with affable, intelligent eyes behind gold-framed spectacles opened the door, brushing bread crumbs from his vest.

The man's eyes slid from Yakima's face to the woman's and back again, his gray-brown eyebrows furrowed skeptically. He kept his weight on his left leg, favoring the right one, the knee of which was bent.

"She twisted her ankle," Yakima said. "It's swollen. Doesn't look broke, but you best take a look at it, Doc."

Again, the doctor's curious gaze swept his unlikely pair of visitors. He hobbled back, brushing more sandwich crumbs from his vest and beckoning with a pale, fine-boned right hand. "Come in, come in. Bring her on into the examining room, and I'll take a look at it."

When Yakima had carried Beth into the office, the doctor closed the door behind them, his voice hesitant as he said, "You're Seagraves's new wife, aren't you?"

"That's right," Beth said tonelessly over Yakima's shoulder as he carried her through a curtained doorway and into an examining room rife with the smell of medicines.

Yakima set her down on the leather pedestal table and stepped back away from her. He was about to say something, but then the doctor came in, using a cane now and yammering nervously, and Yakima swung around and moved back through the curtained doorway and strode across the office to the main door.

He stopped as the mercantile owner, Seagraves, came in looking harried, his long horsey face flushed. He wore a clean green apron. His thin gray hair and string tie were disheveled from the wind.

"My God," he croaked, his eyes homing in on Yakima. "What in holy hell is going on here? I was told you rode in with my wife."

"Don't get your neck up," Yakima grunted. "I found her out in the desert. Horse threw her. She twisted an ankle. Doc's checkin' her out now."

Yakima stepped around the man, pushing the door open.

Behind him, Seagraves said, "Do you know what's being *said* out there?"

Yakima turned a chill look at the man, and curled

a mirthless grin. "The concern's right touching, ain't it?"

He swung around and started down the stairs to the waiting horses.

He stabled Wolf and the paint and then went over to Hopwood's Bathhouse for a long soak.

He didn't normally bathe in town, as he hated paying for what he could get for free out in the tall and uncut, and he preferred moving water for washing his filth away. But there were no near creeks deep enough to soak in around Red Hill, so he paid six bits to the cranky English proprietor who smelled of chocolaty beer malt, hauled his gear into a cedar-paneled bathing room, and let the hot water sear him before he lathered up, then sat back in the water again and lit a cheap cigar.

He smoked the cigar and tried not to think. But the harder he tried not to think, the harder he thought and the sicker he made himself feel.

Christ, why did she have to ride in on that stage? His life had been going all right, memories of Faith not so much diminishing as settling, drawing their barbs in, and he'd been all right with being alone and not giving a shit about anyone, not needing anyone but the occasional cheap whore. But now he couldn't stop thinking about her, the way she'd felt writhing beneath him while he'd hammered against her, her heels and fingers grinding into his back.

And yet, all the while he'd toiled with her, Faith's ghost had been tapping his shoulder. When he'd pulled away from her that second time, he'd looked down into her eyes and it was Faith's cold, dead gaze he saw as she'd hung limp in his arms with the road-house burning behind her.

In his head, he'd heard his own echoing cry: *"Faith!"*

He smoked the cigar down to a nub and looked at the coal. "What you need is a drink and a whore."

He dropped the cigar stub and it sizzled out in the sudsy water. He dried and dressed and headed across town to the Queen of Hearts, where he had two shots of whiskey before he even started to think about a girl, though there were plenty around him, including Janelle though she was currently occupied, riding the knee of a some pilgrim in a green-checked suit with a thick red mustache and muttonchops.

In the back-bar mirror he saw the girl cast him several speculative glances, but he was glad she was occupied. He didn't really want a girl. He really just wanted to suck down some whiskey even though he was well aware of the inherent danger in that, and to brood. The wind howled and moaned outside, giving voice to the demons in his head, and he was glad for the whiskey and the gradually loudening din of the saloon's growing patronage.

He wasn't sure how much he'd had to drink, standing there and glaring at himself in the back-bar mirror, one foot planted atop the brass rail running along the base of the bar, when someone bumped him from behind. He glanced over his shoulder. It was Deputy Stall, who turned to see whom he'd run into, and his big, bearded face flushed suddenly. He glowered.

"Well, if it ain't the breed!" Stall's eyes were bright with drink, and he held a beer in his hand, the other hand draped negligently over his holstered, rubber-gripped Remington. "You know what's goin' around town about you and Seagrave's mail-order bride, don't you?"

Yakima shrugged and slid his eyes to the smaller, wiry, and compact Deputy Silver standing behind Stall, his injured wing tucked against his flat belly. "I don't care."

"You oughta care. That's dangerous territory you're stompin' in, breed. Nobody much cares for old Seagraves, but nobody much cares for you, neither. Ridin' into town with that good-lookin' blonde in tow only made it worse."

Yakima glanced at Silver's arm. "Where'd you get the busted wing, amigo?"

"That's none of your business, amigo."

"You boys weren't skulkin' around out in the wash between here and my boardinghouse, were you?"

Yakima slid his glance between the two men, his nostrils flaring as the color drained beneath Stall's beard. A confused look spread across Silver's lips before the small, muscular deputy tried to cover it with a grin.

Stall narrowed his eyes and flared his nostrils. "If you're spoilin' for a fight, bucko . . ."

"That's what I'm doing."

Before Yakima realized what he was doing but only giving in to the undeniable rage burning through him, he'd sprung forward and grabbed the back of Stall's neck with his own left hand. Pivoting, he slammed the man's face savagely against the bar top. He pulled it back and slammed it down two more times before anyone else in the room even knew what was happening, the heavy crackling thuds resounding above the din.

Stall sobbed and made a strangling sound as, leaving a smear of dark red blood on the polished counter, Yakima pulled his head back once more and drove his right fist into the side of the man's head—two quick, savage blows that tore the ear protruding from the thick, curly, oily mass of the deputy's hair. The half-breed was about to lift his knee to finish off the man when he spied movement out the corner of his left eye.

It was too late to do anything about Silver. His whiskey-soaked rage had swept the man from his mind while he'd tended to Stall.

The blow he knew was coming came—a pistol butt to the back of his head. He felt himself twist around, felt the bar slam against his back and the back of his head. His knees hit the floor. A brass spittoon shone brightly to his right. It bobbed and swayed like a hot air balloon in the summer sun, winking in the saloon's flickering lantern light.

His muscles gave, and he was dropping straight forward into a warm, black pit where all sounds faded to silence.

Chapter 12

The sleep that followed was not restful. Pain followed Yakima into it, and wave after wave of it swept over him, battered him like a small boat on a wind-chopped sea. Only his own whimpering brought him up out of it before he drifted back into it again.

He tossed and turned, heard the loud squawking sounds that after a time he realized deep in his agonized consciousness were bedsprings. Half of his brain wondered where he was. He'd have thought jail. That's where he usually ended up after such a night. But he'd never known a jail cell furnished with a spring bed.

The night was long, long. When he finally shed the clinging, oily fingers of unconsciousness and managed to hold his head above the savage waves, he blinked and looked around, saw the bottle on the table beside his bed. His bed in the boardinghouse.

Only vaguely wondering why in the hell he was here and not in the lockup, he grabbed the bottle, pushed up on his elbows, jerked the cork out of the lip with his teeth, and tipped a long pull. Whiskey dribbled down his lips and chin to dampen the sheets beneath his fully clothed body.

The whiskey hit him a hammering blow, and he squeezed his eyes closed and gritted his teeth against it. As the blows ceased, the pain seemed to recede, and he eased his grip on the bottle, setting it back down on the night table.

Someone chuckled. "You a damn fool—you know that?" Derks said.

Yakima blinked the sleep from his eyes and looked across the small room. Enough light pushed through the shabby curtains over the single window that he could see the old jehu sitting on the side of his bed, his feet, clad in thick, gray wool socks, on the floor. He wore his threadbare balbriggans, and he was leaning his bald head forward, rubbing the back of his neck as he wagged his head slowly.

Yakima smacked his lips. "Don't go thinkin' you're the first to notice." He swallowed to keep the whiskey down, smacked his lips again. "How'd I get here?"

Derks lifted his head and scratched his thick, salt-and-pepper sideburns. "Rathbone was gonna toss ya in the hotbox. I heard the commotion from upstairs where I was givin' that French girl the time o' her life, and I just had a feelin' you was involved."

"Takes a college-educated man to figure that one out."

"So I come down and me and Marv Haney convinced Rathbone and his deputies, one of which left most of his face on the bar top, that you just had a bad day and me and a couple other fellers oughta just take you on back to your room."

Haney was one of the hostlers for the Coronado Line.

Yakima narrowed an eye and tipped his head to the side. "And he went for that?"

"It surprised me, too. Marv shore figured he'd be ridin' shotgun today. Or we wouldn't be runnin' at all." Derks pulled his head back and grimaced his shock and dismay. "When you gonna learn you and fire-water can't dance?"

"I don't owe you any bail?"

Derks continued scowling at his shotgun messenger, then loosed a long, disdainful sigh. He shook his head as he heaved himself to his feet, his old knees popping audibly. "What you can do, though, is haul that big, stupid carcass of yours up outta that bed. We leave in one hour, and you know how Miss Roman gets when we're behind schedule."

Yakima raked his hands down his face. What luck, he thought. He'd figured he'd be in jail, and he'd be drawing his wages from the Romans later in the day. Why wasn't he all that thrilled about how it all had turned out?

The trail beckoned him, that's why. Things were getting too hard here. Too complicated. He had a strong urge to pull his picket pin and give the black his head and gallop on out of here.

Also, apprehension nettled the edges of his consciousness. Letting a man go who'd pummeled one of his deputies was not Rathbone's way. Yakima had come pretty damn close to killing Stall last night. Rathbone's letting him go without even posting bail didn't figure.

Something stank.

What was the sheriff up to? Had he sicced his deputies on Yakima in the wash the night before last? Even beneath the torment in his head, he remembered the looks on the two men's faces when he'd mentioned Silver's injured arm.

Well, there was no time to think about it. Even if his thinker box was working properly, which it wasn't. Thoughts were slippery things. He couldn't get a handle on them. As he heaved himself to his feet, the room tilted, and he had to lunge toward the downside to retrieve his balance.

As Yakima was buttoning his shirt, Derks looked at him and sadly shook his head.

"I'll feel better with some food in me," Yakima said, crouching stiffly for his boots.

"Yeah," Derks growled.

With only one passenger aboard the stage, the two-man crew made it to Apache Gap without incident save battling the wind that hadn't relented one iota.

They pulled into town around two thirty in the afternoon, about an hour before the stage from Las Cruces came rattling in from the dusty little town's opposite side. The spur train had pulled in from Lordsburg that morning, and the strongbox it had been carrying from San Angelo, Texas, was locked in the safe in the Coronado Line's office, which was nothing more than a two-story shack with a sprawling barn and peeled log corrals to one side.

A coyote-dog, whom the clubfooted stationmaster called Titus, patrolled the place ceaselessly, nervously, panting and appearing now and then with a small jackrabbit in its jaws.

That night the creature howled mournfully from the yard's perimeter, so that Yakima, with a still-sore head from his clubbing in the Queen of Hearts, slept only fitfully while Derks snored without surcease in their little room in the shack's second story.

The only good that came from that night was a slight dwindling of the wind.

The next morning, the two breakfasted downstairs on runny eggs scrambled with minuscule bits of rattlesnake meat. Even the coffee was weak. The clubfooted stationmaster had run his Indian wife off the month before, and he'd never learned to cook anything, he said, but fried rattlesnake and an occasional corn dodger.

While the stationmaster stood sentinel with a loaded shotgun out on the shack's front porch, Yakima and Derks transferred the strongbox from the safe to the stage roof and locked it down. Then they secured the U.S. mail pouch beside it.

There were no passengers on this run, which didn't surprise Yakima. Hardly anyone, it seemed, was in a hurry to visit Red Hill, which was even farther out in the high and rocky than Apache Gap, itself not more than the stage office and train depot, with a trading post and a half dozen fleshpots frequented mostly by Mexican horse thieves and renegade Rurales.

By eight o'clock, with the wind suddenly dying as though a furious spirit had finally blown itself out and gone to bed, Derks cracked his blacksnake over the backs of the six-hitch team, and the coach, carrying no passengers, only the strongbox and mail, lurched off into the vast, purple, rocky desert stretching out across the rugged southern slopes of the Coronados.

They stopped at two relay stations, switching horses, and then, in the early afternoon, Derks glanced at Yakima.

"I see it," Yakima said.

"Just makin' sure."

"You just drive. Leave the scoutin' to me."

"Young folks these days," Derks said above the pounding hooves and wheels and the squawk of the coach's thoroughbraces, "don't got no respect for their elders."

Yakima kept one eye on Demon Rock, the other on the terrain off the trail's left side. Owlhoots knew that the most obvious place to attack a stage out here was from the top of the flame-shaped rock formation, so they might try to get a leg up by attacking the stage just before or just after it.

Yakima held the Winchester across his knees with his right hand, while his left gripped the seat's thin side rail.

The trail was washed out and pitted, and his moccasin boots danced atop the floor of the driver's boot as the stage shuddered, rocked, and swayed. Ahead and left, Demon Rock rose higher and higher, sunlight on the top and south side, the east side facing Yakima less clearly limned. As the stage followed the meandering trail, the formation shifted position. As the stage closed the gap and swooped around a sharp bend, it was suddenly looming nearly straight ahead and growing by leaps and bounds, Yakima no longer able to see the top but only the front shoulder.

Yakima had just turned to survey the deep gorge of an ancient river about sixty yards out on the trail's left side when Derks rammed his left elbow into Yakima's side. "See that?"

Yakima followed the old driver's squinting gaze up the formation's shelving, red facade. He saw nothing, only the layered rock and bits of dry, colorless brush and the occasional gaps of small talus slides.

"I don't see—"

Something hot tore through Yakima's upper right arm, and he was instantly filled with a searing pain as the shot jerked him straight back in his seat and nearly caused him to drop the Yellowboy.

"*Ohhh!*" Derks yelped, glancing at Yakima's torn black-and-white calico shirt and the blood pumping from the ragged hole.

"Kick 'em up. Kick 'em up!" Yakima bit out through gritted teeth, fighting back the searing pain and instant nausea as he raised the Yellowboy toward the slight smoke puff he'd spied amongst the rocks about halfway up the formation.

As Derks heaved himself to his feet and whipped the reins over the team's backs, Yakima fired the Winchester, levered a fresh shell, and fired again, the roars rising sharply above the clatter of the coach and the team's hammering hooves. He fired again and again, intending to pepper the face of the formation until Derks could get around it, hoping his shots would forestall an all-out attack.

He watched his bullets blow up dust and chip away rock. As the stage drew up alongside the base of the steep slope, Yakima racked a fresh round and, staring up at the massive pitted and crenellated wall before him, saw a rifleman leap from one rock to another rock several feet lower down. Yakima aimed and fired, but the man was already out of sight, and the half-breed's bullet only trimmed a branch from a gnarled juniper, flinging it straight up as the bullet hammered the shaded stone wall behind it.

Yakima kept firing, wondering why he wasn't drawing more fire. The coach careened off the right-side wheels and then the left-side wheels before slamming violently back down to all four and plowing out from Demon Rock's massive shadow. Yakima twisted around, levering another round into the Yellowboy's chamber to trail the formation with his eyes, vaguely puzzled as to why he saw no one and there were no more smoke puffs.

"*Ah, shit!*" Derks bellowed at the same time that Yakima began hearing an eerie roar.

Yakima whipped back around, and his heart leaped into his throat.

Rocks and boulders were tumbling down the slope

about fifty yards ahead of the stage, on an interception course with the caroming coach. Lowering his rifle and clutching his bloody upper right arm with his left hand, he stared in awe at the dust wafting up from the hammering rocks, hearing the enormous, cannon-like *booms* and *roars* as the boulders bounced and careened over and around each other as though they were all racing to be the first ones to make it to the road.

"Kick 'em up!" Yakima shouted, icy fingers clawing at his neck.

"We ain't gonna make it!" Derks retorted as the two lead horses, seeing the rocks tumbling toward them, jerked suddenly left of the trail and into the brush beyond.

The coach caromed sharply, pitching up on its right-side wheels and bouncing over tufts of brush and shrubs and hammering over rocks with tooth-shattering violence.

Yakima grabbed for his rifle but missed it as the butt bounced off the dashboard, then dropped straight down the front of the stage and disappeared in the soup below of dust and rocks and flying brush. The stage lurched to the right as its left front wheel bounced off a boulder, and Yakima grabbed the edge of the seat to keep from being thrown.

Derks was yelling at the team and trying to haul back on the traces, half standing and half sitting with his feet braced against the dashboard.

Dust boiled so that Yakima could barely see the driver a foot away from him.

Barely managing to hold on with his right arm on fire, Yakima looked to his right just as the first of the bouncing boulders swept through and over the lead horses. His gut twisted in a tight knot as he heard the shrill whinnies and screams, saw in the corner of his left eye the ancient river gorge yawning only a few yards away.

"*Hoooold onnnnnnn!*" Derks bellowed above the thunder of the rocks and the horses' screams.

As the rocks caromed into the other horses including the wheelers, and Yakima glimpsed them being crushed like jackstraws through the broiling dust, the stage jerked sharply right once more. Yakima's right hand was ripped free of the seat. He was pulled as though by the unseen hondo of a cowpuncher's lariat off the stage's left side.

For several agonizing seconds that felt like hours, he was free-falling, watching his moccasins slide up in front of his face while his head and shoulders began slanting downward. Ahead and to his right, he watched the stage get swallowed up by the churning dust and hammering boulders, saw the front dip down sharply as it followed the horses and the rocks on over the lip of the gorge and out of sight.

He had only about a half second to register the horror of what he'd just witnessed, before the unseen ground came up to hammer his back, neck, shoulders, and butt, so that he felt as though he'd been hit by a locomotive. He heard himself give a loud grunt and a groan as he tumbled head over heels down a steep slope, bouncing and pinwheeling, with no way to slow much less stop himself, completely at the mercy of gravity.

First the ground was up and then down and the blue sky spun like a top before there was a tooth-gnashing crunching sound, and total night descended, as cold as the bottom of an ancient grave.

Chapter 13

An aeon passed during which he neither felt nor heard anything.

Then he opened his eyes and saw a blue strip of cloudless sky. He stared at the sky for a time, as though he'd never seen it before. A bird passed high up. Then another. As he slid his eyes to the right, he saw three small, shaggy specks tracing slow circles nearly directly above him.

Then the pain came back, and he felt as though a half dozen devious little men were pounding away at him with chisels and ball-peen hammers. He arched his back and neck, lifted his aching ass from the ground.

"Oh, Christ!"

He dropped his ass suddenly when he felt the fire in his arm well up, as though a flame there had just been doused with coal oil. He grabbed the bloody wound in his gloved left hand, and squeezed, rolling onto his left side and groaning. He clipped the groan when he heard something.

A man's voice. *Men's* voices raised in sudden anger.

The voices originated to his left. Still squeezing the wound to quell the pain as well as the blood flow, Yakima turned his head to stare off down the canyon he suddenly realized he was in, lying sprawled on the brush floor. As the men continued to argue amidst the thuds of tossed wood, Yakima looked up the bank he'd tumbled down. The only reason he wasn't dead, he assumed, was that the brush was thicker here than almost anywhere on the steep bank, and it had cushioned his plunge.

He glanced to his left again. The right side of the bank bulged several yards beyond him. Beyond that bulge must be where the stage had dropped.

He shook his head as if to clear it. The cobwebs remained, however. The fall had brained him. That braining on top of last night's braining had turned his brain to mush. He couldn't get a handle on the situation. He knew the stage had gone over the cliff, likely with Derks aboard, but it was still merely an abstract idea.

He was in shock from the fall and the loss of blood from his arm. And he was already feeling a building fever chill.

He'd just started to wonder if any of the myriad aches in his body were the result of broken bones, when he heard someone thrashing brush nearby. The sound grew louder. He could hear spur *chings*, and then a man in a vaguely familiar voice said, "I'm gonna look over this way."

"Come on, Stall," another familiar voice said behind the first. "You'll never find him. Likely smashed to a bloody heathen pulp!"

Yakima's black brows ridged. Stall. That meant Rathbone and Silver were likely out here, as well.

"Yeah, well, I'm just gonna check over here, anyways!" Stall bellowed, his deep voice cracking angrily on a high note. His voice owned a nasal quality, which was no doubt due to Yakima having smashed the man's face in.

The big deputy was within forty yards, Yakima judged, and closing fast. In less than a minute he'd be walking around the dogleg in the canyon floor.

The half-breed looked around desperately, his heart hammering, wondering if he'd be able to move even if he found a place to move to. Finally, he spied a notch in the chalky, eroded ridge wall just beyond him, on the other side of the canyon. Just a jagged, black gap sheathed in a thin stand of yellow brome grass. Probably snakes in there. The gap was likely too narrow for him, but he dug his moccasin heels into the gravel and pushed himself on his butt toward the bank.

As he heard Stall moving around the curving opposite ridge wall, and caught a glimpse of the man's hat brim and silver belt buckle between the flaps of his dark brown coat, Yakima set his jaws and, skin prickling at the prospect of a snake or spider bite, bulled himself into the gap backward. He grunted as he swiveled his shoulders, worming his way deeper into the cavern that smelled of dust and dry brush.

It wasn't only his bullet-shattered arm that grieved

him. His head still throbbed dully from its unceremo-
nious meeting with Silver's pistol butt. And every bone
and muscle ached; his joints felt as though spikes had
been driven through them. Sharp rocks and goatheads
nipped his ass and the backs of his thighs.

He continued to grind his heels into the gravelly
earth until his feet were inside the gap and he was
behind the screening brush, most of which he'd bent
or torn and which a good tracker would recognize as
a sure sign of his quarry's passage. Yakima dropped
his right hand to his holster and was not surprised the
pistol wasn't there.

It had likely dropped out of the sheath during his
ass-over-teakettle descent of the canyon wall. He could
still feel his Arkansas toothpick sheathed in its usual
position between his shoulder blades, under his shirt
collar, but the knife would do him little good here.

Continuing to squeeze the wound in his arm closed,
Yakima leaned back against a rock and waited, listening. In here, noises from outside sounded flat and hollow. He could hear Stall crashing through the brush, the
man's boots raking rocks and snapping twigs, his spurs
ringing loudly.

Suddenly, the sounds ceased. Yakima canted his
head to one side, saw the big man standing stationary
on the canyon floor, holding a Henry rifle up high across
his chest, turning his head slowly from one side to the
other and back again. His face looked puffy and purple and white plaster covered his nose while a bandage covered his right ear, beneath the brown brim of

his hat, the silver-trimmed band of which flashed in the sunlight.

Yakima lowered his gaze to the bent brush screening his hiding place. Blood smeared the ragged stocks and the rocks behind them. Doubtless, he'd left a trail of it out in the wash, and if Stall continued forward he'd probably see it. He'd also see the gouges Yakima had made as he'd shoved his ass along through the scrub toward the notch cave.

He reached over his shoulder for the toothpick. If the big deputy sniffed him out, Yakima might be able to take him down with the short, razor-edged dagger before Stall could draw a bead on him. That left the other two, but he'd feel better saddling a cloud if he knew he'd taken at least one of these cold-blooded killers with him.

He wrapped his left hand around the toothpick's hide-wrapped handle, and froze. Stall shouldered his rifle, swung around, and headed back in the direction from which he'd come. Yakima released the breath he hadn't realized he'd been holding, and removed his hand from the knife. He could hear Stall's retreating footsteps and the muffled voices from back around the dogleg, but not much more than that. Only the wind and the chitterings of squirrels and birds.

He leaned back once more, gritting his teeth at the pounding and burning in his arm. He felt clammy and sick to his stomach and he could feel cold sweat running down his back and beading behind his ears. Closing his left hand around his upper right arm again, he felt the greasy, warm blood push out between his fingers.

He needed to get the bleeding stopped.

Quickly, he plucked a couple of cartridges from his shell belt. Slipping the toothpick from its sheath behind his neck, he pried each shell open in turn, flipped the bullets aside, and set each cartridge down carefully, open ends up, on a rock beside him. Using the knife's razor-edged blade, he cut his right sleeve off about three inches above the wound, then reached into his shirt pocket for a lucifer. Holding the match in his palm, he raised his right arm until he could clearly see the hole.

Scowling, knowing the pain he was in for, he picked up one cartridge in his shaking fingers and dumped the powder onto the top wound. He slid the match up from his palm to his fingers and raked his thumbnail over it, firing it. Quickly, not allowing himself any time to think about it, he touched the match to the powder.

Whoof!

As soon as the flash had died, the coppery stench of his own scorched flesh and blood assaulted his nostrils. Every muscle in his body was drawn taut. His right arm shook. He glanced at the wound that now looked like red candle wax that had dried on a table.

"Nicely done," he said a little hoarsely, wishing he had a shot of whiskey to help dull the pain.

He lowered his forearm and crooked his elbow, lifting it, to see the bullet's exit wound. That was still dripping blood. Quickly, shivering as though he were battling a high mountain snow squall, he repeated the cauterizing procedure with the exit wound, then removed the bandanna from around his neck and tied it tightly around his arm.

The arm's burning had increased, adding to his overall misery, but at least the bleeding had stopped. It would need to be opened up again, cleaned, and disinfected, but there was no point in thinking of that grisly prospect now. Now he had to work at staying alive long enough to find help. A roof. A bed . . .

But first he needed to find out what had happened to Derks. There was a chance, however slight, that the old jehu had survived the wreck. He might even have survived Rathbone. If so, he'd need help, too.

Reclining on his left arm, cradling the right one across his hip, which was the most comfortable position he could find though it was far from comfortable, Yakima waited, pricking his ears to listen. It shouldn't take Rathbone, Stall, and Silver long to plunder the strongbox and light a shuck from the canyon. There was no point in lingering.

Vaguely, and though it really didn't matter to him now though he knew it would later, he wondered where they'd head to. Back to Red Hill? If they figured both Yakima and Derks were dead, leaving no one to identify them, they might as well. But the money wouldn't do them much good in that backwater, end-of-stage-line, two-horse town.

Where, then? Mexico?

The speculation evaporated beneath the distant rata-plan of galloping hooves. A horse whinnied. Quickly, the quiet sound of the breeze and the birds and squirrels returned.

Yakima fought off his dolor to push off his left elbow and scuttle back out of the gap. Just outside, he remained crouched and looking around carefully, making sure the three killers hadn't tried to trick him out of hiding. When no one appeared except a small rabbit hopping along up the wash's rocky bed, stopping to nibble stalks of grass, Yakima straightened and began striding heavy-footed and weak-kneed down-canyon, keeping his right arm crooked in front of him and biting his cheeks against the pain.

Automatically, he slid his left hand across his belly toward his holster, and remembered that the Colt wasn't there. Swinging around, he went back to the scuffed gravel that marked his plummet down the canyon wall, and found the Colt half buried in dirt and sand beside a sun-bleached chunk of driftwood. He brushed dust off the piece, dropped it into its holster, and snapped the keeper thong closed over the hammer.

He rounded the dogleg in the canyon floor, moving even more slowly now, looking around carefully, listening. As he came around the bend, he stopped and felt the bottom fall out of his stomach.

"Oh, Christ."

He staggered forward, eyes raking the mind-rending scene before him—the stage smashed to bits and scattered around the twisted carcasses of the dead horses, the horses themselves wrapped in the leather ribbons and harnesses. When the stage had hit the canyon floor, the undercarriage had broken out from under it, and it lay nearest Yakima, two wheels still intact, one broken and leaning against a juniper. The fourth had rolled off up the canyon, beyond the dead lead horses that lay with a blood-painted boulder between them.

Yakima stopped near the piled lumber of what had once been the coach, saw the brass rail lining a piece of the roof near a door panel lying faceup with CORONADO TRANSPORT CO. still showing clearly in yellow lettering. The lockbox sat between the brass rail and the door, its lid up. Yakima's eyes hooded darkly as he stared inside, wondering for a moment if he was so addled that he wasn't seeing clearly.

He'd expected to see nothing inside. But, no. There was something inside, all right. The afternoon sunlight washing into the canyon shone on a dozen or so fist-sized rocks piled inside the box.

Yakima blinked sharply, dropped to both knees, and, disregarding his wounded arm, leaned forward and threw both his hands into the box and grabbed a rock in each fist, as though to prove he was only seeing things. They weren't real. He'd be holding only air.

He and Derks couldn't have been carrying rocks. The Romans wouldn't have had them carrying only rocks when they were supposed to be carrying gold coins and greenbacks belonging to the Sand Creek outfit.

Yakima lifted his hands to his face and turned them palm up.

Two dull-colored, nondescript rocks, flecked with bits of mica and oxidized iron, stared back at him, silently mocking.

Yakima looked off across the crushed wreckage and

the twisted bodies of the horses, bells tolling in his ears. Suddenly, he dropped the rocks at his knees, felt a searing fury engulf him. He shuttled his gaze around again, stumbling and turning and shuffling in broad circles, looking for Derks. He tramped through the wreckage and over the horses for several minutes before he found the old man's hatless, bald head and torso protruding from beneath one of the wheelers—a frisky mare who'd been known as Evelyn.

Yakima dropped to his knees beside Derks's right shoulder, heard a sob boil up from deep in his chest. Derks's milky brown eyes were open and staring askance at the ground he was hugging. A thick stream of blood oozed out from the corner of his bloody mouth to slide down his chin and pool thickly on the ground near Evelyn's right foreleg.

Yakima placed his open left hand on Derks's still back. He held it there for a long time. Slowly, he shook his head and stared blankly at the carnage and wreckage before him.

"You sons o' bitches," he said. "Oh, you sons o' bitches."

Chapter 14

"Holy shit in the nun's privy," muttered Lonnie Silver as he, Rathbone, and Stall headed back toward Red Hill, leaving the smashed stage, the dead team, and the dummy strongbox in the canyon behind them.

It was the only thing any of them said for miles as they followed the stage road west in the afternoon heat. Rathbone's own moody silence prevailed over the trio. The sheriff might have been a veteran outlaw, with a good dozen killings behind him, but the mistake he'd just made, wrecking the stage and killing six horses and the old jehu for nothing—nothing but a strongbox filled with rocks!—had left him badly shaken. Shaken and angry.

Not angry. Furious. Enraged.

The face that kept floating up in front of his eyes was that of Rae Roman, her smug smile intact. The bitch had tricked him. How or why, he had no idea. But she'd double-crossed him now just as she had in his room the night before last.

For a time, she'd convinced him she hadn't brained

him and stolen his loot, but she was a liar. She'd
wanted him to think Stall or Silver had done it. If they
had, they'd have left town pronto. Of course, he had
other enemies. Plenty of other enemies. But Rae was
double-crossing him. He was as sure about that as he
was certain the sun would set and the moon would
rise. She couldn't be trusted further than he could
throw her uphill against a stiff wind.

As he rode, grim-faced and bleak-eyed, he raked a
frustrated hand down his dusty, sunburned face. Damn
her! Where was the Sand Creek money? Or maybe
there wasn't any money. No. There had to be money.
If not, she'd have had no reason to send him after the
stage.

Likely, she'd gotten her old man to transport the
money some other way—maybe by armed courier—
and she'd sent him after the stage while she or someone else she'd lured into her double-crossing web had
robbed the courier taking a different route to Red Hill.

Her plan was likely to hide the money somewhere,
as she'd done with the rest of her loot, and bide her
time until she could slip out of town without drawing
suspicion upon herself. She'd wait until her father's
bank had gone belly-up, and the dust had settled, until it would only seem natural that she would leave,
maybe hanging her head in shame for her father's
failings while old Roman himself was left in Red Hill
to muck out stalls or swamp saloons.

Rae would stay to see the old man ruined. She
wouldn't want to miss that. Rathbone didn't know

what motivated her—maybe the girl was just wicked to her rotten core, as some women were—but she'd love it very much.

The sheriff's gut turned as he thought of another possibility—that she'd taken the most recent stolen loot as well as the rest of her cache, and was lighting out for Mexico right now. Right now, as Rathbone and his men dusted the trail back to Red Hill empty-handed, having killed an old man and six horses for no good reason.

"That bitch, that bitch, that fucking bitch," Rathbone muttered.

"What's that, boss?"

Rathbone jerked his head toward Stall riding just off Rathbone's right stirrup. He felt his ears warm. Neither Stall nor Silver knew about Rae Roman's doings in this business. He hadn't told them, because they hadn't needed to know. He didn't want them to know that he and the girl were in cahoots. If they did, they might get worried they'd be double-crossed, and their worries would not be groundless. Besides, neither man could be trusted beyond a certain point. They were liable to get drunk and let something slip in one of the saloons, or blackmail Rathbone or Rae to keep them from letting the town know about their doings.

No, they hadn't needed to know about Rae or anything else. He'd intended to kill both men by now, anyway, after they'd helped him rob the stage, then frame them for the robbery while he'd hid the cache—

the whole thing, without giving Rae her promised cut—and continue on as Red Hill sheriff for another month or so. When the dust of the robbery had settled—and he'd enjoyed Rae Roman's fury, a rage she couldn't act on without incriminating herself—he'd resign his position as county sheriff.

He'd dig up the loot and hightail it for California, where he'd spend his days living high on the hog and possibly even setting sail for Hawaii with a pretty, ripe girl on his arm.

Maybe two girls. He'd have money enough for two. When he tired of them, he'd find two more.

Red Hill rose before Rathbone when Stall broke his own dark silence. "The breed had to be back there. He had to be back there somewhere, and now I'm thinkin' it was a mistake, us leavin' without makin' sure he was dead."

"Forget about the breed." Christ, Rathbone had a hell of a lot more than the breed to worry about. "Take my word for it, you cork-headed fool—he's buried under all that rubble."

Stall shook his head, persistent. "I seen him fall off the coach before it went over the cliff."

"Then he broke his neck and he's lyin' out in the sage somewhere. Forget him, Stall." Rathbone cut a sharp look at the big deputy with his battered face, who was followed closely by Silver, who was no longer using the sling for his wounded arm. "I mean it. We got other fish to fry now."

"You wouldn't find it so easy to forget the son of a bitch who done *this* to your face, boss!" Stall pointed a gloved finger at his swollen, purple nose behind the plaster cast, and his black eyes. "I'm in constant misery here, which no amount of whiskey will relieve. And now I don't even have the consolation of that strongbox loot."

Rathbone reined his horse to a sudden halt. The other two followed suit, their trail dust rising around them. They regarded him skeptically, cautiously.

"Listen up, both of you dunderheads." Rathbone raked his grave eyes between the two men. "Forget the damn strongbox. There'll be more. Now we have to worry about covering our tracks here. Very soon, Roman's gonna want to send out a posse lookin' for the stage. When that happens, you're both gonna have to saddle fresh horses and go."

"Why should we go?" Lonnie Silver said, knitting his black brows. "Christ, I say we pull our picket pins and just light the hell outta here. Let's head fer Mexico and get back into horse stealin'. That was damn lucrative. This here business in Red Hill is fryin' my nerves!"

"I'm with Lonnie," Stall said. "I say we rustle up what we done made outta this business so far and ride due south. I know whorehouses we can stop at all along the way."

He looked to Silver for support, and the dusky-skinned, brown-eyed deputy nodded.

Rathbone sighed, raked his hand down his face once more in frustration. He regarded both men with an expression of strained patience, then chuckled without mirth. "You damn fools. We leave now, we're liable to have a posse on our own asses. We stay, we'll have a shot, a good shot, at another strongbox. Maybe one worth even more than that one was supposed to be."

"Maybe one full of rocks, like that one was," Silver said.

His look of defiance wilted under Rathbone's level stare. His right eye twitched uncertainly. He knew what happened to men who crossed Frank Rathbone. Besides, he'd been with Frank for nearly five years, and the man had kept him at least as wealthy as your average line rider, without having to ride the line. And the opportunities here in Red Hill were right attractive.

"I don't know, Stall," Silver said. "Maybe the boss is right. What's the point of pullin' out now? If we stay another few weeks, we could be set up pretty good."

Scowling, Stall turned toward the buildings of Red Hill rising above the sage-mottled hogbacks. "Ah, hell, I reckon," he said. "If we pull out now, Roman'll wonder why." He looked at Rathbone. "All right. I'm in. But let's get rich inside of a month. I'm damn tired of tryin' to look respectable."

"I'll work on it." Rathbone looked around, then glanced up, squinting an eye at the sun, judging the time of day. "Roman'll likely be callin' on us to ride out after the stage. You rustle up a few men and lead 'em out. I know it'll make for a long damn day, but I'm gonna stay in town and see if I can find out what happened to the loot they was supposed to be carryin'. We might still have a shot at it. If not, I'll try to find out from Roman when the next big load'll be comin' through. And where it'll be comin' through."

"Well, I reckon I can scout around for the breed, then," Stall said, narrowing a speculative eye along their back trail.

"Just don't say or do anything stupid," Rathbone said. "Remember—we were out lookin' for rustlers that been pesterin' the Stillwater Pool ranches. If anyone asks you about it, tell 'em we cut sign but nothing more. We'll be heading out again soon."

When both men muttered and nodded, Rathbone reined his paint forward and gigged it into a lope.

That bitch, he thought. *When I find her, I'm gonna have one hell of a tough time not shooting her.*

Nah, I won't shoot her, he thought as he raced on into the town. *I'll just cut her throat.*

Real quietlike.

He'd no sooner had the thought than he saw her standing out in front of the bank, talking with the mercantiler Seagraves. Rathbone's jaws hardened as he slowed the paint to a walk. His heart turned several hot flip-flops in his chest, and he had to will his hand away from his pistol grips, from pulling the gun and emptying it into the girl's pretty chest as she stood there, coolly chatting business with the stern-faced, apron-clad Seagraves, her pencil protruding from the rich dark hair piled atop her head. She held a thick ledger book down by her side.

As Rathbone approached the bank, she glanced toward him, returned her glance to the mercantiler, then turned back to the sheriff once more, a puzzled little frown—a very nice attempt at fake innocence—wrinkling the skin above the bridge of her nose.

Rathbone gritted his teeth and smiled, lifting his hat straight up off his head as he gave a bow of mock courtliness and said a little too loudly and sarcastically, "Good afternoon, Miss Roman. How are you today, ma'am? Feelin' well in spite of the heat?" He felt his cheeks harden like Portland cement. "Sure is hot out here today. Dang hot!"

When Seagraves frowned over his shoulder at him, Rathbone said, "Wouldn't you say it was hot out today, Mr. Seagraves?"

Trying to get his rage back on its leash, Rathbone kept walking as both Seagraves and Rae studied him now skeptically. The sheriff glanced over his shoulder and scolded himself for that little scene when he saw both his deputies regarding him with much the same expressions as that of the banker's daughter and the mercantiler.

Don't lose your cool now, fool, he told himself. *Keep your temper in check. If you wanna kill her, you're gonna have to do a better job of covering your tracks than this!*

Knowing he might have just blown his chances of making the bitch pay anytime soon—Seagraves had witnessed his odd behavior and curiously aggressive tone—he pulled his horse up to the hitch rack fronting the sheriff's office. His heart was hammering and his blood was jetting hot through his veins.

"You two stay here, keep an eye on things," he growled, raking a hand across his jaw, then reining his horse away from the hitch rack. "I gotta do some checkin' on things."

"What things?" Stall wanted to know as he swung down from his saddle.

"Things!" Rathbone cursed inwardly as he rode away. There he'd gone again—losing his temper in public in broad daylight. Moderating his voice, he said, "I'll be back soon," then gigged the paint into a trot.

A few minutes later he pulled up in front of the Stockmen's House Hotel and Saloon, and swung heavily down from the saddle. He started toward the hotel's porch, but suddenly his feet seemed stuck in quicksand, and he teetered sideways against the paint and had to reach up and grab the horn to keep from falling.

Holding himself there, his horse looking guardedly back at him while twitching its ears, Rathbone felt a tightness in his chest. Good Christ—he wasn't having a heart-stroke, was he? Quickly, he reached up and unknotted his string tie. That seemed to give him some relief. As he took a deep breath, he felt the heaviness in his chest lighten some, and he released his saddle horn.

No. He'd be all right. He'd just been under a lot of stress lately. All his money gone and no telling where the bitch had stashed it. And riding into town after his failed attempt at the strongbox, he'd seen in Rae's eyes that she was going to play games with him again. And now, because he'd made such a spectacle of himself in front of Seagraves and whoever was standing on the street just then, he couldn't even kill the bitch.

Not now, anyway. He'd have to let a day or two pass. Otherwise, folks would remember how odd he'd acted and they'd start wondering if he wasn't responsible for the poor girl's slow gutting and even slower strangling, which was exactly what he intended to do to her.

He sucked another breath with an audible gasp. Looking down, he saw that his fists were both clenched at his sides. Christ, he needed to relax. It took a few seconds, but he finally managed to loosen his muscles and open his fists. Moving forward, he tossed the paint's reins over the hitch rack and began climbing the broad porch steps, taking one deep breath for every step and trying to keep his mind off Rae for the moment and the image of what he'd do to her once he'd let some time pass.

Brushing dust from the lapels of his black frock coat, Rathbone entered the hotel, strode past the unmanned front desk, and through the arched oak doorway beyond it. The saloon was virtually empty—only a couple of cigar-smoking government beef contractors occupied a table in the room's center, playing a desultory game of stud poker and punctuating their conversation with low chuckles. Rathbone had heard they were here to secure a beef contract for Fort Bowie.

The barman, a man named Murphy, stood behind the horseshoe-shaped bar, arms crossed on his chest, looking boredly out the dusty windows beyond his two lone patrons.

As Rathbone headed for the bar, Murphy turned toward him and looked surprised as well as pleased that he had another customer to wait on. "Sheriff," he said, resting his broad, freckled hands on the polished bar top. "Didn't expect you back so soon. How was the hunt?"

Rathbone looked into the man's eyes, frowning. Was that mockery he saw in Murphy's red-browed blues that always looked just a tad bright from drink? You had to be careful around barmen. They tended to know more than they let on.

No, he decided, tossing his hat onto the bar. Murphy was just making conversation.

"Cut some sign," Rathbone said. "Not much more than that. Big country out there. If I had a few more deputies . . . or deputies who could track." He snorted. He made it a habit of talking his men down, making sure the town knew who was really in charge. "Brandy."

Murphy reached under the bar without looking, and hauled up a flat-faced bottle. He produced a snifter from the bar, then popped the cork from the bottle and filled the glass.

"Any trouble in town?" Rathbone said.

"Nah." Murphy set the bottle on the counter. "Pretty quiet. Just waitin' on the stage. Maybe get some business then."

Rathbone's gaze flicked to the man again sharply, suspiciously. But Murphy only appeared bored. Rathbone always figured the man had few worries. Murphy had a cut of the hotel, but the hotel seemed to be doing well. Rathbone envied the man. Jesus, what would a worry-free life be like?

What would it feel like, not wanting to kill a woman so badly you were constantly grinding your back teeth down to a fine powder?

Rathbone felt his hand shake as he threw down half the drink in one swallow, then leaned forward and probed the goose egg on his temple with the first two fingers of his left hand and sighed.

"How's the head?"

"Better than the Mescin's." Rathbone had told Murphy earlier that a drunken Mexican had hit him with a beer bottle. That was his story for anyone who asked.

He conversed with Murphy for a while, then threw back the rest of the drink and enjoyed the feeling of calm that began to pacify the snakes coiling and uncoiling within him.

"Think I'll head upstairs," he said, donning his hat, then grabbing the bottle and the glass and swinging toward the door. "I need me a good, long nap. See ya, Murph."

"See ya, Sheriff."

He climbed the carpeted stairs to his room, finally feeling calm enough for a long snooze.

The calm didn't last long.

When he got to his room and opened a shade, he sensed someone behind him. Not again! He spun around, drawing his big Colt quickly and ratcheting back the hammer.

"Don't shoot, Frank—it's only me."

Rae Roman lay propped up in his bed, her back against the headboard. The covers were pulled down around her white belly. Her hair fell to her shoulders, and her breasts were bare.

"I'm afraid I owe you an apology," she said, and crossed her arms on her chest, cupping her heavy, sloping breasts in her hands.

Chapter 15

Yakima had one hell of a tough time climbing up out of the canyon. The climb was tougher and longer, albeit less painful, than the descent.

When he finally reached the trail above, he dropped to his knees, holding his wounded right arm in front of him, gripping that wrist with his other hand while he caught his breath and tried to blink the cobwebs from his vision. The soft, dusty colors of the desert washed around him like mirages. He was hot and then cold by turns, his calico shirt pasted against his back.

He looked at his arm. Blood trickled out from beneath the bandanna he'd wrapped around it. He'd have to get that stopped soon. First things first. Heaving himself to his feet, he walked up trail until, after nearly twenty minutes of fervent searching, he discovered the Yellowboy lying in a patch of scrub. He dropped to his knees again, resting, and scooped the rifle up out of the caliche. He rested the gun across his thighs, running his left hand down the length of the fore stock and brass receiver in which a bear had been scrolled, rising on its haunches to fight off several hungry wolves in knee-high grass.

His Shaolin-monk friend, George, had won the rifle in a poker game. George had been a man of peace, so, having no use for the weapon himself, he gave it to Yakima. The half-breed prized the rifle almost as much as he cherished his stallion, Wolf, or his memories of George, who'd been a father to him for one bright, halcyon moment in his otherwise bitter past.

There were several scratches in the fore and rear stocks but the receiver had made out all right. A little hog tallow would take care of the scratches in the wood, and a liberal rub of Patriot's gun oil would bring a shine back to the receiver. He thumbed cartridges from his belt, sliding them into the Winchester's loading gate, racked a shell to check the action, then depressed the hammer and rose, resting the rifle barrel across his left shoulder.

He looked around to see if there happened to be any travelers in the area. Spying nothing but a small dust devil climbing a distant, eastern hogback, he swung around and began tramping west toward Red Hill. Diamondback Station was only a few miles down the road. If he could hold to a steady pace in spite of his aching body and pounding arm, he should make it before sundown.

One step at a time, he told himself, when he began climbing the second hill along the stage road and his feet were starting to feel as though rocks were bound to his ankles.

One step at a time . . .

Nearly a half hour later, he stopped suddenly and blinked, pricking his ears. He'd heard something. Hoofbeats. As the muffled thuds grew more and more distinct and a high clatter joined them, he realized the sound of the approaching riders was coming from straight ahead and from behind the next low rise.

His heart quickening, he worked his way to the top of the hill and stared down the other side to see two dust plumes growing before him, a small wagon and a horseback rider pulling them around a hat-shaped bluff. The wagon driver was whipping his reins across the back of the gray horse hitched to the singletree.

Cautiously, Yakima drew the Winchester's hammer back to half cock, loosened his Colt in its holster, and continued forward, a skeptical glance to his green eyes set deep in their red-brown sockets. The lines in his forehead planed out when he recognized the long nose set in the horsey face of Chick Bannon driving the spring wagon. Bannon's Mexican hostler, Ivano Santiago, rode the white-socked dun a little ahead of the wagon, the man's chaps flapping against his denim-clad legs.

Santiago and Bannon drew up in front of Yakima, and the Diamondback stationmaster's eyes were sharp with dread. "Don't tell me . . ."

Yakima tossed his head backward as he said, "Owlhoots drove us into a canyon."

Bannon frowned as though Yakima were a vision he was trying to make out from a distance, several questions bouncing around in his head at once.

Yakima answered one of them, "Derks is dead."

Bannon swallowed and his flat leathery cheeks rose higher beneath his eyes. "Hellfire. A good man—Avril." He wagged his head. "And . . . the strongbox?"

"It's still there," Yakima growled. "Someone filled it with rocks. Never did have any money in it. The Romans pulled a fast one, outfitted us with a dummy box." He strode forward, holding his right wrist against his belly, biting back the pain. "Good businesspeople, the Romans. Used us for decoys. Must be havin' the strongbox hauled in by another means."

Yakima spat to one side in distaste, slid his rifle onto the floor of the driver's boot, and climbed up onto the seat beside Bannon, who was still regarding him like some strange creature fallen from the sky. "You get a look at the robbers?"

"Nope," Yakima lied. He didn't want it getting around to Rathbone that he was onto him. Prey was easier to hunt when it didn't know it was being stalked.

"How far?"

"About two miles. You'll see the rocks across the trail."

Bannon glanced at Santiago, who stared grimly down from the saddle of his dun, both the hostler's gloved hands resting on his broad, California-style saddle horn. "Check it out, Ivano. Fetch Derks back to the station. The mailbag, too. We'll haul him to town tomorrow."

The Mexican nodded, pulled the dun's drooping head up, then spurred it into a gallop up the trail. At the same time, Bannon swung the wagon around and headed back toward Diamondback Station. "How bad you hit?"

Yakima leaned forward to remove the pressure of the seat back against his arm. His pinched voice belied the pain and nausea that gripped him. He felt himself weakening and was having trouble keeping his head up. "I'll live."

"I'll drive you straight into Red Hill. Think you can make it?"

Yakima nodded, leaned his head back, and closed his eyes.

"I best report to the Romans and Sheriff Rathbone."

"You do that."

"Damn," Yakima heard Bannon say above the clomps of the gray's trotting hooves. "The Romans sure ain't gonna like losin' a stage, a good driver, and six horses. A dummy strongbox, you say? I'll be damned."

"Yeah. Me, too."

Yakima gripped the seat so he wouldn't bounce out. He felt himself slipping into unconsciousness in spite of the wagon's jouncing, and let himself go.

He didn't go far enough to relieve the pain, however. And the jolting ride kept bouncing him back to wakefulness. It wasn't long before every inch of his body registered every rock and thorny shrub he'd hit on that tumble down the mountain, and his arm once again felt as though it had been slathered in hot tar.

Bannon stopped at Diamondback Station to hitch a fresh horse to the wagon and to grab a full canteen, and then they were off again, hammering over the low ridges and caroming around jutting cliff walls. Crossing rocky washes was twice the misery of the general trail, and Yakima heard himself groan when Bannon put the horse a little too briskly up the steep bank of Soldier's Gulch.

"Sorry," he muttered when Yakima drilled him with a one-eyed glare, and shook the reins over the horse's back.

Yakima had semi–drifted off when he felt the wagon lurch to a halt and heard Bannon bellowing, "Whoo-ahhh!"

He lifted his chin from his chest and looked around. There was only a little natural light left on the main street of Red Hill, and the oil pots fronting the saloons had been lit. The sky over the town was dark green. Men were milling along the boardwalks—many more than normal for this time of day.

In most towns across the frontier, there was a big turnout for the drama of a late stage.

The seat bounced as Bannon climbed down from the wagon's driver's boot and pounded up the steps of the doctor's office, using the rickety railing and yelling, "Doc Mangan? Doc—you in there? Got a wounded shotgun rider out here!"

Yakima looked up the street. He could see the shadows of a half dozen or so mounted men milling in front of the sheriff's office directly across from the bank. Two other people stood in the street near the riders. From this distance and in the failing light, it was hard to tell for sure, but the two standing in the street appeared an older man in a suit and long coat, and a woman with her hair up and holding a cape around her shoulders.

None of the group had apparently heard the wagon clatter into town. All heads were turned toward the jailhouse, where Yakima could hear Rathbone's familiar voice rising above the crowd's din. Beyond the milling riders, a tall, slender, black-clad figure silhouetted by lit flares attached to the jailhouse's porch posts jerked this way and that.

Yakima ground his teeth but tried to keep his rage on a leash. Later.

Later . . .

"Help me get him up there, Doc," Bannon hollered from the top of the stairs.

As he started down, his boots clomping loudly and his spurs ringing, the man and the woman on the street before the sheriff's office swung their heads toward the doctor's second-story office. The umber torchlight bathed their faces and glistened in their eyes. The Romans, all right—father and daughter. Yakima felt a burning desire to shoot both of them, as well, though he supposed he couldn't really fault their business decision. The decoy strongbox had been a wise move, if a heartless one—throwing two men, albeit a black man and a half-breed, as well as six good horses, to the wolves for nothing.

He'd let them go. If there was a God, they'd answer to him. Rathbone, Stall, and Silver, however, would answer to Yakima.

As Bannon dropped down the stairs to the street, the Romans glanced at each other in complicity, and then, by ones and twos, the horseback riders started turning toward the doctor's office, as well. As Bannon reached up to help Yakima down from the wagon, the Romans began walking toward the office, and one of the riders swung his prancing horse around and pointed.

"Hey, it's Roman's breed!"

Yakima reached under the wagon seat for his rifle, then eased his weight against Bannon as the Diamondback Station manager helped him over the front wheel and down to the ground. The crowd was moving in a mass toward Yakima's side of the street, converging on and surrounding the Romans.

"Bannon!" Roman called, the banker moving choppily on his short legs, his unbuttoned camelhair greatcoat flapping against his thighs. "Henry, that you? Good Lord—what happened?"

Yakima glanced sidelong at the station manager. "You tell him."

He pulled away from Bannon and started up the stairs. The doctor had come halfway down. He held a hand-carved bamboo cane in his right hand, and his gold-framed spectacles glinted in the light from the flares and burning oil pots.

"I can't help you, young fella," Mangan said, frowning down at Yakima. His southern accent was as soft and rolling as the Tennessee hills in springtime. "I got a bad hip and knee. Can you make it?"

Yakima climbed the steps, passing the sawbones, who then turned and followed his patient up and inside the doctor's office, where a black German shepherd with a long gray snout waited, just inside the door. The doctor backed up as Yakima moved inside, and the dog watched him with attentive, cautious eyes, groaning.

"Back, Buford," the doctor said, waving the dog off. "Go on back to the examining room, son. Straight back. You know where it is."

"Buford?"

"Named after my commanding officer at Gettysburg. Don't tell these carpetbaggers around here, or they'll shoot him." He waved to the dog that followed Yakima, head in the air and nose working as he smelled the fresh blood. "Go lie down, you impertinent cuss!"

Buford gave a frustrated yip and turned around several times before plopping down in the nest of empty feed sacks abutting the doctor's rolltop desk in the office's central room, where a thick cigar smoldered in an ashtray amongst a mess of scrap paper and medicines in jars and bottles of every shape, color, and size. Yakima went into the examining room and eased himself down on the horsehide-upholstered pedestal table.

"Where's Derks?" the doctor asked as he lifted a lamp chimney and raked a match across the top of a washstand.

"Dead."

"Lord!" Mangan touched the match to the wick he'd just raised, then lowered the wick back down a notch and set the chimney over it. "What happened?"

"Owlhoots hit us with a rock slide. Sent the stage into a canyon just the other side of Diamondback Station."

"Oh, for pity's sake," Mangan clucked, drawing the

door curtain closed on the main room. "I've never heard the like. What are things coming to?"

Yakima stared at the red-curtained window behind the lamp that the doctor had just lit. He kept seeing the stage disappearing into the dust fog as he heard the horses screaming and Derks bellowing. Then the front of the stage pitched abruptly forward, and the last thing Yakima saw was the rear luggage boot jerking sharply up, then following the rest of the stage into the rocks and dust over the edge of the cliff.

His chest ached and his throat constricted.

Old Derks was gone. Just like that. . . .

Yakima felt his chest tighten even more, and then the flames of fury wrapped his heart, as well, and he tightened his jaws until his cheeks dimpled as he imagined how it was going to go for Rathbone and the sheriff's murdering deputies.

Suddenly, he realized the doctor had slowly waved his hand in front of his face, frowning at him curiously.

"I asked you what you did here." Mangan had his hand gently wrapped around Yakima's wounded arm. "Are those powder burns?"

"Yeah."

"Good thinkin', young man. I've seen fellas burn themselves good, cause a bigger problem than the one they started with. But it looks like you kept the powder in the hole."

Yakima felt himself loll back as he weakened from exhaustion.

"That's all right," the doctor said. "You lie back.

I'm gonna have to open that wound up and swab it out. Don't want infection setting into the bone, or you'll lose the arm. I've chopped enough arms off during the war for one lifetime."

"Do what you need to, Doc." Yakima lay slowly back, rested his head on a pillow covered in blue-striped ticking, and stared up at the pressed tin ceiling. "Do whatever you need to." He had to get sewn up well enough to go after Derks's killers. The sooner the better.

"Holy Christ!" the doctor said in astonishment when he'd unbuttoned Yakima's shirt and pulled it open. He stared down at Yakima's chest and belly.

Yakima lifted his own head to follow the doctor's gaze. Nearly every inch of his torso was scraped or nicked or gouged, with scattered thorns protruding from his thick hide the color of old saddle leather. Plum-colored bruising was beginning to rise over and around his ribs and across his shoulders, edged with a sickly yellow-green resembling a stormy midwestern sky.

"I'm a fast healer, Doc. Been through it before."

"I see that," Mangan growled as he brushed a blunt-tipped finger across one of the knotted knife scars. "And I hope you are a good healer. You're gonna need—"

Buford's sudden bark cut the doctor off. There was the click of the outside door opening, and a man's voice called, "Doc? It's Sheriff Rathbone. Me and the Romans are here to see the breed."

Chapter 16

Mangan frowned over his glasses at the examination room's curtained doorway. "You're just gonna have to wait, Sheriff. I'm tending this man at the moment."

Mangan gave a caustic chuff as boots pounded in the outer office, and Buford whined and groaned, the dog's toenails clacking on the wooden floor. "Get outta the way, dog," Rathbone ordered.

He drew the curtain aside and poked his head into the examining room, frowning, all business, his five-pointed sheriff's star winking in the lamplight. "Good— he's conscious."

"Sheriff," Mangan said, Yakima's bloody bandanna in his hand, "I told you—"

"It's all right, Doc." Yakima turned to Rathbone and tried to maintain a passive expression as he said, "Come on in, Sheriff. The faster you get after those owlhoots who ran us down, the better."

He saw the look of relief dull the anxiety in the sheriff's eyes. Yakima knew the man had been wondering if he'd gotten a look at him and his cold-blooded compadres when they'd attacked the stage. Now he drew the curtain wide, glanced over his shoulder, and moved on into the examination room, sauntering officiously, rubbing down his soup-strainer mustache with one hand, then sniffing and dipping his fingers into the pockets of his paisley vest.

Rae Roman moved into the room behind him. She was followed by her father, who looked concerned more than bereaved, his fleshy face mottled, eyes hooded. The loss of two men, a coach, and a team was much easier to swallow than a strongbox. Men and teams could be replaced. The loss of money could ruin a man.

Yakima couldn't keep his anger out of his eyes as he studied the two Coronado Line owners.

"Bannon told us what happened, Henry," the sheriff said, standing off to the far end of the examination table as Mangan continued to examine the two bullet holes in Yakima's arm. "What happened? They take you by surprise?"

Yakima nodded. "Yep. Took us by surprise. Rock slide. I was thrown off the coach before it went over the cliff. Rolled down into a little ravine. Woke up with one hell of a headache." He glanced at both Romans standing beside him, both looking over his battered torso with looks of barely concealed revulsion. "I suppose Bannon told you that Derks went into the canyon with the coach?"

The Romans nodded gravely. "What a shame," the woman said, pursing her lips and shaking her head.

"You didn't get a look at the attackers?" Delbert

Roman said, planting his fists on the side of the table and leaning over his battered shotgun messenger.

"No." Yakima looked at Rathbone, who was studying him with a vague unease in his eyes. "I saw neither hide nor hair of any of 'em. Judging by the tracks I saw later, there were three. They appeared to be headed in the direction of Red Hill."

That was just to give Rathbone a little jolt of apprehension. Keeping his expression plain, Yakima added, "They mighta turned off somewhere between there and here, though. Or—who knows?—maybe they're amongst us right now."

He looked innocently at the Romans, but he thought he could hear Rathbone's heart thudding hard in the sheriff's chest.

Delbert Roman turned to Rathbone, as if waiting for the sheriff to start doing his job. Rathbone cleared his throat, drew a deep breath, and furrowed his brows. "Three, you say? Headed toward Red Hill, huh?" He looked at the Romans. "I'll have my men keep an eye out for strangers. In the meantime, I'll send the posse out to try and cut sign. Might as well wait for light, though, now."

As the doctor stoked the room's sheet-iron stove, Yakima scowled at Rathbone, playing out his role as vengeance-hungry shotgun rider while keeping the sheriff in the dark as to whom he was really hunting. "I'd like to volunteer to ride along with that posse tomorrow, Sheriff."

The doctor, who'd just filled a copper pan with

water and set it on the stove, tossed a caustic laugh over his shoulder. "You won't be going anywhere for several days, Mr. Henry. Those bruises all across your body are going to hurt considerably more tomorrow and likely for the next week or so. I'm guessing you have cracked or maybe broken ribs. And you'll have to keep that arm in a sling for a time, give it time to heal. The bullet nicked the bone."

The doctor narrowed a gray-browed eye to emphasize "bone," then turned back to his water, into which he dropped a small scissors and a scalpel.

Rathbone held his gaze on Yakima. "Bannon knows where we'll find the stage?"

Yakima nodded.

Rathbone sighed and looked at the banker. "Well, I reckon that's about all I need. I'll pass the information on to the men, have them set out first thing tomorrow."

Rathbone pinched his hat brim to the Romans and headed out the door. Yakima smiled inwardly at the man's charade, and at the smooth way he, Yakima, felt that he'd pulled off his own. How he really felt would very soon be all too clear.

In the outer office, Buford barked and the dog's toenails made a wild scraping sound across the wooden floor as he leaped at Rathbone.

"Goddamn dog!" the sheriff barked, scuffing his heels and ringing his spurs. "Mangan, if you don't heel this cur, I'm gonna shoot him!"

"At ease, Buford," the doctor called over his shoul-

der, the grin stretching his cheek betraying his amusement. "At ease, at ease."

The dog groaned. The door clicked open and slammed
shut, and Rathbone was gone.

Yakima looked at both Romans staring guiltily down
at him. He knew what they were thinking, and he
didn't want to make it easy for them. "The dummy
strongbox was a real good move."

"Yes, well, it was my own decision, Mr. Henry,"
Roman said, a deep red flush rising in his cheeks and
broad nose. "Mine and the foreman's from the Sand
Creek outfit. He wanted me to guarantee the safe de-
livery of his money, so I cooked up a plan to have
it delivered by a freighter who runs regularly between
Apache Gap and Red Hill. It came in yesterday. Safe
and sound."

He glanced at his daughter, who continued to look
down at Yakima's arm as though in shame. At least,
she appeared ashamed. It was hard to tell what the
stone-faced young woman was ever thinking.

Roman pursed his lips with satisfaction and nodded.

"I'll be drawing my wages," Yakima said. "You can
hold 'em for me till I'm ready to ride."

Roman frowned. The doctor turned away from the
pan that was beginning to sigh as the water heated.
Yakima lifted his head from the pillow and glared up
at his former employers.

"I don't like the way you two do business. I reckon
it's good business. For you. But Avril Derks went into
this job believing if he died doing it, he'd be dying for

what you had in the strongbox. And putting rocks in that strongbox without letting us know about it was the most low-down, dirty, rotten bit of hornswoggling as I've ever seen. I won't work for ring-tailed polecats. Now, if you'll excuse me, my arm hurts."

Delbert Roman looked at his daughter as though for private council. Rae Roman kept her blandly oblique stare on Yakima. Finally, his face turning even a darker red than before, the banker scowled at his former shotgun messenger, his nostrils pinching and turning white, his jowls quivering.

"Well, I'm sorry that's how you feel about it, Mr. Henry. You do know, however, that if you had been doing your job correctly, you might have prevented the stage's being dumped into that canyon in the first place."

Yakima narrowed an eye at the man. His own eyes blazed now, and his Indian-dark face turned umber. "You just make sure you give ol' Derks a respectable send-off. A nice, big stone with his name carved in it, and a preacher to say a few words over him. You do that, or I'll see you about it personally."

Rae Roman gasped and stepped back. "I told you, Father. This man is a savage!"

"Come on, Rae." Scowling indignantly at Yakima, the banker turned his daughter around by her shoulders and gave her a gentle shove toward the door. He followed her into the main office, where Buford groaned but did not bark. Roman glanced back once more at Yakima warily, then, straightening his beaver hat on his head and pursing his lips in mute outrage, followed his daughter out of the office and slammed the door behind him.

Buford gave a single bark at the racket but remained in his nest beside the desk.

The doctor was standing before the stove upon which the kettle was steaming, and began rolling up his shirtsleeves. "I don't blame you for what you said to those folks, Henry. But you'd be well advised to light a shuck out of town as soon as you're well enough. The Romans are powerful people. And powerful people make formidable enemies."

"I've had enemies before."

Mangan glanced at the scars beneath the bruising on Yakima's belly, chest, and shoulders, and nodded. "I see that."

Chapter 17

A mountain-sized giant slammed the anvil he held clenched in his wagon-sized fist deep into Yakima's rib cage, and the half-breed snapped his eyes open as he sat up in bed suddenly, groaning. He reached for his ribs with both hands, and that reignited the fire in his upper right arm.

He tipped his head back on his shoulders, and his painful grimace opened a cavern in his face. He tried to suck a breath, but that increased the pain in his ribs even more, and then he vaguely realized that wide bandage had been wrapped taught around his torso. His right arm was in a cotton sling.

"Oh, Yakima, easy!" said a female voice. "Rest back, now . . . *gently*. I know it hurts. Shall I call the doctor?"

Yakima opened his eyes. His brows knitted curiously. Beth Seagraves stood crouched before him, her hands on his shoulders, gently pushing him down. In her left hand she held a cool, damp cloth. A ladder-back, hide-bottom chair was angled beside the bed, and on the chair was an enamel basin of water.

The woman's blond hair was entwined in a thick bun atop her head. She wore a plain cream dress with tan squares and lace seams, and it was buttoned all the way to her neck, the collar held fast with a cameo pin. It was pulled taut across her breasts that were rising and falling heavily as she breathed.

Yakima relented to the pressure of her hands, and slowly lowered his head to the pillow. He glanced around the room as he drew shallow draughts of air into his chest. He was no longer in the examination room. This room was small, but he was in a real bed, and there was a dresser in a corner with chipped red paint and a cracked, rust-spotted mirror. Shabby blue curtains were drawn over a four-paned window. Behind them was a watery wash of afternoon light.

He could hear muffled sounds from outside.

As the pain slowly gave some ground, Yakima opened his fists and sucked a little more air into his lungs.

"You've several cracked ribs," Beth said. "The doctor's been keeping you on pain medication—laudanum, mostly. He said I could give another spoonful if you woke."

Yakima stared up at her questioningly, unable not to admire the creaminess of her skin that seemed lit from inside, and the glow of her hazel eyes in the soft light angling against her from the window. She canted her head to one side, and her red lips lifted a gentle smile. "I'm working for the doctor as of yesterday. Don't worry—I may not have any formal training, but I know what I'm doing. I worked part-time for a doctor back in Iowa."

"Good to know." Yakima frowned. He reached up with his left hand and traced with his middle finger a slightly swollen, half-inch cut on her upper lip, on the far right side of her mouth. She lowered her eyes, color rising in her cheeks, and she raised her hand to Yakima's, closing her smaller one over his broad, thick, rope-scarred paw.

Her voice was a murmur. "Please, don't."

"Seagraves?"

Her eyes found his, and a boldness blazed there. "I've left him. I've moved into a room with Mrs. Purdy— Calvin and I. I intend to work long enough for a stake, and then I'll leave."

Yakima lowered his hand, felt a tenderness for the woman rise up above his own throbbing aches. "Where?"

"I don't know. Back to Grand Island, I suppose. It's home. I'll find something there." She turned and walked over to the window and slid the curtain aside with one hand. "This is such a lonely, dusty place. A savage place. No place to raise a boy. He doesn't like school here. He refused to call Mr. Seagraves 'sir.' Thus, he's sporting a black eye."

"Is that why the bastard hit you?"

Beth let the curtain fall back into place and turned toward Yakima. "Would you like some laudanum?"

"Not just yet." Yakima looked around the room, saw his clothes and hat hanging from a spike in the wall near the curtained doorway. His gun and shell belt hung from a spike, as well. His Yellowboy stood in the corner near the dresser.

He squirmed around, feeling a heaviness under the

pain in all his limbs and the sluggishness of pent-up blood. "How long have I been here, anyway?"

"This is your third day. The doctor kept you out, when he saw how bad off your were. That must have been a terrible tumble you took."

"I've ached before," he groaned, shifting his weight around, trying to relieve some of the soreness in his rump. "But not like this."

"Dr. Mangan said he removed nearly a hundred cactus spikes from your backside."

"I can believe it."

Beth walked over to Yakima's shell belt, reached up, removed the keeper thong from over his Colt's hammer, and slid the gun from the holster. She carried it over to the bed and handed it to him.

"You'd better keep this under your pillow, now that you're awake."

Yakima arched a brow at the woman.

"One of the sheriff's deputies has been hanging around outside the doctor's office. He wanted to pay you a visit yesterday, but the doctor wouldn't let him."

Yakima stretched a grim smile. "Stall?"

"I believe that's his name. The big man." Beth soaked the cloth in the basin atop the chair and dabbed at Yakima's hot forehead. "I heard about what happened in the Queen of Hearts, between you and him. You'd best be careful."

Yakima reached up and slipped the pistol beneath his pillow. "Thanks."

She dabbed at his face for a time. The cool rag felt nice against his chin.

"They bury Derks yet?"

"Yesterday. A nice funeral for a black man. The Romans are even having a chiseled stone set at the head of his grave." Beth glanced down at him, amused, then continued dabbing at his brow.

"Rathbone still around?"

She glanced at him again, faintly curious, then nodded. "He sent a posse out to look for the men who ran the stage off the cliff." She shook her head grimly and wrung the cloth out in the basin once more. "They came back empty-handed. The long riders are probably way up high in the Coronados by now. I suspect they'll be back, though, after another strongbox. A filled one, this time."

Beth lifted the cloth from his swollen left cheek and frowned down at him. He realized then that he'd been staring hard at the ceiling, and that his expression must have been hard, cold, grave. He'd been imagining how he was going to settle his and Derks's debt with Rathbone.

"Yakima," the woman asked. "What's your quarrel with the sheriff?"

He feigned a quizzical smile. "Quarrel? I don't have any *quarrel* with the man at all."

No, not a quarrel. A *reckoning*.

He winced as an Apache war lance rammed through his left side and out the right. "You know, I think I'll take a sip of that laudanum now."

Yakima slept until later that night, when Beth came in with a bowl of soup. He was weak from both physical pain and the laudanum, so she tied a bib around his neck and fed him. It made him feel like a child or an old man, but there wasn't much he could do about that. He needed food to get healthy again.

Besides, in spite of the mental anguish she caused him, bringing up memories of another pretty blonde who was now dead and buried north of here, he enjoyed her company. The way she looked in her tight dress, the clarity of her eyes, the sureness of her slender hands, the sound of her breathing. She smelled of rosewater and talcum—a distinctly female smell.

He wondered, as she spooned soup into his mouth and he ate past his point of being full, if he would ever fall as deeply in love again as he'd fallen for Faith. If he'd ever go to bed with a woman, wake up with her, work with her, share with her the joys and sorrows of daily living, and watch the days roll away together like waves beating against a sandy beach.

He squeezed his eyes closed to waylay the tears.

No. They said that for every man there was really only one woman. Well, he'd had his. The woman before him now resembled Faith in many ways, and she was lovely, to be sure. And the man in him yearned to lie with her again and enjoy her body writhing with his. But he could never love her the way he'd loved Faith.

He could never love any woman again the way he'd loved Faith.

"More laudanum?" Beth said, holding the spoon away from his mouth.

Yakima opened his eyes. She studied him, saw the

brightness there in his narrowed eyes that stared across the room, unseeing but glistening like rain-washed chunks of jade. Slowly, she lowered the spoon.

"Whoever she was," she said softly, dropping the spoon into the bowl, "she was a very lucky woman."

"She's dead."

"I had a feeling. And I know how it feels."

She rose and started walking to the door. She stopped suddenly, set the bowl on the dresser, and sat down on the edge of the bed. Slowly, she leaned toward him, wrapped her arms around his neck, and kissed him softly on the lips, moving her lips tenderly, lovingly against his while caressing his cheeks with her fingers.

She pulled away, smiling, then rose, retrieved the bowl, and left the room.

Yakima squeezed his eyes closed and cursed.

Later, Mangan came in, removed the bandage on his arm, and inspected the wound carefully, muttering to himself in a satisfied manner before swabbing the wound with alcohol that burned like hellfires, and re-wrapped the bullet holes with gauze and a length of clean linen, then returned the limb to the sling.

"How long before you think I'll be able to walk out of here?" Yakima asked him as Mangan washed his hands with alcohol.

"When you feel good enough. A couple of days, probably. With those ribs and the amount of blood you lost, you're probably going to feel like holing up in bed for a while, taking it easy." Mangan glanced over his shoulder and shifted his eyes to Yakima's pillow. "What's the gun for?"

Yakima turned his head slightly, saw the horn-gripped handle protruding slightly from beneath the pillow. He reached up with his left hand and poked the gun out of sight. "What's a gun usually for?"

Mangan was still looking at him over his shoulder as he rubbed his hands down with alcohol. "Don't give me any trouble, Yakima."

"Who said I was going to bring trouble?"

"A man like you." Mangan shook his head. "They always bring trouble. Don't take this the wrong way, son, but I'll be glad when you're gone."

"You're getting owly in your old age, Doc." Yakima waggled his head around, stretching the kinks out of his neck. "Or maybe you've seen Deputy Stall hanging around outside your office."

Mangan lowered his shirtsleeves and began buttoning the cuffs. "You and Stall save whatever you have between you for after you leave here."

He gave Yakima a hard look, then pushed through the curtained doorway.

Later, when Mangan had gone home after dark, Beth returned to keep an eye on Yakima, to swab his face when the fever returned and to help him with the chamber pot. She cooked him a savory stew and served it to him with bread that her landlady, Mrs. Purdy, had baked. He was able to feed himself while she sat near the bed, knitting a sweater for Calvin.

They talked for a time about the boy and Mrs.

Purdy and the landlady's garden, which she'd gotten Calvin to help the woman weed. She said nothing about Seagraves but only that she hoped to be leaving soon, that she missed Nebraska and the family she had left there—a sister, some cousins, and a couple of aunts. Her husband's parents were still there, and she thought she could live with them for a time, until she could get back on her feet again.

Her own folks had died in a cyclone.

After Yakima had finished the stew, he slept but was awakened by the rumble of thunder. Rain pelted the roof and battered his window. Silver water cascaded off the porch overhang, dropping into darkness. He listened for a time before the somnolent sounds lulled him to sleep. He woke again to a male voice raised in anger, and jerked his right hand up without thinking.

He groaned as an iron crab chewed into his arm, then half turned and pulled the gun out from beneath the pillow with his other hand.

"I told you, Sylvus," he heard Beth say in the doctor's main office, above the rattle of rain against his window and the frequent thunder rumbles, "I've changed my mind. I will not be the wife of a man who can never love me, can never love my son!"

"Your son," Seagraves said in a tight voice that trembled with barely controlled rage, "has shown no respect but only disdain for me. You've set a right bad example for him, Beth, right away telling him that he could sleep downstairs after *I'd* told him that he'd have his own room upstairs in the attic!"

Yakima hadn't been out of bed except to use the chamber pot and to shuffle over to the window a few times, and he felt as though his muscles had atrophied. He grunted and groaned as he heaved himself to his feet, keeping his right arm in the sling, then shuffled over to the spike where his clothes had been hung. He was naked save for the bandage around his torso, and now as he walked across the wooden floor, he realized that even his feet hurt.

In the outer office, he could hear Beth and Seagraves continue to argue over the boy, Beth explaining that Calvin had been afraid to sleep on a separate floor from his mother since his father's death, and that a little boy couldn't be expected to work nearly full-time in Seagraves's store when he was also attending class at the Red Hill school every day.

"And he certainly shouldn't be expected to start working such a schedule the very day after his arrival in Red Hill and his mother's marriage to a man neither she nor her boy had ever even met!"

"And why not, pray tell!" Seagraves demanded as Yakima pulled on his threadbare long-handles as quickly as he could in his condition.

"You don't want a son or a wife," Beth retorted, her voice rising sharply. "What you want, Mr. Seagraves, is a pair of *slaves*!"

"How dare you speak to me like that! You show me some respect, Beth!"

"You don't deserve any respect. Now go on and get the hell out of here. I've an appointment with an attorney in the morning, and I fully intend to have the marriage annulled as soon as possible."

"Oh, no, you don't. You will not make a laughing-stock of me here in my own town! No more than you already have, damn you!"

Beth gave a pained yelp, and Yakima, his long-handles unbuttoned, pushed through the curtained doorway, tramped down a short hall and into the main office. On the office's far side, the door was open, showing lightning flashes and the rain that was hammering the outside staircase, the bullet-sized drops splashing silver in the lantern light. Wet footprints shone on the thick rug fronting the door and beyond it, tracing an arc.

Yakima heard another groan and a whimper, and he turned to his left.

Seagraves, clad in a yellow India rubber rain slicker and sodden high-crowned felt hat, was crouched over Beth, whom he had down on her knees, near the doctor's rolltop desk. Seagraves had his hand wrapped around her right wrist and was twisting her arm around.

Beth sobbed and stretched her lips back from her teeth in misery, her hair tumbling down from the neat bun atop her head. Tears washed down her cheeks and over her chin to join the raindrops that had dribbled off the brim of Seagraves's hat to the floor at his rubber boots.

"You can't!" Beth cried. "You can't make me come back. I'm taking my money out of the bank, and Calvin and I are leaving!"

Seagraves laughed and twisted Beth's wrist harder, evoking a louder, shriller cry from the woman. "You just try it! That money is mine for all the work I did in preparing the house—"

Seagraves stopped when he heard the loud, ratcheting click, then turned sharply to see Yakima's cocked Colt aimed in Yakima's extended left hand at a spot between the man's two predatory, yellow-gray eyes.

The eyes snapped even wider as Seagraves barked, "How dare you aim a gun at me, you half-breed heathen!"

Yakima kept the gun aimed at the mercantiler's forehead, his nostrils flared with fury. He looked down at Seagraves's hand that was still wrapped taut around Beth's wrist, and the man suddenly let her go. His face paled slightly, and the fear in his eyes turned instantly to apprehension.

"You got three seconds to haul your ass out of here, Seagraves."

"This is none of your affair!"

Yakima narrowed an eye and steadied the gun in his fist. "One . . ."

Seagraves jerked back suddenly, as though he'd been slapped. Yakima tracked him with the cocked revolver.

"Two . . ."

The mercantiler backed to the door, his wet boots squeaking on the floor, and cast another searing glare at his mail-order bride. "Why . . . I wouldn't have you back now if you begged me. You're nothing but a *trollop*!"

"Three."

Seagraves wheeled and fairly ran through the open door, and turned sharply to his left. He bolted down the steps, angling down beyond the sashed window left of the door, making the stair rail leap and jerk as a witch's finger of lightning flashed over the next rooftop, and a peal of thunder made the room shake. Yakima shuffled over and closed the door.

Beth was on the floor, knees raised to her chin, her face in her hands. Her shoulders jerked as she sobbed.

Yakima went over to her, laid his gun on the floor, and wrapped his arms around her.

He held her for a long time as she cried not only over Seagraves's assault, Yakima knew, but also over the general lousy course her and her son's lives had taken. Yakima wished there was something he could do for her.

For her and the boy. Something to make them happy and feel that the world wasn't so cold and dark.

But all he could do was hold her and let her cry while the rain beat down and the thunder rumbled like cannons.

Chapter 18

Lightning flashed in the windows, illuminating Rathbone's wafting cigar smoke so that it glowed like cobwebs in reflected sunlight. A moment of silence, like a held breath. Then thunder echoed like the gods flinging boulders across a canyon high in the Coronados.

The naked sheriff sat back against the headboard of his bed in the Stockmen's House Hotel, and stared across the room, through the billowing smoke, to where Rae Roman stood before his dresser, clad in only a gauzy wrap and silk slippers as she ran a tortoiseshell brush through her hair. She was illuminated by the violet bracket lamps on the wall before her, silhouetting her curvaceous body deliciously. The shaded sides of her heavy breasts bulged out darkly, delightfully.

Rathbone felt a tightness in his chest, a thickness in his throat. He could never get enough of this woman. Every minute, every hour with her only made him want more, more, more. Thank God she'd been able to convince him she'd had nothing to do with that dummy strongbox, that that had been her father's and the Sand Creek manager's planning, and she hadn't known about it until long after Rathbone and his men had ridden out after it. The Sand Creek manager had wanted the secret kept between himself and Delbert Roman, with not even Rae or Elmwood, the loan officer, knowing.

Thank God she hadn't crossed him as he still found himself fearing she had or might still. He'd have killed her and missed out on tonight, tomorrow night, and all the nights hereafter. . . .

"Frank, I'm hungry," she said into the mirror, her voice a purr, barely audible above the drumming rain.

"I've got something to take your mind off it."

"Already had that."

"The night is young. And, like you said, the old man's in a poker game." Holding the stogie in one hand, Rathbone rose from the bed and walked toward her. "Take my word for it, having been in on those stud marathons of his myself, he'll be there till breakfast."

"God, you're tireless."

Rae stared at herself in the mirror, the luminous dark eyes, the full breasts that the wrap did not so much conceal as accentuate and make all the more inviting. She'd always been proud of her breasts, and in spite of the disgusted looks she customarily gave the men she found stealing peeks at them even with their wives present, or outright ogling them as though they were freshly polished, melon-sized pearls, she'd always basked in the attention. And it wasn't just the attention she savored. Her body had always given her a certain sense of security, knowing that in the world of lustful men, no matter how poor she got, or down-trodden, or how desperate to leave this godforsaken hellhole, she could always rely on her figure to dig her out.

As long as she had it, that is. As long as she had her relative youth. Neither would last forever. And she saw what became of women who'd weathered on past their prime.

She had to use her natural endowments now to her best advantage, and set herself up for the rest of her life, for the days when her face grew wrinkled and leathery, her belly bulged to an unfashionable degree, and her breasts sagged like half-filled bladder flasks.

The thought was a cold breath along her spine, and she gave a shiver as she stared at that horrific image of herself in the mirror.

She jerked again when hands slid around her sides from behind.

"Ooh," Rathbone breathed in her ear, his breath sour with the stench of brandy and cigar smoke. "Catch a chill, my dear? Let me warm you."

His hands groped her not altogether unpleasingly, and she tilted her head away from his, watching his hands in the mirror. "Later, Frank. After you've ordered up a couple of steaks from the kitchen."

He snorted in frustration as he nibbled her ear, the nibbles growing smaller until he gave her lobe a little, last tug, his mustache scratching against her ear and neck. "All right, all right."

He looked at her over her shoulder in the mirror and

lowered his hands to her hips. "But first, before the
T-bones—when're you and the old man gonna get another stage up and running? More importantly, when're
you gonna get another one up and running and hauling another strongbox? I assume the Sand Creek boys
done picked up the one the old bastard had hauled in
here by Arnold McGinnis's bull train."

She raised her arms to gently shove his away from
her, and resumed brushing her brown hair out in the
mirror, lifting a shine that the lamplight caused to glisten.
She waited till a loud clap of thunder had passed, then
said primly, "Well, you're wrong in your assumptions,
my dear Frank."

What a simpleton he was. She'd known all along,
having eavesdropped on her father's conversation with
the Sand Creek manager, that the stage would be carrying a dummy box and that McGinnis's outfit would
be hauling it. She'd simply wanted Rathbone to go
after the stage in hopes that the savage Yakima Henry
would kill him or that he would kill Yakima Henry.
She needed both men out of her way. In the meantime, she'd sent a couple of professional gunmen after
the bull train, but, not knowing the country, the fools
had gotten lost and missed the train altogether.

So, now she needed Rathbone again to help her
get the money out of the bank. When he'd done that,
and turned over her cut, she'd have him killed and then
take his cut, as well. What she was going to do with
the other two men she had in her employ and who
were still hanging around town, awaiting her orders,
she had no idea. She'd think of something. If she were

a man who was good with a gun, she'd simply kill them.

Sometimes she really hated being female. At least the limitation had caused her to hone her wits as well as her wiles to a razor's edge, and she'd benefited from that as well as been distracted from the tawdriness of this ramshackle, backwater town.

Rathbone had turned his head to frown down at her. "How was I wrong?"

"The money's still in the bank."

"Still in the bank?"

"All this rain has likely flooded the river that runs between here and Red Hill, and the Sand Creek manager hasn't been able to get a contingent of armed men through to pick it up. We'll likely have a couple of days or until the rains let up and the flood waters recede."

Rae's eyes met Rathbone's in the mirror again.

"Before those waters recede, my darling Frank, we need to get the money out of the bank. Quietly."

"How the hell we gonna rob a bank quietly? You got the combination to the safe?"

"I already told you I don't." Rae put some steel into her voice. Her father hadn't given the combination to her, but only to the loan officer, because the combination was changed every two weeks and he didn't want her "pretty head cluttered up with such nonsense." She'd always wondered if it was because deep down he really didn't trust her.

"Ronald Elmwood has the combination," Rae continued, speaking softly now beneath the clattering storm.

"Today is what—Friday? I say Monday morning you and your men meet Ronald at the bank. He's always the first one there, sometimes as early as seven o'clock."

"He'll know it's us," Rathbone said in a menacing singsong.

Rae's eyes were cool, flat as a lake at sundown. "Yes, he will, won't he? And what can he possibly do about it?"

She set her brush down and placed her hand against his face, continuing to stare at his mirror image gravely, darkly, with a pasteboard smile stretching her lips. "Rest assured that if you try to double-cross me, Frank, I'll have you hunted and killed like the rabid cur you are. There'll be nowhere for you to hide."

She dug her long fingernails into his cheek and made a rasping sound as she raked his beard stubble. "It might take me months, or even a few years. But you'd better plan on keeping a careful watch over your shoulder while you're spending our money, because eventually you'll pay dearly for every penny you stole from me!"

Rathbone smiled, then ran his hands up her sides and slid them forward to brusquely grab her breasts. He kneaded them hard and nuzzled her neck so roughly, raking her unblemished skin with his mustache, that she gave an indignant yelp.

"Touché, my tulip," Rathbone warned. "Just remember—the same goes for you."

The next morning, Rathbone and his deputies sat down to a breakfast of steak and eggs in the dining room of the

Stockmen's Hotel. Quietly, when the waitress was out of hearing in the kitchen—only two other tables were occupied, as Saturday mornings at the hotel as in all of Red Hill were usually sedate—the sheriff informed Stall and Silver of the plan for Monday morning.

"Any packing you need to do, any last-minute business, needs to be taken care of this weekend. Once we're out of town with the money, we're out of town for good."

Silver shoved the last bit of egg into his mouth and sat back in his chair, frowning across the table at Rathbone. "How do you know that horse money's still in the bank, boss?"

"You seen any Sand Creek men in town lately?" Rathbone asked.

Silver and Stall glanced at each other, shrugging.

"I figure they won't be in till the river's gone down," the sheriff added, swabbing the steak grease from his plate with a thick wedge of toast.

"If we run out, folks're gonna know who stole the loot," Stall said. "They'll put it together right quick. Maybe we best just kill ole Elmwood as planned, then stash the loot like we done with the rest of it, and wait for the dust to settle. Then we can say we all done got an offer for better jobs up north or down south, and light a shuck without nobody the wiser. If we play it like you said, boss, we're likely to have a posse on our asses."

Sure, if they played it like he said, thought Rathbone with an inward smirk. But it wouldn't exactly be played the way he'd said.

He intended to kill Stall and Silver and then head off to St. Louis with the loot. He'd wait for Rae there, and split the money with her. He wouldn't double-cross her as he'd once intended. Not that any sense of honor restrained him. It was the woman herself. That body had gotten under his skin. Maybe more than that. God, he hoped not, but he was beginning to wonder if his hatred for her coupled with his animal cravings had somehow transmogrified into a weird, perverted form of love.

He just couldn't imagine not having her in his arms every night.

After her father had been ruined—the lost coach along with the stolen Sand Creek money would likely be the straw that finally broke Roman's back—Rae would pull out and join Rathbone in St. Louis, where they'd both change their names in case anyone put them together with the stolen loot, and make their way farther east, where'd they live like king and queen. He'd have preferred California, but, hell, he wasn't picky.

If Rae wanted to go East, they'd go East. As Mr. and Mrs. Rasmussen, Rathbone thought. He liked the ring of that. That had been his mother's maiden name. Seemed only fitting. Frederick and Racine Rasmussen.

Rathbone grinned behind the coffee mug he held high before his face. "You two just leave the thinkin' to me," he scolded. "I've done right by you so far, ain't I?"

Stall and Silver looked at him uncertainly. Something about that didn't sound right to the big deputy, but he had more important things on his mind.

"All right if I take care of the breed first, boss?"

"I wouldn't have it any other way, my friend." Rathbone swallowed a mouthful of lukewarm coffee and set his cup down with a sigh. "Just make sure there're no witnesses. I don't want anything, not even the score you got with the breed, to interfere with our plans for Monday morning."

Stall and Silver looked at each other with hard looks of complicity.

Chapter 19

"Well, I'll be damned," Yakima said to himself about midmorning the next day. "They really did it."

With Beth's help, he'd managed to dress. Now, with his right arm in a sling, he stood in the small boot hill cemetery on a high hill just north of the village, staring down at the freshly mounded and rock-covered grave fronted by a tombstone that appeared to have been set there just that morning.

He shook his head and gave a bemused snort. He'd thought he'd come up here and see the grave marked by only a small wooden cross, if that, and he'd have to stroll over to the bank and slap the demon shit out of Delbert Roman.

But they'd really done it. Nicely chiseled, too:

Avril Derks
B: ?–D: September 21, 1878
Driver for Coronado Transp.
RIP

Yakima squatted on his heels and doffed his hat, dropping his eyes from the marker to the rocks that neatly covered the grave. He set the handful of desert wildflowers he'd picked earlier into a little cavity amongst the rocks. The bright blues, yellows, and reds added a nice touch of color to the drab brown mound, just as they'd colored the desert so nicely after the hard monsoon rains.

Yakima's pleasant surprise at finding the tombstone here, just as he'd ordered, dwindled, replaced by a whirlpool of anger churning beneath his battered ribs, swelling out and riffling into his belly. A raw burning, like that which he'd felt upon finding his Shaolin monk friend, George, hanging from the cottonwood simply because the man had outsmarted others who'd thought themselves much smarter at poker.

The waste of it all.

A good man dead—one who'd suffered a long, hard life and worked his ass off and shown undeserved loyalty to a company who'd taken him for granted—because Rathbone and his outlaw deputies were after the empty strongbox. They'd run Derks into that canyon like a troublesome animal they were merely trying to get out of the way.

Yakima's hands kneaded the edge of his hat brim as his eyes bored into the rocks of the driver's grave. Self-recrimination added to the mix of sharp-edged emotions. Rathbone had gone to such extremes, he knew, because of Yakima himself. He was why Derks was dead. Rathbone had likely not arrested Yakima so the run wouldn't be canceled or the big shipment postponed. He couldn't be faulted for doing his job, but if he hadn't done it so well, or hadn't come to this damn jerkwater in the first place, and seen that "help wanted" sign in the German Café, Derks might still be alive. Barring the Diamondback bushwhacking, that is. . . .

Yakima heard a tearing sound, and looked down. His big hands were giving the hat a going-over, and he'd made a small rip in the edge of the brim. He cursed, smoothed the brim under his fingers, and set the hat on his head.

He pushed up to his feet with a wince at the aches in his ribs and his joints, and the barks of the bruises that covered nearly every inch of his body.

"Nice ridin' with you, pard. Rest easy."

His face hard as granite, he swung around to face the town at the bottom of the long, gentle slope.

It was Saturday, and there weren't many people out. Late-breakfast fires had spread a blue haze over the rooftops. The air was golden clear after the rain, and even the smell of the privies and trash heaps had thinned out beneath the purifying tang of wet sage and cedar.

He'd done all he could to the Romans to make them pay for their part in Derks's death. He'd shamed them and made them open their pocketbooks for the marker.

But he hadn't even gotten started on settling up with Rathbone.

He'd moved back over to the boardinghouse earlier. After a few more days' rest, he'd settle up that part of the bill, as well. It shouldn't take long. Men like Rathbone, Stall, and Silver deserved only to be shot down like rabid dogs. And dumped in the nearest ravine. Then Yakima would ride the hell out of here. To where, he had no idea.

One place was as bad as another.

He headed on down the narrow footpath lined with rocks. It wound around several spindly cottonwoods to the valley bottom and the town. The main street was deserted save for a couple of ranch hands in rough trail garb, riding a couple of rangy cow ponies down the middle of the street, heading toward Yakima. They'd made a Friday night of it, and now they rode with hunched shoulders and hanging heads, their horses' hooves plodding in the mud of the wet street. Yakima hugged the north edge of the street as the riders passed him and he made his way westward toward his boardinghouse beyond Bayonet Creek, intending to take another long, healing nap.

Boots thumped on the boardwalk to his left and he saw a big figure in a gray duster walking toward him. The man was obscured by the shade of the awning over his head, but the plaster over the man's nose and the bandage over one ear identified him. He stopped suddenly and lifted his rifle in both hands defensively as Yakima kept moving, a droll smile lifting the corners of the half-breed's mouth.

"Mornin', Stall."

"Breed . . . ," the deputy grumbled, turning his body slowly to track Yakima as he passed him, heading in the opposite direction.

"How's that nose?"

Stall's eyes widened and he hardened his jaws in anger. "You know how the nose is, you son of a bitch."

"Yeah, I reckon I do." Yakima chuckled and continued walking, keeping his head turned toward the deputy, who remained where he was, in a defensive position, scowling after him.

Yakima kept his right hand pressed flat against his belly, the sling restraining his movements, but he'd slip the arm free and reach for the pistol thronged on his thigh if he had to. Even in his condition, he'd make short work of the big deputy.

Stall knew that, too. That's why he did nothing but stand there, watching Yakima dwindle into the distance.

As the half-breed began angling south across the street, he glanced again over his shoulder. Stall was still standing where he'd left him, watching. Turning forward and continuing his stroll, Yakima wondered what the man was waiting for. And then it dawned on him that Stall was waiting to see where he was headed.

Likely considering following him and ambushing him somewhere there wouldn't be witnesses.

Smoothly, as though he'd been heading there all along, Yakima angled toward the feed barn where he'd stabled Wolf. He wasn't sure how well he could ride with his bruised ribs, but he'd ridden gimped up before. This was too good of an opportunity to turn his back on.

If Stall wanted to ambush him, Yakima would make it easy for him. Too easy.

He went in the livery barn's side door and informed the hostler, who was mucking out a stall and looking bleary-eyed from Friday night high jinks, that he was taking his black out for a run. Wolf was in the rear corral, separated from the other stallions and mares, and he was so eager to be sprung from his confines that Yakima didn't even have to rope him. Grunting against the pain in his grinding ribs, Yakima saddled and bridled the snorting, prancing, tail-switching beast, then grabbed his rifle, which he'd left hidden in the barn earlier when he'd fed the horse a breakfast of oats and parched corn. He'd gone out to rustle up some wildflowers for Derks's grave, and, his being mostly one-handed, the rifle would have gotten in the way though he hadn't liked leaving the prized piece behind where it might get stolen and when he was liable to get bushwhacked by the broken-nosed Cordovan Stall.

Leading the horse out of the corral and into the still-quiet main street, he took the reins in his hands and cast a quick, furtive glance over to where he'd left the deputy. Stall was still there, in front of the German Café, leaning against an awning post and cradling his rifle in his arms. He was looking toward Yakima, the darkness around the man's eyes contrasting sharply with the white plaster of Paris cast on his nose.

Yakima grabbed the saddle horn with his left hand and awkwardly swung up into the leather, the twisting movements causing his ribs and arm to sing out. The half-breed edged the horse ahead into the street, and again he cast another sidelong look back in the direction from which he'd come.

He grinned.

Stall had just stepped off the boardwalk and was angling across the street, his back to Yakima though he continued casting eager glances over his left shoulder as his duster swung about his stout legs and he held his Henry low in his right hand. He was heading for the sheriff's office, moving fast, sort of run-stepping as he swerved around mud puddles, gobbets of the wet dung and sand churning up behind him.

Yakima pressed the heels of his moccasins against Wolf's ribs and neck-reined the horse to the left, trotting on past the sheriff's office, which he did not so much as glance at now, not wanting to give any indication he was up to anything untoward but only taking his stallion out to run the stable rough out of him and get some fresh grass into him to relieve the green heaves caused by too much grain.

He felt good even with his aching ribs when the last outlying shacks of the town tumbled away behind him, and he and Wolf were loping along the two-track ranch trail into open country.

The air was sweet, perfumed like the boudoir of a high-priced whore. The caliche was brick red between the cactus plants and mesquites and cedars, the foliage itself greener than before the rain, with here and there a scrubby little desert wildflower offering a splash of red or lilac or lemon yellow. Vapor slithered across the ground and rose into the slowly warming air.

Yakima reined Wolf down to a walk. He wanted to blow the horse out, get him as well exercised as he could, but his own ribs wouldn't stand for it. He'd have to keep him slow. That was all right. If anyone aimed to shadow him, he wanted to make sure they didn't have much trouble keeping up.

A mile from town, he swung the black off the trail's right side and followed a game path up into the rugged bluffs and treacherous escarpments of the lower Coronados. He kept looking back over his shoulder to make sure he was leaving plenty of sign.

"Hold on, cork-head," said Deputy Lonnie Silver about fifteen minutes later, pointing to the shoe marks that angled off the main trail and into the scrub. "He headed off into the desert."

Stall, who had ridden several yards down the main wagon trail, overlooking the sign, wheeled his big sorrel quickly, looking at once incredulous and hungry, his small mouth set tight and his nostrils pinched.

"Some tracker," Silver chuckled.

"Shut up, pepper belly," Stall said, spurring his horse into the desert. "I want any shit out of you, I'll squeeze your head!"

They followed the half-breed's trail across a shallow wash, up a steep incline, and then over a bench. The hills around them were covered in saguaro cactus, juniper, cedar, and wild oaks, with clumps of buck brush choking the washes. Doves cooed and occasional hawks gave their raspy hunting cry as they lazed on the cool morning updrafts.

"Easy, Cord," Silver said when they'd followed the trail about ten minutes. "He's ridin' slow. Don't wanna ride up on the son of a bitch."

"Why not?"

"'Cause the way you're ridin', he'll hear us and be waitin' for us."

"Yeah, well, me an' that rock-worshippin' son of a bitch got us a conversation to have."

The wiry, muscular Lonnie Silver, who'd removed his arm sling though the wounded wing still pained him, chuckled. "Yeah, it's been pretty one-sided so far."

Stall cast an owl glance over his shoulder, gritting his teeth savagely. Turning his head forward, he cursed in frustration and halted the horse near a split-trunked saguaro angling its roots down the sides of a recent cutbank. Silver was right. He had to slow down, take his time, keep his eyes and ears open. Holding his rifle across the pommel of his saddle, he sleeved sweat from his broad forehead and stared ahead across the bench that rose slowly to barren, rocky ridges. The half-breed seemed to be headed for a notch between the mountains. A good place to get bushwhacked in there.

Stall swung down from his saddle and dropped to a knee beside a shoe print. He ran his gloved finger along the edge of the print, then stared across the slope.

"Hell," he said. "He is takin' his time. He ain't more than five minutes ahead of us."

Stall looked back at Silver. He didn't like to admit

it, but the half-Mex deputy had the cooler head. "Think he's leadin' us into something?"

"Could be." Silver swung down from his own saddle and shucked his carbine from his saddle boot. "I say we move ahead on foot. If he gets too far ahead, we can come back for the horses. But if he's got a dry-gulch planned, I for one don't want my head stickin' up too high above cover."

Stall drew a deep breath through his mouth—his nose was still sore to take anything but the shallowest breaths through—and led the sorrel into a nest of rocks and scrub. He looped his reins over the branch of a dead cedar. Silver tied his own horse to a willow growing up around jimson weed, then squinted a brown eye at the sun, judging the time. As an afterthought, he grabbed his canteen from his saddle horn and looped it over his neck.

"Let's mosey," Stall said, levering a cartridge into his Henry's breech, then lowering the hammer to half cock.

He moved out of the rocks and headed up the trail, following the prints of the half-breed's black stallion. He hadn't gone thirty yards before the heat lay like a blanket across his shoulders and he felt the sweat rolling down his back. Barely pausing, he shrugged out of his duster, laid it beside the half-breed's trail, then adjusted his suspenders on his thick shoulders and quickened his pace.

Soon, as they followed a narrow, gravelly wash up the steepening grade, he and Silver were both breathing heard. They were grateful when the wash swerved to the northeast and a volcanic dyke rose up to block the sun, offering refreshing shade.

A rifle barked, echoing.

Stall stopped in his tracks and crouched down, his skin crawling as he awaited a bullet. He turned to Silver, who stood in much the same position about twenty yards behind him, the smaller deputy pressing one hand against the stone wall beside him while holding his Winchester in the other, looking around warily and stretching his lips back from his brown, crooked teeth.

"Where'd that come from?" Stall said, his dry mouth tasting like metal.

As if in response, the rifle barked again. Again, the shot flatted out across the rocky slopes rising all around the two deputies.

"Hard to tell with that echo," Silver said. "Maybe east. Maybe west."

The rifle barked two more times quickly, and both deputies got down on their hands and knees, staying as low as they could while jerking their heads around wildly, both now holding their rifles up high across their chests.

"You think it might not be him?" Silver said. " 'Cause whoever it is don't seem to be shooting at us."

There was a low rumble. It sounded the way the thunder had sounded as it paced around Red Hill over the past several days. Stall looked around wildly again, a cold hand pressing flat against his lower spine.

Ahead and right, gray dust rose as several boulders tumbled down the ridge they'd been resting on for aeons. They were heading straight down the slope and into the steep-sided wash in which Stall and Silver now stood, frozen, jaws hanging.

"No," Stall muttered, his tongue like a flap of dry leather in his mouth. "He ain't shootin' at us. He's shootin' at them rocks up there."

When the rocks and boulders reached the bottom of the wash, they'd have nowhere to go but down the wash's steeply sloping floor.

"Mierda!"

Silver threw down his rifle and ran.

Chapter 20

Stall followed his half-Mexican partner back down the wash, stopping once to turn and insanely trigger his rifle at the rocks and boulders that were caroming toward him, making the ground leap beneath his boots. The rifle's bark was snuffed by the ever-loudening roar of the slide. Cursing, Stall threw down the rifle and continued running, pumping his arms and legs, heart pounding, casting frequent, desperate glances back over his shoulder.

The rocks hammered toward him, doubling in size before his eyes every second so that he could see their clarifying pits, knobs, and fissures, and individual grains in the dust licking up around them.

Stall heard himself wail as he continued running, unable to keep up with the smaller, lighter Silver, who was twenty yards ahead and gaining. The wash's banks were too steep to climb here, but fifty, sixty yards farther down they were shallower and more manageable.

Stall heard himself sob again as he glanced back once more and realized he wouldn't make it. He stopped suddenly and leaped wildly onto the left-side wall, bellowing now and swinging his arms up and digging his boots into the wall's cleft, trying to haul himself up. The boulders hammered toward him, bouncing, the cannonlike explosions making his ears shudder. His hand slipped from a notch and he fell straight down the wall and faced the raging onslaught of ancient stone, opening his mouth to scream as the first wagon-sized boulder slammed into him and turned him instantly to cherry pudding, not hesitating in the least as it and the dozens of others behind it continued on down the wash toward Silver.

The light-footed half-Mexican, however, managed to heave himself up the wash's five-foot-high right wall just as he felt the chill breath of the landslide caress his neck, as the dust that the rocks swept in front of it billowed up around him. He scrambled for all he was worth, kicking with his feet, pulling with his hands, grunting like an animal.

Atop the bank, ignoring the bite of prickly pear thorns in his arms and thighs, he dug his high, undershot boot heels into the chalky ground and heaved himself forward with a great burst of desperate energy. He hit the ground ten feet beyond and rolled back behind a fringe of shielding escarpment, hearing the dinosaurlike screech and raging roar of the landslide careening on past him. Rising onto his knees but keeping his head low, he edged a look over the side of the scarp, his brown eyes narrowed against the dust and flying grit.

Most of the rocks and boulders remained within

the confines of the wash until the slide had hammered a good fifty yards beyond Silver's position. Then the rocks and boulders fanned out, spilling out across the bench before slowing and settling. Belching sounds continued, the scrape and bell-like clangs, as, here and there, rocks continued rolling over one another as gravity continued to shift them over and around one another.

Far off past Silver, the last moving rock tumbled down the side of a larger one and rolled slowly about twenty feet into the desert before slowing even more and coming to a final rest against an insignificant chunk of sun-bleached driftwood.

Silence descended.

Dust billowed.

Silver choked on the grit in his throat and brushed it out of his hair with both hands. Somewhere in the wash he'd lost his hat; it was likely buried under several tons.

Giddiness overcame him, a great lightening of his chest, as he pushed himself to his feet and stared at the rumble-filled wash before him. At the great tumult that had come within a hairbreadth of hammering him into jelly and burying him where not even God could find him.

Poor Stall. . . .

Silver chuckled. As relief swept over him with nearly as much force as the rocks he'd so narrowly avoided, he hunched his shoulders and threw his head back, sending great guffaws toward the brassy sky into which the sun climbed like a swelling lemon.

He laughed a long time.

Only when the laughter dwindled did he sense someone behind him.

Silver jerked his head to one side, saw a tall black-hatted shadow behind him, long jet hair fluttering around broad shoulders.

A soft voice teeming with menace said, "This ain't gonna bring Derks back, but it might make him rest a little lighter."

Silver wheeled, his right hand dropped toward the Smith & Wesson revolver holstered on his right hip. His fingertips only started to rake the handle before the big figure in front of him leaped suddenly high in the air, the half-breed's face twisting while the green eyes remained fixed and hard on Silver's face. Suddenly, the big savage's back was facing Silver, and then a moccasined foot was careening toward Silver's head from the left.

A stillborn scream escaped Silver's lips in the form of a croak a sixth of a second before the half-breed's heel smashed into the side of Silver's head. Silver's head smacked the side of the escarpment like a pumpkin thrown by a powerful arm.

A dull wooden thump sounded as the wiry deputy bounced off the stone wall, leaving a broad stain of thick red blood on the rock face before the man's body crumpled like a puppet from which the strings had suddenly been cut. He piled up at the base of the scarp, blood oozing from every orifice, wide eyes still owning the shocked look that would be fixed there until predators scampered in and dragged the body off later on in the afternoon.

Yakima stepped back from Silver's heaped carcass and dropped to his knees, folding his arms across his screeching ribs. "God," he groaned, hardening his jaws as he glanced at Silver once more, "did that feel good!"

Yakima fetched Wolf back from the little box canyon in which he'd secured the stallion, then rode him out to where he'd watched through his field glasses as Stall and Silver had tethered their own mounts. There, as the three horses contentedly cropped jimson weed around him, he built a fire from driftwood sticks, brewed a pot of green tea, and sat back in the shade of an overhanging rock, sipping the brew for which he'd acquired a taste while working with George, and smoking a cigarette.

After all that—even though he really hadn't had to put forth much effort save from triggering a few pills at the rocky ridge—he needed a rest. He should have just shot Silver, or rammed the butt of his Yellowboy against the man's head. That high kick had really riled his ribs, cost him some healing time.

But it had been worth it. He'd savor that look of shock and horror and disorientation in the Mex's eyes for a good long time. Couldn't wait to tell Derks about it, in fact.

When he'd finished his tea, he kicked dirt on the fire, then slid his Yellowboy into his saddle boot and gathered up the reins of all three horses. Mounting Wolf, he led the other two back down the washes and canyons to the main trail snaking in from the west. The town was a little more active, he saw a half hour later, as he rode past the Queen of Hearts, all three of its hitch racks packed with horses, mostly ranch ponies, with one lone prospector's mule.

As Yakima angled over to the sheriff's office, he was glad to see smoke rising from the adobe brick dwelling's chimney abutting the west wall. A shadow moved in the sashed window right of the door, and a moment later Rathbone stepped out, donning his black John B. and removing the thick stogy from his teeth.

As he closed the door behind him, he scowled over the unpainted porch rail at the two riderless horses flanking Yakima. "Terrible news," the half-breed said evenly, his deep voice vaguely threatening. "Rock slide. Your deputies didn't make it." He tossed the reins over the hitch rack and rode on up the street, feeling Rathbone's eyes boring holes between his shoulder blades.

As Yakima put Wolf up the main ramp of the livery barn, he heard a voice say behind him, just barely loud enough for him to hear, "There's that damn half-breed. What you suppose he's up to, anyway?"

Raw fury sparked behind Yakima's eyes. He whipped Wolf around tightly and ran him back down the ramp and across the street, where the two government beef contractors stood casually outside one of Red Hill's seamier whorehouses, the Red Hill House—a small two-story brick building with upper- and lower-story verandas with brightly colored wooden railings. Three bored-looking doves slumped on the second-story porch, half dressed and smoking, a dreamy-eyed redhead enjoying a clear bottle of what appeared to be Mexican *baconora*.

Slipping his right arm free of its sling, Yakima reined Wolf to a halt and glared down at the two men—the pinch-mouthed Buttercup and the long-haired, long-faced Slater—who each stood holding up a lower veranda support post, smug looks on their faces. They both looked freshly bathed, their suits laundered, white shirts crisply starched and pressed.

"You got something you wanna say to me, Buttercup?"

His right hand, fingers splayed, rested over the soft brown holster thronged on his right thigh.

The expressions on the two men's faces shifted from arrogant sneers to cautious, skeptical scowls and back again. They slid their eyes to each other, then returned them to Yakima, whose own eyes burned out of his flat-planed face like jade backlit by the flames of an awakening volcano. The dark-haired Buttercup licked his lips and worked his mouth as though attempting to speak, a sudden apprehension making it hard for him to get the words out. He held one hand above the polished walnut grips of the Smith & Wesson positioned for the cross draw on his left hip, a gold watch chain brushing the edge of the handle.

Yakima stared at him, his lips stretched savagely, challenge in his eyes. Buttercup returned the look. His left eye twitched. A vague gray shadow slid across the brown, gold-flecked cornea, and the man's lower jaw loosened. He dropped his hand away from his pistol.

Suddenly, mindless of his wounded arm, Yakima jerked his Colt up out of its holster, and the gun exploded twice, blowing dirt and shit up from the street and throwing it back across both contractors' polished half boots and crisp tweed trouser legs.

"God *damn*!" Slater intoned as he and his partner bolted backward, leaning forward, spreading their arms indignantly, and casting shocked gazes down at their pants.

Yakima holstered the smoking Colt while drilling the men with one more warning scowl. "Why don't you men contract for your beef and go the hell back to where you came from? You're starting to annoy the hell out of me."

He reined Wolf around, heeled the horse back across the street, clomped up the ramp and through the livery barn's broad open doors.

When he'd unsaddled the stallion and put him into the rear paddock, he headed back outside. Neither of the contractors was anywhere around, and he was glad. He was itching for a fight though he knew it was Rathbone he was itching to fight with, and he'd have to wait for the sheriff.

He wouldn't hunt him down. Not yet. Yakima wanted the man to think about those two empty saddles. Think about them real hard. Then, when Rathbone was ready and came looking for Yakima, Yakima would make himself real easy to find.

Then he'd get the hell out of Red Hill.

He'd never known a town he wanted to leave so badly.

He tramped across the wash to the dilapidated end of Red Hill and stopped across the wet, rutted trail from his boardinghouse. Planks had been set across the street, and they, too, now were mud covered. One led up to the porch of the boardinghouse upon which Delbert Roman sat on a bench, his crisp beaver hat on his knee. The well-dressed banker appeared to be waiting for someone, and when his eyes found Yakima, they held there.

The banker rose as Yakima walked across the street via the sodden planks, the boards making squelching sounds in the mud beneath the half-breed's weight.

He stopped at the bottom of the three porch steps and set a moccasin on the second one. "You're kind of backwatering it these days, aren't you, Roman?"

"I wanted to talk to you, Mr. Henry."

"Mr. Henry?" Yakima snorted. "That sounds right polite."

"Please," Roman said seriously. "I'd like to speak in private."

Yakima only frowned at the man.

"I'd like to make you an offer," Roman said with an impatient pitch to his voice. "Please, Henry. I'm a desperate man."

"Yeah," Yakima growled, walking on into the boardinghouse ahead of him. "There's lots o' them around Red Hill these days."

Chapter 21

"All right," Yakima said, when they'd entered his room and Roman had quietly closed his door. "Spill it."

Delbert Roman looked around, still holding his hat in his hands with an embarrassing and uncustomary look of subservience on his pale, fleshy face. Especially given his surroundings—the shabby, cramped room in which Derks's gear was still piled on his bed. Yakima hadn't had the heart to throw it out yet. He figured he'd turn it over to Ma Prate when he left.

A whiskey bottle and two dirty glasses stood on the washstand, inside the chipped enamel basin, there being no other available surface. Mangan had taken Yakima off the laudanum, so he was relying on whiskey to quell his pain.

The banker hesitated a moment as he took in the shabbiness of the room, then went over and sat on the edge of Derks's cot and set the hat on the bed beside him. Yakima remained by the door, the thumb of his good hand hooked behind his cartridge belt, his rifle leaning against the wall nearby.

"Look," Roman said. "I've lost a coach and six horses. I'm in the process of having another stage driven into Apache Gap from Las Cruces. I'm also hiring a new driver, and I'm acquiring six more horses. I can handle the financial loss of the coach and the horses, but I cannot risk any more holdups. I need a man—a good man—to ride shotgun."

"What for? Seems to me you've found a better way to haul the strongboxes."

"That won't work forever. Soon, even the freight trains will be getting held up, and they'll be refusing to take the risk without more compensation than I can afford. No, I have to continue hauling the strongboxes on the stage. That's my business, after all. And I can't afford people, potential customers, to lose confidence." Roman swallowed, his jowls quivering, his pale blue eyes beseeching. "If you'll agree to stay with Coronado Transport, Mr. Henry, I'll pay you the reward money for the men you brought down last week at Diamondback Station."

Roman reached into his coat and removed a folded wad of greenbacks. He set the money on the bed. "There's five hundred dollars. Consider it a token of my faith in you, and of my appreciation for services rendered. I can see by the look in your eye that you're feeling nothing but disdain for me. For that, I suppose I can't blame you." He looked out the dirty window to his right, and seemed to study something out there for a time, narrowing his eye corners slightly, before turning back to Yakima. "I'd like you to take the five hundred dollars and take some time to consider my offer. If you decide not to accept, the money is still yours."

"I won't consider it."

"You *must* consider it," Roman said, his tone growing brittle. He gave an incredulous laugh and held the money up, shaking it. "Five hundred dollars! An entire year's pay! For God's sake, man"—he dropped the money back down to the cot and kept his fervent, beseeching gaze on Yakima—"where will you go? What will you do? A man like you . . ."

"If you're trying to get on my good side, you got a peculiar way of doin' it."

"I don't mean to insult you, only reason with you. This town, this job must certainly be as good as another. You're not out on the range every day in the blistering heat. You have days off, a couple of good saloons, whorehouses with some nice-looking doxies . . ."

When that tack didn't seem to be working, Roman hurried to say, "Did you see the marker I put on Derks's grave?"

Yakima walked across the room and splashed whiskey into one of the dirty glasses. "I saw it." He threw back the shot and turned to the banker sitting on the dead jehu's bed, knees spread, broadcloth trousers drawn up above his black silk socks. He was once more holding his hat in his hands, like a recalcitrant but truckling schoolboy. "The marker's the least you could have done, throwing us to the wolves like that."

He extended the hand holding the glass at the

banker, pointing. "Get out of here, Roman. I'll be pull-ing my picket pins soon, and I don't want your face bein' the last one I see. Makes my stomach turn."

"Look, Henry." Roman stood, leaving the pile of greenbacks on Derks's cot, and moved over to Ya-kima, stopping about three feet away and looking up at him with urgent pleading, maybe even trepidation, in his eyes. "Let me speak plainly. I've become some-what suspicious of Sheriff Rathbone."

Yakima worked hard at not laughing, at keeping his expression plain. He said nothing.

"I've heard around, late at night, that Rathbone was a fairly formidable road agent south of the border and over in Texas. He's always seemed very inter-ested in my business." A dark, brooding look washed over the man's features. "As well as my daughter. Someone recently has seen him snooping around my house when I wasn't there—only Rae. Anyway, I'm beginning to wonder if he hasn't had a hand in the recent holdups that have been plaguing my line. If so, I'll need a man as . . . as . . . "

"Savage?"

"As formidable a gunhand as Rathbone himself is," Roman said, "to combat him and whoever else he might be bringing in to prey on Coronado Transport. There have been a lot of strangers coming and going around Red Hill over the past several months. I'm wondering if they've been working for the sheriff. And, possibly, someone else. . . . "

Yakima turned to splash another shot of whiskey

into his glass. His hand shook slightly, and he knew he should be going easy on the strong stuff. In his state, there was no telling what he might do, and he only wanted now to kill Rathbone and get the hell out of here in one piece. More immediately, he wanted this simpering, little businessman to get the hell away from him. He had no intention of working for the man. Or of taking his five hundred dollars.

"Look, Roman," Yakima said, his back to the man, throwing back the shot, "I don't think you're gonna have to worry about Rathbone much longer."

When Roman started to speak, Yakima cut him off quickly. "Don't ask me how I know that, goddamnit, just take my word on it and get out of here." Yakima wheeled, holding the glass down by his side, squeezing it. "Get the hell out of here now!"

Roman rocked back on his heels as though he'd been slapped. He stepped backward and scowled pensively up at Yakima.

"Now!" the half-breed shouted. "And take your money."

Roman wheeled and stomped over to the door. He grabbed the knob, turned back to the half-breed, and, his jowls and pitted cheeks turning pink, pointed at the money he'd left on the bed. "Consider that your last wages and, like I said, payment for your consideration. Don't let the whiskey do your talking for you, Mr. Henry. Tomorrow, when you're feeling better, you count that money!" The banker gave an odd little, superior half smile. "And consider my offer."

Roman hurried out and closed the door.

Yakima's heart swelled with raw fury. He threw the glass at the door. It shattered loudly and sprayed across the floor.

"You already got my answer, you *son of a bitch*!"

As he glowered at the door panel, to which shards of glass clung like bristles, he heard low voices in the hall, beneath the sounds of Roman's retreating footsteps. Another set grew louder, these softer, halting. A single knock on the door before the knob turned and the hinges squawked as the door pushed open two feet.

Beth Holgate or Seagraves, or whatever she was calling herself these days, poked her head through the gap. Her hazel eyes found Yakima, and the skin above the bridge of her nose wrinkled. She glanced at the glass-littered floor, then stepped into the room cautiously, closing the door behind her and quipping, "Drop your drink?"

"What do you want?" He hadn't meant to sound so angry, but that was how he was feeling. Angry and out of sorts.

Beth carried a small beaded purse in one hand, a handful of gauze and white linen in the other. The cloth was wrapped around a small brown bottle of rubbing alcohol.

"Dr. Mangan sent me to change the bandages on your arm."

Yakima kept his back pressed against the washstand. As he stared at the beautiful woman before him, whose cream-colored dress with tan lace was lower cut than her usual attire, he felt his anger transform, shift from a burning in his temples to a warm heaviness in his loins. "Mangan sent you?"

She dropped her eyes briefly and nibbled her lower lip. "That's right."

"I don't believe you."

The skin above her nose wrinkled once more.

"He told me he'd be out of his office till Monday." Yakima strolled toward her. "He told me he was heading to Apache Gap this weekend, to tend some miner's widow giving birth."

Beth just stared at him, her lips slightly parted. His shadow passed over her as he stopped before her, inches away. She leaned back slightly as he leaned toward her and placed his left hand against the door behind her.

"Tell me that ain't altogether true," he said in a low, thick voice. "Tell me you came here because you wanted to see me." He sniffed her hair, her neck, pressed his nose against the lobe of her right ear.

Her breasts rose and fell heavily.

"Yakima . . ."

"Tell me."

"I . . . we can't." Beth placed a hand on his own heaving chest and turned her face away from his, her voice thin as she said, "There's no point. . . ."

"Yeah, there is. You know what it is, too." Yakima lowered his head and pressed his lips to the deep furrow of her cleavage, took a deep sniff of the womanly scent of her. The warm, womanly want in her . . .

He pressed his lips to it, shoved his face down deeper into her bodice, felt her lean away from him again, groaning, dropping both her purse and the gauze on the floor and pressing her hands against his head, running her hands roughly through his hair as he kissed and nuzzled her breasts, feeling her body coming alive against him.

Later, in the waning hours of the afternoon, he dropped his bare legs over the side of the bed, sitting up. Beth rose sleepily, her blond hair in shambles about her slender shoulders. She drew her long legs in and raked her toes against his arm as she stood and, tucking her hair back behind her ears, walked carefully on her bare feet to where she'd dropped her purse and the fresh bandage makings.

He watched her bend over to pick up the bandages, and gave an inner groan of renewed desire.

She walked back over to the bed and sat down beside him. She set the bandages on the bed between her legs and canted her head to inspect the wound in his upper arm.

"Needs changing," she said, adding ironically, "You're lucky I came when I did." She took a small scissors from the pouch between her legs and cut away the old bandage as Yakima dropped his elbows on his knees and ran his hands through his hair, which was slightly sweat-damp from their lovemaking.

Beth glanced at the money that had gotten knocked onto the floor as they'd undressed each other. "If that's the time you drew from the stage company—I passed Roman in the hall—you're leaving a mighty good job, I'd say."

As she dribbled alcohol onto a folded piece of gauze, Yakima leaned down and scooped the money up in his left hand. Beth gently swabbed his wound, and Yakima tidied the stack of greenbacks on the cot beside him. When she finished cleaning the wound, and had wrapped it with fresh gauze and linen, he extended the money to her.

"For services rendered."

Beth looked down at the proffered stack. "Which services? Never mind. I wouldn't get that much for either."

He shook the stack at her. "Take it."

"No!" Beth looked indignant as she stood and began gathering the clothes that Yakima had strewn about the room. "I did nothing to earn that money."

"I meant the medical services. Not . . . the other." Yakima shook his head in frustration. "I want you to take it and get the hell out of town. Hire someone to take you and Calvin to Apache Gap. From there, hop the train back to the Midwest. Take some more advice, and stay there."

She bent over to step into a pair of pink lace panties. "I won't take your money, Yakima. I'm not a whore."

Yakima groaned and heaved himself to his feet. "I'm not payin' you for anything. It's a gift, for chrissa—"

He was two feet from her when something pinged through the window to his right and plunked into the door to his left. The bullet had screeched through the air between them, and now the rifle's bark reached Yakima's ears, echoing hollowly.

Beth gasped and jerked back.

Yakima grabbed her shoulders, swung her around, and threw her onto the bed as two more bullets shattered the window, one hammering the door again while another pinged loudly off a hinge.

Chapter 22

Beth bounced on the bed and rolled up against the wall.

Yakima threw himself to the floor as another bullet screeched through the air over his head, smashing into the wall left of the door, and grabbed his rifle. Loudly racking a shell into the chamber, he crawled to the room's outside wall and heaved up off his heels to press his bare back against the window frame, shaking his long hair back from his face and edging a look into the boardinghouse's backyard.

A figure in a dark suit was scurrying through the brush and rocks of the desert south of the boardinghouse, keeping his head low.

Yakima raised the rifle, poking the barrel out the broken window, and fired three times, triggering and levering, watching his slugs blowing up rocks and sand around the fleeing bushwhacker. The empty casings clattered onto the floor behind him, rolling around his feet. A fourth slug tore the branch off a paloverde tree.

The shooter leaped into a distant wash, and Yakima ejected the spent casing, racked a fresh shell into the chamber, and stared after the man for nearly a minute, keeping his rifle pressed taut against his cheek.

But the man was gone.

Yakima lowered the long gun and looked at Beth, who lay with her back to him, knees drawn up to her chest. She wore only the pink panties, and her hair was a disheveled mass hiding her shoulders. Slowly, she lowered her arms slightly and rolled onto her back, turning to look at him, incredulous, indignant, keeping her hands close to her face.

From downstairs, Ma Prate wailed, "Yakima Henry, what in tarnation is goin' *on* up there?"

Ignoring the old woman, Yakima kept his eyes on Beth. "Give me a few minutes to track him, make sure he's gone. Then get dressed and get outta here." Yakima leaned the rifle against the dresser and grabbed his summer long-handles, gritting his teeth as he glanced at her, his sweat-damp hair flying about his face, "And take that money!"

"Who was that?" she said from the bed, her voice strangely calm.

"Friend of mine."

"Who, Yakima?"

"Rathbone, I think."

"Why?"

He stumbled around, pulling his buckskin trousers up over his long-handles. "I reckon he's piss-burned I killed his deputies, left 'em both rotting out in the desert."

Beth just looked at him, her gaze stricken, horrified. What was she seeing now? he vaguely wondered. A savage? Feeling her eyes on him, he sat on the edge of the cot to pull his moccasins on. He leaned down to press his lips against her forehead, then stood and wrapped his cartridge belt around his waist.

"Remember—stay here but keep your head down. When you're sure the coast is clear, hightail it."

She leaned back against the wall, raising her knees, cupping her breasts in her hands almost defensively. "I don't know what to think about you, Yakima."

"Yeah, me, neither."

He donned his hat, grabbed the rifle, and, thumbing fresh cartridges from his shell belt into the Yellowboy's chamber, went out. He slammed the door behind him, then slid one last shell into the rifle's chamber as he dropped quickly down the stairs, Ma Prate waiting at the bottom with a look of exasperation on her craggy features, one hand draped over the wolf's head ball of the newell post.

"You'll pay for shootin' up my place, you half-breed son of a bitch!"

"Yes, ma'am," Yakima muttered obediently as he strode quickly across the small parlor and out the boardinghouse's front screen door.

He knew the shooter—whom he was certain was Rathbone though he hadn't gotten a good luck at the man—had hightailed it well away from here by now. But hoping he'd be able to track the ambusher back to his lair, where he could finish his business here in Red Hill once and for all, Yakima tramped out into the desert, heading for the wash in which the son of a bitch had fled.

Sitting with his shoulder pressed against the ruined stable's crumbling adobe wall, Rathbone watched the half-breed step out from behind a one-armed saguaro cactus about twenty yards beyond him. Moving at an angle while following Rathbone's tracks before the sheriff had doubled back, the half-breed turned, sliding his rifle around cautiously. As he turned to face the stable but kept on walking catlike away from it, Rathbone jerked his head back behind the front door's empty casing, hearing a frightened gasp leak up from deep in his throat.

He clutched the cocked pistol in his lap, and waited, gritting his teeth. His rifle lay on the stable's straw-littered floor, the receiver snugged against the sheriff's right hip. The damn thing had jammed, was useless now. He had only the pistol.

He'd led the breed out here hoping for a good, close shot, but that didn't look as though it was going to happen. He could squeeze off a pill from here, but the half-breed was too far away for the short gun. Likely, and the way Rathbone's luck was holding, he'd either miss the man again entirely or only wing him, bring the flames of hell down on his own head.

And that would be the end of the sheriff of Red Hill.

Rathbone pressed his back against the wall and gritted his teeth harder. The breed had stopped; there was no continuing crunch of gravel beneath his moccasins. Had he heard Rathbone's gasp? Or, having a keen savage prescience, did he just *sense* Rathbone in here, hiding now like a damn rabbit with a wolf on its trail?

With nothing but a pistol, a jammed rifle, and an empty brandy flask. . . .

Rathbone waited, pressing his back harder against the stable wall, his sweaty palm greasing the ivory handle of his .45. Shortly, the soft crunching of the breed's footsteps started up again, gradually dwindling. Rathbone slid a glance around the door casing. The breed was moving off through the scrub.

Rathbone released the breath he hadn't realized he'd been holding. He tried to relax his shoulders, but they were as unyielding as a yoke. Flipping the lid off the brandy flask, he raised it to his lips. Empty. He managed to shake two small drops onto his tongue, and he savored these, pressing his tongue to the roof of his mouth, smearing the brandy around until it had dissolved into his saliva, and he swallowed it and lamented the total lack of satisfaction it gave him.

He returned the flask to his coat pocket and leaned his back against the wall. *Christ* . . . What the hell was happening to him?

His nerves had been in knots for days. But they'd been growing steadily tighter since earlier that morning, when the breed had ridden into town with those two riderless horses trailing him, and he'd tossed the reins over the hitch rack fronting the sheriff's office and ridden away. Giving Rathbone his broad back in silent, sneering challenge.

That had been an unexpectedly hard blow to Rathbone's morale. He'd kept a hard, cold look in his eyes, but he'd gone into the jailhouse, fished a brandy bottle out of his desk drawer, and, watching out his window the two suddenly orphaned horses standing hangheaded at the hitch rack, obliviously twitching their ears and drawing water from the stock trough, nursed the bottle while brooding until he'd taken down a good third of it.

Rathbone had always seen himself as a tough hombre. One of the toughest men he'd known. But the blows here in Red Hill, including his having had his loot stolen out of his hotel room—which had been the harshest blow of all, he thought now as he fingered the goose egg on his temple—were turning him into a drunken, babbling idiot.

Spineless and afraid. Doubtful of his own abilities as a man, a sheriff, and as an outlaw.

If the half-breed had been able to turn both Silver and Stall toe-down so easily—and both had been formidable men in their own rights—he certainly wouldn't have much trouble bringing Rathbone down, as well. Especially now, after failure upon failure, self-doubt, and his wretchedly subservient desires for Rae Roman had turned him into a whipped dog.

Christ . . . what the hell was happening to him?

The answer appeared as an image before his eyes.

Of course.

Rae. Before he'd met her, he'd been sure of himself. Confident in his strength. But now, having known her, having enjoyed the intoxicating pleasures of her flesh, he felt as pliable as India rubber. Doubtful. Halting. Tormented. Suspicous of the woman . . .

In love with her.

And afraid of death!

He heaved himself to his feet, groaning, yearning for another drink. Even if he had another bottle stored away in his office or his hotel room, he couldn't return to either place. The breed would find him there. He had to leave the stable soon, before the breed realized he'd backtracked.

He'd head for a saloon.

No. He couldn't be seen in public in his condition. He needed to drink and think in relative seclusion where he could summon back his toughness and get another rifle to finish the breed once and for all. Then, Monday morning, he'd secure the strongbox from the bank and follow through with his and Rae's plans for starting a new, rich life together!

Rae . . .

Cautiously, Rathbone looked over the stable's crumbling walls, making sure the breed was nowhere near. Then, moving quickly now, his heart thudding anxiously, desperate for another drink and to see, to feel Rae, he scrambled through a glassless window and headed back toward Red Hill, intending to take a roundabout way to the Roman house.

Rae should be there on a Saturday. Delbert would likely be at the bank. Rathbone and Rae would be alone, and he'd find both of what he needed there. . . .

Fortunately, it was a relatively quiet Saturday afternoon, and he was confident that he'd managed to cross the main drag on the south end of town without being noticed. He certainly didn't want to have to talk to anyone in this frazzled, half-drunk state he was in. If they didn't smell the brandy on him, they'd likely see the folly in his eyes.

Rathbone stepped over the short picket fence that Rae had put up around the flower bed encircling her and her father's house, all the flowers there dead from lack of watering, and pressed his shoulder against the house's southeast corner. He looked around to make sure no one was out here, pricking his ears to see if he could pick up Delbert Roman's voice from inside. As he began to move out from around the corner and head for the house's front door, he stopped suddenly, flinching and turning his head toward the stable off to his right.

He'd heard a clattering sound. Now he watched in horror as one of the two large white stable doors swung open. With a startled grunt, he leaped back behind the corner of the house. From the stable, he heard hoof clomps, the squawk of heavy leather, the grind of iron-shod wheels, and the faint rattle of a bridle bit. He also heard a woman's voice talking to the horse, cajoling the mount in a clipped, hard tone.

Rathbone edged a look around the side of the house just as Rae Roman swung up into the front seat of her black leather surrey. She was dressed in a long, spruce green riding skirt with a vest of the same color over a white, lace-up, puffy-sleeved blouse. Pinned to her richly piled hair was a broad-brimmed straw hat bedecked with silk roses.

Rathbone's heart lightened. Just as suddenly, when Rae looked back over the front seat into the buggy's rear, back-facing seat, apprehension took hold of him, and he restrained himself from calling out to her. She seemed preoccupied. Now as she turned forward and shook the ribbons over the tall roan gelding in the buggy's traces, she had a severe, determined, almost furtive expression on her pale face. She lifted her eyes, sweeping the area around her, and Rathbone again jerked his head back behind the house.

He heard the fast thuds of the roan's hooves, and his chest constricted as he hoped against hope she would not pull the surrey around the rear of the house and see him standing out here like a Peeping Tom or, worse, a drunk, lusty, desperate sheriff. But, no— the thudding and the wheels' grinding dwindled into the distance.

Rathbone looked out from around the house to see Rae pulling the buggy around and heading north toward a secondary trail that wound around the town and eventually climbed into the forbidding reaches of the Coronados.

Rathbone frowned. Where in the hell was she going?

His eyes dropped to the back of the surrey. Was that a streamer truck lashed to the cargo carrier extending off the back of the rig? Suspicion bit at him again, for the moment shouldering aside his lust for the woman. On its heels came the white heat of raw fury.

What was she up to?

He stared after her until the surrey disappeared around a hillock covered in saguaros and barrel cactus, and then he, heart thudding desperately, began looking around wildly for a horse. He had to follow her. If the bitch thought she was going to run out on him before he could replenish his own cache, she had another think coming.

Spying no horses except three unsaddled ones in a small pasture to the east, Rathbone strode quickly back toward the main part of town. He didn't care who saw him now. His mind was on Rae. On *only* Rae. Hoping she wasn't double-crossing him, that she *hadn't been* double-crossing him but silently vowing that if she was, she'd know the full fury of his wrath.

He headed down a side street, found a cantina before which a single dapple-gray gelding was tethered—a rangy, black-stockinged horse that stood with one back foot cocked. Rathbone cast an angry, defiant gaze at the cantina, then quickly tightened the horse's latigo straps and slipped the hanging bit into its mouth.

Quickly, before anyone could take note of the Red Hill sheriff in the act of horse stealing, he swung up into the leather, reined the incredulous mount northward, and rammed his spurred heels into the horse's ribs.

Obviously, the ranch pony wasn't accustomed to being treated so shabbily. It gave a little, indignant buck-kick, then, to avoid more of the same treatment, broke into a reluctant, tight-muscled lope, shaking its head and snorting.

Chapter 23

Rae turned the roan off the main trail and onto a rocky little trace that threaded the mouth of a box canyon. She jerked back on the reins suddenly, and when the horse and surrey had stopped, she took a cautious look around.

There was only the wind nudging the cedars and tossing red dust and sand this way and that. No shadows moved amongst the rocky ridges.

Relieved, she shook the reins over the roan's back and continued on into the box canyon, the variegated walls rising around her. A large jackrabbit bolted out from behind a rock and startled the roan, who whinnied, causing Rae to grit her teeth and look behind her once more. As the jack ran on across the trail and into the brush, the woman put the horse ahead, and they crossed a deep wash that ran with dirty red floodwater before reaching the canyon's high back wall.

Rae set the brake, wrapped the ribbons around the handle, and climbed down, careful not to trip over her skirts. Reaching up, she plucked a pair of leather gloves from beneath the surrey's seat, then, adjusting her hat for as much protection as possible from the bright noon sun, made her way around the horse to the canyon wall.

Low on the wall were a series of natural stairs. They rose around a rock tank filled with fresh water, which, judging by the tracks in the mud, had recently sated the thirst of desert animals. She couldn't identify the tracks, but some were large with pads the size of men's thumbs, and they bore the indentations of what must have been claws.

A bobcat? A wolf, perhaps? The thought gave her a shiver, and she looked around her immediate area again cautiously.

What a savage country. She'd heard of men from Red Hill being attacked by such creatures, and there had been little left of them. She was getting out of here soon. Very soon. Just as soon as Rathbone and his deputies managed to secure the Sand Creek money from the bank vault, and were themselves killed by Buttercup and Slater. She wanted to have her stash nearby, ready to go at a moment's notice.

As she climbed the rock shelves awkwardly in her elastic-sided shoes, holding her skirts above her ankles, she gave a caustic chuff. Rathbone. The man was as weak as her father. Weaker, maybe. He was actually convinced that she was going to run away with him, maybe even marry him.

She had no intention.

As soon as her hired gunmen had killed him, all the money would be hers. Aside from the gunmen's salary, that is. She just hoped Buttercup and Slater wouldn't be a problem. They were professional killers, after all, and killers, she'd heard, as a general rule were more trustworthy than thieves. Besides, they'd been recommended by a saloon-owner from Apache Gap whom she trusted, and killers got by on their reputations.

Rae didn't see herself as a thief, of course. Only a woman driven by circumstance beyond her control to make a better life for herself. If she had to kill a few men in the process—well, the world could do with a few less men in it. Especially men like her father and Sheriff Rathbone . . .

A couple of feet above the highest rock tank, Rae crouched, pulled her gloves on, and looked around once more. The bowl-shaped canyon was empty. There was only the roan and the buggy parked below her, the horse watching her skeptically, occasionally shaking his head at black flies. When she'd pulled on the second glove, she began removing stones from the opening of a small notch cave. One by one, she tossed the stones aside until the crescent-shaped opening shone before her. She straightened, kicked gravel into the hole, and listened.

When no diamondbacks rattled a warning, she squatted down before the hole once more, and reached inside. She pulled out a large, dusty burlap sack, loosened the rope she'd tied around the top, and peered inside.

He heart lightened. Her lips spread in a satisfied grin.

Tightening the rope, she straightened and gave a grunt as she lifted the bag by its mouth.

"Need help with that, Rae?"

"Oh, God!" She jumped with a start and lifted her head. *"Father!"*

Delbert Roman stood before her, decked out in leather riding breeches and corduroy jacket over a blue wool shirt, a red neckerchief knotted around his thick neck. Her heart thudded and the look of shock and horror on her face was tempered by one of resentment when she saw that her father was flanked by none other than the gunmen—*her* gunmen—Buttercup and Slater.

Rae's mind reeled, as did her vision. The ground pitched around her, and she had to spread her high-heeled, elastic-sided shoes to keep from falling. The burlap sack hit the ground with a thud, dust rising.

Roman scowled at her, a hurt, incredulous look in his washed-out, old eyes. Buttercup's lips curled a sneer. The taller, long-faced, long-haired Slater merely canted his head to one side, waiting, hooking his thumbs behind his black cartridge belt. He had the vaguely bored, faintly eager look of a man waiting to get into a particularly busy brothel.

"You know," Roman said with an anguished sigh, "it's taken me until this very moment to fully comprehend and believe what's been going on here." When Rae said nothing but only continued to stare at him, stricken, he added, "My own daughter. Destroying me!" He glanced to either side. "In case you're wondering, your hired killers here, Mr. Buttercup and Mr. Slater, are both undercover operatives. Lou Stillwater in Apache Gap informed me of your intention of hiring two shootists, and I wrote to my friend Alan Pinkerton in Denver. He arranged all this, and sent two of his finest detectives."

His smile in place, Buttercup pinched his hat brim. Slater just canted his head to the other side, keeping his thumbs hooked behind his cartridge belt, his right hand near the big, ivory-handled Colt holstered high on his right hip.

Rae looked off over the canyon, saw a switching horse tail in the dry wash she'd crossed on her way to her cache. Her father and the detectives must have been close behind her, followed her into the canyon, and dismounted in the wash. How had she missed them? She realized now that the roan hadn't been shaking his head at flies but at the men sneaking up on her.

What a fool she was!

Her ears rang. A giant fist squeezed her heart. As she stared at her father, realizing suddenly that the jig was up, the game over, anger welled up from beneath her confusion, and she felt tears of fury dribble out from her eyes and roll down her cheeks as her jaws hardened and her lips quivered.

"*I* destroyed *you*? Ha! What do you think you did to Mother when she learned you were bedding charlatans, and everyone in Philadelphia knew about it but her?"

"That was between me and your mother!"

"And what do you think you did to me when you dragged me out here only to discover you were the same womanizing fool you'd been when you'd killed

Mother and bankrupted yourself back home?" Rae gritted her teeth and shook her head slowly. "*Destroyed?* You don't know the meaning of the word!"

Roman's pitted cheeks reddened, and his eyes blazed. "You know nothing of our relationship—your mother's and mine. Why didn't you ask me, Rae? I'd have told you how stiff, how cold she was even in the—"

"No!" Rae screamed, dropping to her knees and holding her hands over her ears. "I won't listen to your lies, you womanizing *scoundrel*!"

Buttercup stepped forward, reached down for the mouth of the burlap sack. "We'd best get the money back to the bank, Mr. Roman."

"As for your daughter," Slater said, running a thumbnail across the blond beard stubbling the side of his face and scowling down at Rae, who continued to sob uncontrollably at her father's ankles, pressing her hands to the side of her head. Her straw hat had fallen off, and her hair was tumbling down her shoulders. "I'd say she has a date with a judge."

"A *federal* judge," Slater said. "Seein' as how she and her friend the sheriff have stolen bonds from the U.S. mail."

Buttercup reached down and grabbed the woman's arm.

"No," Roman objected, holding up his hand. "I'll see her down to her buggy." He added grimly, harshly, "Then to Rathbone's jail, though you men better find him first."

"We'll see to the sheriff's arrest, now that we have

his accomplice under wraps," Buttercup said, holding the bag over his shoulder as Roman dropped to a knee beside his daughter.

"You will, will you?"

Rae lifted her head at the unexpected though familiar voice of Rathbone. Her eyes had just found the man before the gun in his hand flashed and roared, kicking up a high-pitched ringing in her ears. Buttercup screamed and sort of leaped forward, twisting around and dropping the gunnysack, his left shoulder bloody.

Blam!

Slater didn't have time to turn around before the second bullet tore through his back and out his chest before it spanged off a rock to Rae's left. Slater stumbled forward, legs wobbling. He raised one weak arm to his chest before he dropped to both knees, staring dumbly into the distance on the far side of the canyon.

Buttercup was balancing on one foot, trying to slide his S & W from its holster and half facing Rathbone.

The sheriff narrowed an eye as he aimed down the long, smoking barrel of his .45 once more, his mouth stretching a hard, amused grin. The gun in his outstretched hand roared once more.

Buttercup's hand dropped away from the pistol in his holster, and the Pinkerton detective piled up in the rocks fronting the notch cave, quivering as the life drained out of him. At the same time, Roman screamed and lurched up and off his heels, propelling himself wildly forward. Inadvertently, he kicked Rae with his right foot, tripped, and hit the ground behind her on a shoulder. He twisted around, eyes terrified, and turned his face up to Rathbone, who stood several yards away, where the slope began dropping toward the canyon floor.

The sheriff was still holding his pistol straight out from his shoulder, his mustached lips stretching away from his yellow-brown teeth, eyes blazing with a crazy, wild amusement. Rae had lifted her head, and she was sliding her befuddled gaze between the sheriff and her father. Her eyes were brightening, her own lips stretching a savage, delighted grin, her hair hanging dusty and disheveled about her shoulders.

"Frank!" she cried. "Oh, Frank. Thank God!"

Rathbone kept his eyes on Roman, who lay back on his elbows, grimacing, the terrified look continuing to twist his fleshy, pink-mottled cheeks.

"Thank who?" Rathbone chuckled.

Rae pushed to her feet, swept an untidy lock of hair back from her face, and turned toward her father. "Don't shoot him, Frank. Let's just leave him, grab the money, and get out of here."

"Nice stash you got there." Rathbone toed the bag. "That looks like considerably more than your cut of the loot. You don't have mine in there, too—*do you, Rae*?"

A stricken look washed over her once again, her plain face bleaching. Demurely dropping her eyes while a blush found its way back into her otherwise smooth, pale cheeks, she reached for Rathbone's arm. "Frank . . ."

"Quite a pair you two make," Roman growled, one leg curled beneath the other.

"Shut up, you old fool!" Rae snapped at him. "You're getting exactly what you deserve!"

"And what are you getting, Rae?" Rathbone stared at her, that menacing grin locked on his lips, his eyes cobalt with barely restrained fury. "And me—what am I getting?"

"Why, Frank," she said. "I have to admit that I have been rather . . . *overly cautious*. But what you'll be getting, my darling"—she reached up and ran a hand through his hair, beaming at him, a ridiculous parody of a coquette in her conservative, dusty traveling basque, and with her hair hanging in dusty tangles about her shoulders—"is me."

Rathbone jerked the gun back behind his shoulder. He snapped it forward. The butt slammed against the woman's right temple, and she flew backward against the canyon wall with a scream.

"How's it feel?" Rathbone gritted his teeth at her. "How's it feel, Rae?" He looked down at the money. "We had an agreement, you an' me. We would have split all the loot between us, and we would have grown old together. Back East or wherever the hell you wanted to go!" His voice cracked with emotion, and his eyes shone. "It would have been good, Rae. It would have been real good. Only you had to play me for the fool, and you robbed me. Twenty, thirty thousand dollars wasn't enough for you, huh?"

"Please, Frank," Rae cried, crossing her arms on her chest and clutching her shoulders. "I didn't know if I could trust *you*. I merely took your share of the stolen money as a precaution against your abandoning me!"

"You know what you bought with that money, Rae? Huh? You know what you bought for your time and trouble?"

Delbert Roman said weakly, "Please, Sheriff . . ."

Rae Roman stared at Rathbone, her chest rising and falling heavily. Her eyes acquired a sharp, fearful cast, and she dropped her gaze to the .45 that the sheriff was extending straight out from his belly, his savage grin in place.

"Frank." Rae's voice sounded wooden as she continued to stare at the gun in Rathbone's clenched fist. "Please, Frank—we can work this out between us."

"Don't do it, Sheriff," her father beseeched.

Rathbone's mouth opened wide, loosing a string of loud guffaws, his eyes flashing like daggers. "What you bought, you crazy bitch, is several ounces of lead!"

With that last, the gun leaped in his hand, barking, smoke and flames stabbing from the barrel.

He fired again, again, and again.

Until the hammer dropped with a ping on an empty chamber.

Chapter 24

"Oh, you crazy son of a bitch!" Delbert Roman screamed, staring at his daughter lying in a bloody heap against the gaping, open mouth of the notch cave. He turned his bleached face and terror-bright eyes on the sheriff, who stood holding his smoking, empty pistol down by his side, head lifted, laughing loudly.

"*You crazy son of a bitch!*" Roman wailed again, lunging off his heels and, keeping his head down, bolting toward Rathbone, spittle flying from between his quivering lips.

Rathbone raised his pistol negligently, still laughing. As Roman caromed toward him, the sheriff swiped the Colt's barrel across the banker's left temple, opening a bloody gash in the man's forehead. Rathbone stepped aside, and Roman went stumbling off into the rocks, arms flapping like wings, before he banged a knee against a boulder and fell in a great tumult of wafting dust and crunching cactus stems. He rolled onto his side, tried lifting his head, squinting his eyes. They rolled back into his head, and he collapsed on his back.

Out.

Rathbone stood staring down at the man, his own chest rising and falling heavily. He looked at the dead Pinkerton agents, then at Rae. She lay twisted on one side, one leg curled beneath her, her skirts forming a shroud of sorts over the lower half of her body. Blood shone on her chest and belly, glowing brightly in the midday sun.

"You stupid bitch," Rathbone snarled at her, his exhilaration over what he'd just done now waning. Another feeling edged it away. Sadness. A tragic sense of loss.

Why had she double-crossed him? He really had loved her. He'd never loved anyone else in his entire life. Had never known what love was, in fact. But he'd be damned if he hadn't loved the stupid, crazy bitch lying dead before him now. She hadn't loved him back, however. Hadn't known how to. All she'd cared about was the money.

Rathbone dropped to a knee beside her. Her eyes stared up at him. But they didn't see him. He felt a tightness in his chest, a burning in his belly, when he saw how still she lay before him. Remembering how she'd once writhed beneath him, groaning and sighing and digging her fingers into his back . . .

"Oh, Rae." A sob bubbled up from deep in his throat.

He set his gun down, placed a hand on her forehead. He slid the hand down her face, lightly closing her eyes. Then he folded her arms across her bloody belly, laid one of her hands atop the other.

He knelt there for a time feeling as though he were slowly being hollowed out, then grabbed his Colt and heaved himself to his feet. Holstering the empty pistol, he grabbed the money sack and stood staring down at Roman once more. The man's chest rose and fell as he breathed, and his lips were stretching painfully, eyelids fluttering. The three-inch gash across his left temple was oozing blood that dribbled down around his eye and onto his pale, pink-mottled cheek.

Rathbone kicked one of the man's riding boots. "Come on, Roman. Git up."

Roman lay there, eyelids fluttering.

"I said git up, Roman!" Rathbone kicked the man again, harder. "You an' me are goin' to the bank. It's about time you and your daughter paid me for all my trouble."

He laughed at that, but he did not feel any humor. The laugh sounded hollow even to himself. He felt wretched. Wretched, suddenly, with greed. The money in the sack would be enough to set him up for a few years in San Francisco, but the money in that last strongbox, the one tucked away in the Red Hill Bank & Trust, would get him through the rest of his wretched life quite nicely.

"I said get up!"

He reached down and pulled the banker to his feet. The man yelped, groaned, and sobbed, his knees buckling as he staggered around, Rathbone holding him up with one hand while he grabbed his money sack again with the other.

"Get your ass down to the buggy and climb in." He

shoved Roman out ahead of him. Too hard. The man stumbled down the hill and dropped to his knees. "Up!" Rathbone raged. "Get up or I'll brain you again, you fat, rich son of a bitch!"

He jerked Roman to his feet once more. As the man staggered down the shelving cliff face before him, meandering around the rock tanks, Rathbone snarled, "How in the hell did you raise such a daughter? Such a greedy bitch? Huh, Roman? You know what she's been doin' to you, the whole past year? She's been beddin' me to get to you and your *money*!"

"Oh, God!" Roman groaned. "Oh, sweet Jesus!"

"Jesus ain't gonna help you, you fat, stupid bastard." Rathbone laughed. "There ain't no one gonna help you. Only me, Roman. I might just let your sorry ass live if you open the bank vault without giving me any more trouble!"

Roman dropped to his knees beside the buggy, the roan turning its head to inspect the man warily. "I can't." Roman dropped to all fours and let his head hang between his shoulders. Blood dribbled from the gash in his forehead and onto the sand beneath him.

"My head hurts," he said, raking in a deep, pained breath. "Oh, Jesus . . . I'm seeing double. I think I might be sick."

Rathbone tossed the money onto the buggy's backseat, then glanced at the canyon mouth to make sure no one else had decided to join the dance. He doubted the half-breed would track him here, but you never knew about a breed. Especially the one the Romans had hired. Sliding his pistol from his holster, he quickly plucked all six spent casings out, refilled the chambers with fresh, and spun the cylinder.

He lowered the gun, ratcheting the hammer back loudly, and pressed the barrel against the back of the banker's head. "Get into the buggy."

"You have enough money there in the bag, Rathbone." Roman shook his head wearily. "Please. Just take it and go. Let me be."

"If I leave here, Roman, I'm going to be leaving a fourth corpse. Make up your mind. You're either getting into the buggy or I'm gonna kill you right here."

In the end, the banker pulled himself onto the left-side buggy seat. He leaned forward, elbows on his knees, holding his head in his hands, as Rathbone climbed aboard, glanced back at the money bag, then grabbed the reins and turned the roan back in the direction from which it had come.

As he crossed the wash, muddy water splashing up around the buggy's red wheels, Rathbone kept a sharp eye on the widening canyon mouth before him. He loosed a relieved breath when he finally sped through it and turned onto the trail, an old miners' road, and saw no one waiting for him in the broad canyon beyond.

The sheriff chuckled. He glanced over at Roman. The banker was still leaning forward with his head in his hands, blood dribbling down from his forehead and cheek and onto the dusty toe of his left riding boot.

"Cheer up, Roman." Rathbone reached over and patted the man's back as if in sympathy. "I'll be on my way soon, and you'll get your forehead patched up. The doc'll give you something to ease your pain."

"I'm finished," Roman said, slowly shaking his head. He lifted his head and leaned back in the seat, reaching into a back pocket of his trousers for a red handkerchief with little white stars on it. He folded the cloth and pressed it against his bloody temple. His voice sounded wooden, toneless as he said, "My daughter . . . Rae . . . dead."

"Well, look at it this way. You know what she was."

Roman looked at him, revulsion and hatred in his eyes. Rathbone saw the look, realized how he must appear to the banker—callous beyond belief, strong, an indomitable adversary—and he laughed. Yes, he was strong. He didn't need Rae to make him happy. He'd make himself happy. Of course, all the loot in the bag and in the bank vault would help.

The bitch really shouldn't have done what she'd done. If she hadn't gotten so greedy, she'd not only have had the money, she'd have had him!

Rathbone laughed again and gave the roan its head as it high-stepped around a sharp curve in the trail between two narrowing cliff walls and clomped on back toward town. As the ragged fringe of Red Hill appeared beyond the last wash, Rathbone cast another sharp-eyed gaze into the scrub around him. He didn't want to be seen driving Rae's buggy, her father himself sitting beside him with a bloody forehead. He turned off the main trail and took a small side street that was little more than a gravelly trace between stock pens and corrals.

When the trace fizzled in a brush-choked arroyo near a small adobe house that was home to a large Mexican family, he swung over to a plank bridge, crossed the arroyo, and turned onto a bona fide though sparsely populated side street. He was on the street for only a hundred yards before he threaded the gap between the schoolhouse, quiet on a Saturday, and a ruined Spanish church.

A minute later, having seen no one but a few old women out hanging wash on their lines or beating rope rugs hanging from porch rails, he pulled up to the rear of the Red Hill Bank & Trust. He jumped to the ground and went around to the other side, where Roman was staring off almost uncomprehendingly as blood continued to dribble down from the gash in his temple.

"Dead," he said breathily. "My daughter is dead."

"Get down from there, Roman."

The banker looked at Rathbone, frowning. "You killed her."

"I'll kill you, too, if you don't haul your fat ass down out of there." Rathbone grabbed the banker's arm and pulled. Roman scrambled down, holding on to the short brass rail along the side of the carriage to keep from falling. Still, when he hit the ground, he got his feet twisted, and he dropped to one knee.

Rathbone jerked the man back to his feet and pushed him ahead of him. They stopped at the bank's rear door. Rathbone glanced around cautiously. "Open it."

"I don't have the key with me."

Rathbone sighed, slid his revolver from its holster,

cocked it, and shoved the barrel up against the underside of Roman's chin. "Yes, you do. You've always got the key with you."

Roman winced at the barrel's pressure, then shoved his right hand into his pants pocket, hauling out two brass keys dangling from a small brass ring. He swung around to the door, poked the key in the lock, and turned the knob. Rathbone shoved the man inside before looking around once more, then followed Roman into the bank's small rear foyer, instantly smelling the varnish that shone on the structure's oak-trimmed interior.

Rathbone closed the door and flicked the locking bolt home. He shoved Roman ahead, into the afternoon shadows, and the sheriff was glad that no one was here. Of course, he'd let no one keep him from getting his hands on the strongbox, but the bank's being vacant this afternoon made his job a whole lot easier.

He poked and prodded the heavy-footed, wobbly-legged Roman on through the bank's office area, through the gate in the low, wooden railing, and into the main business area complete with tellers' cages and a small alcove that served as the Red Hill Post Office. He kicked open the unlocked wooden door with a frosted upper glass panel that separated the tellers' cages from the lobby, and shoved Roman up against the vault's heavy gray iron door.

"Open it."

"Oh, Jesus." Roman sagged down against the door to his knees. He groaned and clutched his head in his hands. "I can't think . . . the combination . . . Christ—I just can't remember it!"

Rathbone hardened his jaws and pressed the Colt's barrel taut against the side of the man's head. "You *better* remember it."

"I don't!"

"Roman, we've come this far. Do I have to kill you now?"

Roman looked up at the sheriff, his eyes wide and glassy with exasperation, the blood on his left temple glistening in the gold light angling through the tops of the front windows that the drawn, tan shades did not cover. "You scrambled my brains, Rathbone. I can't think straight, and I'm seeing double!"

Rathbone pressed the barrel harder against the banker's head, just above his ear, and twisted it, pressing Roman's head up hard against the vault. "Well, you start seeing straight, or you're gonna have a hole in your head—one that's a whole lot bigger than that little crease I gave you!"

"All right!" Roman spoke through gritted teeth. "Give me a minute to think!"

Rathbone pulled the gun away from the banker's head. "You got fifteen seconds, you son of a bitch."

A shadow moved across the drawn shades covering the bank's front windows. A bowler-hatted figure with the silhouette of a cigar protruding from the pedestrian's mouth. Rathbone's belly tightened, and he unconsciously held his breath when he saw the man stop before the door, which was also covered by a shade.

The door rattled. There were the clicks of a key in the lock.

"Who the hell is that?" Rathbone whisper-shouted.

Blinking his eyes as if to clear them, Roman looked at the door in which the hatted shadow stood, slightly crouched, both hands held in front of him.

"Oh, no. Elmwood always works for a few hours on Saturday afternoon."

The door lock clicked.

Rathbone grabbed Roman's collar and jerked the man back into the lobby. "Get rid of him!"

The door opened. Elmwood stood there in the opening, silhouetted against the afternoon light behind him, a long black cigar smoldering between his lips. His round spectacles flashed dully above his carefully trimmed, ginger-colored beard. He frowned at Roman. Then he glanced at Rathbone peeking out around the door that led to the vault.

He returned his gaze to Roman, and then, just as he said, "What on earth is going on here, sir?" Rathbone remembered the nasty tattoo on the banker's forehead. The sheriff's heart kicked like a mule in his chest and before he knew what he was doing, he raised the Colt at Elmwood and fired.

"No!" Roman cried.

Rathbone's Colt barked twice more, throwing the dapper loan officer out the open door and into the street.

Chapter 25

Rathbone stared out the open door, through the thick cloud of his own powder smoke, where the young loan officer lay quivering bizarrely as the life bled out of him. There had been several men standing around outside the Queen of Hearts Saloon, and now they were beginning to wander haltingly toward the bank, sort of crouched and holding their hands over their holstered pistols.

"Calvin!" came a woman's cry.

Rathbone shifted his gaze down the cross street before him. The blond mail-order bride of the mercantiler, Seagraves, was walking toward the bank, as well. Dressed in a plain cotton housedress, she lifted the hem of her skirt above her ankles and increased her speed, calling, "Calvin!" over and over again and staring worriedly toward the main street.

Rathbone looked up and down the street, saw more men in small, scattered groups headed in his direction, and cursed. What the hell was he going to do now? He just realized that Roman was in front of him, staring out the door and muttering, "Oh, my God! Oh, my God!"

"Shut up!" Rathbone lurched forward, and slammed the bank's front door closed on the loan officer lying several feet beyond the boardwalk, limbs akimbo, as though he'd fallen from the sky.

Rathone looked around the bank as though at the walls of a large prison cell. His pulse hammered in his ears and the smell of the wafting smoke was a pungent, cloying odor in his nostrils.

"Oh, my God!" Roman said once more, turning his stricken eyes to the sheriff. "What are you going to do now, Sheriff? Huh? What are you going to do now? Kill the entire town? They're coming! Did you see? They're all heading this way and you'll be surround—"

Bang! Bang! Bang!

More smoke puffed in the air between Rathbone and Roman. The banker was dead after the first shot, however, but the next two bullets plowed through the man as he flew straight back against one of the teller cages, the grillwork of which was painted red by the banker's own blood. Roman bounced off the cage, staggered forward, eyes already glassy and vacant, and fell facedown on the floor without even trying to break his fall with his hands.

Outside, the woman was fairly screaming the boy's name as male shouts rose from up and down the street. Spurs began *chinging* as men trotted or ran toward the bank. Rathbone slid a shade back from one of the windows with his pistol barrel, saw the woman moving into the street from the southern cross street as well as a dozen or so men hustling in defensive postures toward the bank, most now with guns in their hands and looks of exasperation on their faces.

"Shit!"

Rathbone stepped back from the window and turned to the vault. The iron door was as immovable as solid stone. He imagined the strongbox sitting on a shelf behind the door, and frustration gripped him hard. He raised his hands to his head, rammed the butt of his pistol and the heel of his other hand against his temples, sobbing angrily.

Outside, the voices and spur *chings* and the thuds of running feet were growing louder.

Rathbone had to get out of here. He had to take what loot he had in the buggy—Rae's loot—and make a break for it. He'd head in whichever direction seemed the clearest, and he'd get the hell out of Red Hill and make a fresh start somewhere else, under an alias.

Quickly, as boots thumped on the bank's front boardwalk, Rathbone dashed to the rear of the building, opened the door, and looked around. He jerked back when he saw a figure out there, near the buggy. He raised the Colt, drawing the hammer back, but held fire. It was the boy—the mail-order bride's little freckle-faced brat—standing out there between Rae's buggy and the bank's two-hole privy. The kid held a short, vaguely pistol-shaped stick in his hand, and he stood stock-still now as he stared at Rathbone, anxiety lifting a flush in his cheeks and brightening his light brown eyes.

"You're not a robber," the boy said dully, frowning. "You're the sheriff. . . ."

Rathbone looked around. There was only the boy out here. So far.

"Yeah, that's right. I'm the sheriff." He strode quickly out into the bank's backyard, switching his pistol to his right hand, then wrapping his arm around the boy's waist and lifting him off his feet. "Why don't you hop in the buggy, there, little feller? I'm gonna need some help tracking them bank robbers. I think they lit out the front!"

Calvin grunted and groaned as the sheriff carried him brusquely over to the buggy, then tossed him up onto the seat like a twenty-pound sack of grain. "I don't think I better," the boy said, frightened now as he watched the sheriff climb up beside him, holster his pistol, and grab the ribbons from around the brake handle. "That's my mom callin', and I think she's worried about me."

"Pshaw!" Rathbone said, turning the roan around. "You help me bring the bad guys in, you'll be a hero, young feller!"

He could hear the voices growing louder as the men surrounded the bank.

"Hold on tight, Deputy!" Rathbone barked as he pulled the roan out past the privy, aimed him south, and then shook the ribbons fiercely over the animal's broad back.

"Calvin!"

As the buggy rattled and bounced through the weeds and onto the side street, Rathbone glanced to his left.

The woman was running down the middle of the side street, holding the hem of her skirt above her ankles, her pretty, light-complected features creased with dread.

"Calvin, no!"

"Mama!" the boy screamed, flinging an arm back over the seat toward his mother.

"Calvin!"

Rathbone shook the ribbons over the roan's back and turned once more to the woman to yell, "You keep them men here in town, ma'am. If I see anyone on my trail, you'll get this little critter back in *pieces*!"

The roan whinnied, and the buggy hammered off down the trail, heading north toward where the Coronados rose stark and rocky against the horizon, their lower slopes turning burned orange in the severely olanting sunlight.

"*Maww-maaaa!*" the boy screamed.

"Oh, my God—Cal-*viiinnnnn!*" his mother wailed, stopping suddenly in the middle of the side street and clenching her hands beneath her chin.

Hooves thudded behind her, and Beth turned to see Yakima barreling around the bank atop his big black stallion. The half-breed had been saddling Wolf in the livery barn with the intention of riding out after Rathbone, when he'd heard the shooting. Now he slowed the stallion a tad as he stared off to where the buggy was dwindling into the desert, following the side street that became a trail, which would take a rider high into the Coronados if he followed it far enough.

"I'll get him," Yakima growled, grinding his heels into Wolf's flanks.

"No!" Beth lunged for Yakima's leg. "Rathbone said he'd kill him!"

Townsmen were moving around them, shouting, arguing, a few standing over the dead loan officer, a few others moving into the bank cautiously, guns drawn. No one seemed to know what was going on, just that Rathbone had killed Elmwood.

"Beth," Yakima said. "If he gets too far from town, we may never get Calvin back, anyway. I'm gonna follow him, but I'll keep my distance."

She stared up at him, flushed and wide-eyed. Slowly, she nodded her head, then stepped back away from the horse and followed the half-breed with her gaze as he trotted on down the street and into the desert beyond.

Yakima watched the buggy disappear over a distant rise, but even though the sheriff of Red Hill was out of sight, he resisted the urge to give the stallion its head. Rathbone was crazy enough to kill the boy if he saw a man on his trail. Especially, Yakima thought, if he saw the half-breed himself on his trail.

Frustrated, he kept a tight grip on the reins, holding them up high against his chest, his long hair dancing around his stony cheeks. He'd follow the man at a distance, bide his time, wait until dark to ride in and get the boy back. Then he'd kick Rathbone out bloody and get the hell out of here himself.

Up and down the hogbacks he rode, climbing gradually into the Coronados via dry washes and around looming mesas. The trail forked several times, but the furrows of the buggy wheels were easy to follow in the still-damp ground. As he rode up a gentle slope, meandering around cedars, barrel cactus, and boulders, a horse whinnied somewhere ahead of him.

A boy screamed. There was a tooth-gnashing clatter, like that of a buggy rolling over.

Dread flooding Yakima's belly with bile, he heeled Wolf into a ground-eating lope. He curved around a cabin-sized boulder and started down a slope along the shoulder of a long spine of upthrust volcanic rock. Down where the slope flattened out, the buggy lay on its side, two wheels spinning, facing a broad ravine. The horse was racing off beyond it, along the ravine's twisting back, trailing its reins and the double-tree.

Yakima heard the boy screaming though he couldn't see him. The half-breed gigged the black into another ground-churning run down the dyke's shoulder, Wolf's hooves thudding in the packed, damp caliche, throwing gravel up behind him. On the other side of a knob from which a gnarled mesquite grew, Rathbone was down on his hands and knees, crawling desperately after the greenbacks that had apparently spilled from the gunnysack lying nearby. A breeze had picked up, blowing the paper money in all directions.

Yakima checked Wolf down and looked around wildly, shucking his Winchester and cocking it one-handed. "Where's the boy, Rathbone?"

The sheriff had been so distracted by the money that he hadn't noticed Yakima ride up and stop near the buggy. The sheriff—hatless, bloody scratches on his face, hair hanging across his forehead—jerked his gaze at the half-breed.

"Where is he?" Yakima snarled.

Rathbone's eyes snapped wide. His Colt came up in a blur. He was faster than Yakima realized, and he almost let the man get off a shot before he took a hasty, one-handed aim from Wolf's back, and triggered the Winchester.

The bullet slammed through the sheriff's belly. Rathbone yelped and triggered his Colt into the ground in front of him, blowing up a wad of greenbacks that went dancing off on the wind. The sheriff bent forward, pressing his forehead into the turf and bellowing.

Yakima leaped out of the saddle and looked around wildly. "Calvin? Boy, where are you?"

A weak cry was carried on the breeze. "Help!"

Yakima looked toward the ravine, then, hearing another, even weaker cry, broke into a run. To his left, a pistol popped. The bullet screeched behind Yakima, who stopped and wheeled. Holding one hand across his bloody belly, Rathbone was raising his pistol once more, bellowing incoherently.

Yakima quickly racked a fresh cartridge into the Yellowboy's chamber, pressed his cheek against the rear stock, and lined up the sights on the sheriff's forehead.

Rathbone triggered his Colt a quarter-second before Yakima drilled a quarter-sized hole through the man's forehead, punching him back into a patch of Spanish bayonet over which several greenbacks fluttered.

"Help!" came the boy's weak cry again.

Yakima took another step toward the canyon, felt a hitch in his side. He looked down. The side of his buckskin shirt was torn and blood-spotted. Yakima cursed, continued on to the edge of the ravine, and looked down

Calvin was dangling over the edge of the deep canyon from an arrow-shaped rock that jutted out from the canyon's wall about twenty feet down from the top. The boy was kicking, trying to dig his shoes into the canyon wall, but the wall was just beyond the reach of his short legs. His little hands were wrapped around the edge of the rock. They were bone white, and they were slipping.

He was looking down, chin dipped to his chest.

"Calvin, look up here!" Yakima called, leaning his rifle against a rock and casting his gaze around for the best way down the cliff. "Keep your eyes up here, and hold on! You hear me, boy?"

Bells tolled in his head as he continued to urge the boy to hold on. He thought of Beth as he began making his way down the steep wall, planting his feet against rocks and small, wiry shrubs as he dropped six feet down from the top, then ten. The boy was all she had. She, all the boy had.

As he turned to face the wall so that he could use his hands as well as his feet, images of Faith from that last night at Thornton's roadhouse, the flames reflected in her dead eyes, kept floating up in front of his retinas. He blinked them away, kept his eyes on Calvin's little hands that were slowly sliding off the rock below him, his little brown shoes inching farther and farther into the gaping emptiness below him.

"Hold on, boy," Yakima urged. "Just hold on. I'm comin' for you."

The boy said nothing. Too weak to talk. That wasn't good.

Yakima saw the boy's left hand slide down off the side of the rock and disappear. Then the right one slid off, too, and Yakima crouched and thrust his own right hand out just as the boy started to drop. The half-breed's big brown hand wrapped around the boy's thin, pale wrist and squeezed.

"Gotcha!"

Yakima felt an angry hitch in his side as, with one hand, the other hand holding another rock while he kept his moccasins clamped down hard in a shallow trough, he lifted the boy up beside him. Calvin lunged for purchase on the canyon wall. He was sobbing, shaking.

"You're all right, boy. Now we just have to get back up the wall and out of here."

Yakima wrapped his right arm around the boy's waist and, gritting his teeth against the pain in the arm as well as his side, began climbing. He and Calvin were halfway to the top when Yakima looked up and saw Beth Holgate staring down over the side, her blond hair blowing in the wind. She said nothing but only watched, tears careening down her cheeks, as Yakima hoisted Calvin up and over the lip of the ridge and into his mother's engulfing arms.

She knelt down and held her son tightly, sobbing

and bawling and rocking him, Calvin's own little arms wrapped taut around his mother's neck, his scratched, bruised, and blood-streaked face buried in her bosom.

Beth held the boy for a long, long time. Pulling away from him slightly, she pressed her lips against the boy's head. "Oh, Calvin. What would I ever do without you?"

The boy looked up at her. His own eyes were bright, his cheeks flushed and wet. "That was close," he breathed. "If it hadn't been for Mr. Henry, I reckon I'd be a goner, Mom."

"Yes," Beth said. "Oh, Yakima, thank . . ."

She let her voice trail off as she looked around. There was only the overturned buggy, the windblown greenbacks, the saddled pinto she'd borrowed in town, and Rathbone. The sun was going down, and this flat area between the western slope and the ravine was cast in slanting golden light and purple shadows.

"Yakima?" she said.

Then she spied movement on the opposite ridge— a horse and rider lunging up the side of the rocky dyke.

Beth rose to her feet and strode quickly toward where the slope began rising from the flat. "Yakima?" Her call was torn this way and that by the chill wind.

She raised a hand against several bright though fast-dying rays of light and kept her eyes on the horse and rider approaching the crest of the scarp. *"Yakimaaaah!"* she shouted.

She waited, watching. He kept riding, the horse lunging off its powerful rear legs, Yakima crouching over the pommel of his saddle, his long black hair streaming out behind his shoulders.

Beth held the back of her wrist across her forehead, the last rays of the sun gilding her face, flashing in the tears rolling down her cheeks. Her voice was soft, pleading, almost inaudible. "Please, don't go."

Horse and rider were silhouetted for a moment against the umber western sky. They dropped down the other side of the ridge, and were gone.

ABOUT THE AUTHOR

Frank Leslie is the pseudonym of an acclaimed Western novelist who has written more than fifty novels and a comic book series. He divides his time between Colorado and Arizona, exploring the West in his pickup and travel trailer.

For Western action this thrilling, this authentic,
there's only one Frank Leslie.
Read on for a special preview of

REVENGE AT HATCHET CREEK

Coming from Signet in June 2011. . . .

Yak-yak-yak-yak-yak-yak-yak . . . !

The caterwauling of the Gatling gun seemed to be echoing the first syllable of Yakima Henry's name as the big half-breed himself cranked the handle and stared out over the revolving canister and through the billowing powder smoke. The .45-caliber rounds being slung from the six blazing maws tore the rough-clad posse riders out from behind their covering rocks, and spun them into the spindly Dakota bunch grass like rag dolls caught in a cyclone.

Yakima couldn't help grinning, his green eyes sparking at the thrill of the kill. This bunch had been dogging him too long, and they'd intended to use the Gatling gun themselves to shoot him off the canyon's north cliff, where they'd had him trapped like a cow-killing wildcat. And they almost had . . . until he'd gotten around them early this morning and taken the gun over for his own retributive purposes. . . .

Yak-yak-yak-yak-yak . . . !

The chest of one of the posse riders opened up like a

tomato smashed against a barn door. The man screamed, showing pale yellow teeth beneath his bushy black mustache. He flung his rolling-block Remington rifle over his head and turned a backward somersault over one of the boulders strewn along the shore of War Hatchet Creek.

Yakima spied movement to his right and spun the gun toward the ridge. A rifleman had leaped onto a flat-topped boulder sheathed in dry grass and gnarled burr oaks, but before he could raise his Winchester to his shoulder, the Gatling's hot lead puffed dust from his heavy sheepskin coat, and blew doggets of blood, flesh, and spine out his back. He screamed as he triggered his rifle into the rock he was standing on, then twisted around and fell back off the rock and out of sight.

Yakima released the Gatling's trigger.

He stared out over the red-hot barrel, through the webbing smoke hanging in a heavy, fetid cloud over the back of the buckboard farm wagon, in which the Gatling was perched. The wagon sat between the base of the chalky, boulder-strewn ridge and the muddy waters of War Hatchet Creek, on the trail that led south from the little town of Wild Rose. Around the wagon, three men lay dead.

They were the first of the seven- or eight-man posse that Yakima—having bided his time over the long, cold night—had taken down when he'd stolen up on the wagon and taken over the Gatling gun. He could see parts of two other dead men peeking out from behind a cottonwood stump on his left and a boulder about forty yards downstream, along the bank of the creek.

It was just after dawn, and the canyon was all soft gray light and purple shadows. The creek moved darkly in its meandering bank, gurgling softly. The fall yellow leaves of the cottonwoods standing tall along the creek scratched in a rising breeze.

Yakima kept his finger on the Gatling gun's trigger. He'd taken down most of the men who'd been hunting him after he'd left Wild Rose like a mule with its tail on fire, but three or four still hadn't been accounted for.

Suddenly, a rifle barrel poked up from behind a boulder on the right side of the trail, about thirty yards beyond the wagon. The entire rifle appeared in a man's gloved hand. The hand waved the rifle slowly from left to right.

"Holy Christ—don't shoot no more, mister," a man yelled. "I give up!"

A man's tan-hatted head appeared from behind a flat-topped boulder halfway up the ridge on Yakima's right. The man's face was a dun oval beneath the hat. A red knit scarf was wrapped around his neck.

"Same here, breed. Hold your fire!"

The Gatling gun's swivel rod squawked as Yakima trained the deadly weapon toward the man on the ridge. "Throw your guns out. Both of you."

Each man tossed a rifle out. The man near the trail tossed out what appeared an old cap-and-ball Colt with a wooden handle held together with rawhide. The man on the ridge tossed out two newer-model pistols and a hunting knife. The knife clattered when it hit the gravel, and rolled nearly all the way down to the trail.

"That all you got?"

"That's it for me," said the man on the ridge.

"That's all I'm carryin' right there," said the man nearer the trail.

All night, Yakima had been pinned down about three-quarters of the way up the ridge. From there, he'd seen the posse tether their horses in a cottonwood copse about a hundred yards upstream, toward town, and on the other side of the creek. All the horses were likely still there, though it looked as though all but two wouldn't be bearing riders for a while.

They'd brought the deadly Gatling gun in just after sundown. They'd stood around, drinking whiskey and firing at Yakima hunkered behind boulders along the ridge, taking bets on who would kill his wild half-breed ass and arguing over who'd get his long black scalp. They'd been having a real good time.

Not such a good one now . . .

"You'd better not have so much as a pocketknife on you—either of you!" Yakima warned. "Now crawl the hell out of there and vamoose!"

The man nearer the trail rose from behind his rock, hands raised high above his head. He was a stocky, chubby-cheeked man with a black beard. Yakima remembered seeing him spinning the roulette wheel in the Dakota Plains Saloon when the deputy sheriff had slapped iron on Yakima, and Yakima had been forced to dispatch the fool.

"Can we gather our dead?" the chubby-cheeked man asked. "Trail 'em back to town?" He squinted an eye at the sky behind Yakima. "Looks like a storm's buildin'. Don't wanna leave 'em out here to get covered up."

"Go ahead," Yakima growled. "When I'm outta here."

He turned his head to one side, stuck two fingers into his mouth, and whistled for his horse. He hadn't seen the mount since he'd climbed the ridge to try and bushwhack the men who'd chased him out from town but had ended up getting bushwhacked and pinned down himself. Not his best moment. He hadn't expected such a big group to trail him. Especially not one wielding a Gatling gun. The deputy must have had a lot of friends.

Where in the hell had they gotten ahold of a Gatling gun out here in western Dakota Territory, anyway?

Yakima looked at the trail, following the stream's course, twisting off behind him. He saw no sign of the horse, but he was sure the black stallion was lurking around here somewhere. Wolf never strayed far without Yakima. They'd been together a long time, been through a lot.

Yakima turned forward, waiting, listening for the horse's thudding hooves. He heard instead the wagon groan slightly, felt it jerk a little.

Something moved behind him. He felt a hot pricking sensation on the right side of his back. He grunted and jerked forward, then turned his head to see the man whom he thought he'd killed when he'd slipped into the wagon—the man who'd been wielding the Gatling gun—scowl at him from about two feet away.

In the man's right hand was a short, bloody knife. The blood on the knife was his own, Yakima realized, as the heavy burning sensation nearly blinded him with scalding fury.

He pivoted, swinging the Gatling gun around, and fired.

Yak-yak-yak-yak-yak!

The .45-caliber rounds, fired from point-blank range, nearly tore the knife-wielding man in two before flipping him back and over the wagon's tailgate. Grinding his molars against the pain in his back, Yakima spun the Gatling back toward the other two men, both of whom jerked with starts when they saw the savage fury in Yakima's eyes.

"Hey!" yelled the man nearest the trail, stumbling back a step but keeping his hands raised as though to grab one of the fast-scudding gray clouds. "Come on, now—that was Raymond Woodyard. Lassiter's cousin. We got no stake in his doin's. We're done, breed!"

Lassiter was the name of the deputy sheriff whom Yakima had sent to his reward.

The man on the side of the ridge stood where he'd been standing before, also reaching for the sky that was fast darkening with storm clouds. He stared at Yakima, who saw the man's throat move as he swallowed.

Hoof thuds sounded. Yakima looked behind him. His black stallion with four white stockings was galloping toward him from the other side of the creek. The stallion shook its head and snorted, and then crossed the stream in three lunging strides, the reins whipping along behind it. The big sleek black came up through the cottonwoods, and Yakima released the Gatling gun. He grabbed his Winchester Yellowboy repeater, which he'd emptied along with his horn-gripped Colt .44 when he'd been pinned down on the ridge, and touched his back.

He looked at his hand, saw the thick blood smeared there, and cursed.

He glanced once more at the two surviving members of the posse, then stepped over the tailgate and onto the black. His saddle was loose, but he'd adjust it later. Slipping the Yellowboy into its saddle boot on the horse's right side, Yakima reached for the dangling reins. He turned the horse downstream and touched the heels of his high-topped, fur-trimmed moccasins to the black's flanks. Wolf gave another blow, shook his head, and lunged off down the trail, away from the carnage and the two men who stood staring after him, both still reaching skyward as though in some bizarre religious ritual.

Yakima looked at his bloody hand again, and grunted. Goddamn that deputy and the extra jack he'd found in the card deck they'd been using for poker—or claimed to have found. Yakima knew the man was piss-burned because Yakima had been lying over in Wild Rose for three days, and holing up with the soiled dove whom Deputy Lassiter himself had put his stamp on. Besides, the man had obviously been prejudiced against half-breeds. Yakima's green eyes, red-brown skin, and long black hair betrayed his mixed-blood heritage to the unreasoning, knee-jerk disdain of many.

So Lassiter himself had slipped the jack into the deck and accused Yakima himself of the subterfuge.

Yakima had told the man to go fuck himself and then his ugly sister seven ways from sundown. Worse than being called a low-down, dirty half-breed, he hated being called a cheat.

Lassiter had given a grim smile and reached for the big Remington positioned for the cross draw on his left hip.

Yakima had heard Lassiter's reputation for being fast, so Yakima had drilled the deputy from beneath the table—shooting from *up through* the table and taking the point of the man's chin off. The second shot had drilled him through his heart and left him flopping around on the floor of the Dakota Territory Saloon like a landed fish, the blood pool spreading ever wider and wider across the rough wooden floor.

"Law, law!" the bartender with the west-Texas drawl had exclaimed, shaking his head and widening his eyes in horror. "Now you done it, ya crazy half-breed. That's Wes Lassiter you drilled, an' before he's done saddlin' a cloud to ride to the Great Beyond, you're gonna be stretchin' hemp from one of the cottonwoods along Hatchet Creek!"

Now Yakima grimaced as he felt a cold wind blow against him, peppering his face with chill raindrops.

He rode tall in the saddle, refusing to give in to the burning wound in his back. He didn't think the cut was deep—at least, not more than five inches, the length

of the blade he'd seen in Raymond Woodyard's hand.
Of course, he'd have to get the bleeding stopped, but
he needed to find shelter first. Where he'd find that
out here, he had no idea.

As he followed the trail up out of the canyon and
onto the rolling tableland beyond, all he saw was dun
hogbacks turning darker and darker under the darkening sky from which a cold rain was slanting down.
The trail rose and fell before him like a thin ribbon of
pale string amongst the tawny grass, with not a cabin
anywhere in sight.

A lone cottonwood or oak here or there, but those
were the only features. All the rest was rolling prairie
with its carpeting of autumn brown grama grass and
sky.

He was alone out here. As alone as he'd ever
been. He could feel his blood leaking from the stab
wound and dribbling down under his shirt, turning
cold against his skin. He wore a denim jacket over his
buckskin shirt, long-handles under the shirt and his
buckskin breeches, but he'd need to don his sheepskin
coat soon.

The sky, for as far as he could see in the east, north,
and south, was the color of ripe plums. An early-winter
snowstorm was blowing across these stark northern
plains. It would get cold soon. Freezing cold. The rain
would turn to snow, and the snow would get so thick
he wouldn't be able to see much farther than his horse's
ears.

He knew how it was up here. He'd worked in this
country before. He'd tried to stay clear of it since, but

a job had brought him back two months ago—a job delivering freight to Winnipeg up in Manitoba—and he hadn't had enough sense to hightail it south as soon as the job was done.

He was in trouble.

Real trouble.

As he rode up and down the hogbacks, letting Wolf follow the trail on his own, Yakima felt himself getting weaker and weaker. The rain turned to snow. It whipped like chunks of ice against his face, clung to his brows and the long hair falling down to his shoulders and curling around his bear-tooth necklace. He paused to don his coat and to tie a scarf under his hat, to keep his ears from freezing, and then he continued riding, hoping that soon the trail would lead to a farm or a ranch or possibly a roadhouse—anywhere he could get warm and get someone to patch his wound before he bled dry.

The horse stopped.

Yakima lifted his head. He hadn't realized he'd slept. He stared out over Wolf's twitching ears and into a vast canyon filled with a wide black stretch of flat water. The Missouri River. Had to be. There was no other watercourse that large and imposing out here.

Shit, he'd come to the end of the line. There was no way across the Big Muddy, especially not now when the water temperature was likely near freezing.

Yakima had barely noted the passage of such troubled thoughts across his brain before his heavy lids closed down over his eyes. His hands released the saddle horn, which they'd been clinging to for the past two hours, and he fell down the side of his horse and into the heavy, damp snow that was piled as high as Wolf's hocks.

The snow piled higher and higher as the wind whipped it sideways on its descent from the nightlike, storm-tossed Dakota sky.

From

Frank Leslie

THE KILLERS OF CIMARRON

After outlaws murder his friend and take a
young woman hostage, Colter Farrow is back on
the vengeance trail, determined to bring the woman
back alive—and send the killers of Cimarron
straight to hell.

THE GUNS OF SAPINERO

Colter Farrow was just a skinny cow-puncher when
the men came to Sapinero Valley and murdered his
best friend, whose past as a gunfighter had caught
up with him. Now, Colter must strap on his
Remington revolver, deliver some justice, and
create a reputation of his own.

THE KILLING BREED

Yakima Henry has been dealt more than his share of
trouble—even for a half-white, half-Indian in the
West. Now he's running a small Arizona horse ranch
with his longtime love, Faith, and thinks he may
have finally found his share of peace and prosperity.
But a man from both their pasts is coming—with
vengeance on his mind...

**Available wherever books are sold or at
penguin.com**